W9-BDW-096

TRAVELS WITH MY AUNT

"It is as if Shakespeare, after the tragedies, had chosen to write not 'The Tempest' but 'Charley's Aunt.' After 18 novels variously described as entertainments, authentic modern tragedies or murky theological melodramas, Graham Greene has at last put himself onstage in a comic masterpiece . . . The funniest book in many a long glum year."

—Time

"Entertaining . . . Highly civilized fun, an 'Auntie Mame' for somewhat higher brows."

—Saturday Review

"An altogether new and different Greene—mellower, constantly and hilariously funny, a stylish tongue-in-cheek farceur who seems at times to be parodying some of his own most somber moments."

—Book Week

"The funniest sexual satire since 'Portnoy's Complaint,' which, of course, it resembles not at all . . . A completely fresh romp through Graham Greeneland."

—San Francisco Chronicle

BRIGHTON ROCK
A BURNT-OUT CASE
THE COMEDIANS
THE CONFIDENTIAL AGENT
THE END OF THE AFFAIR
THE HEART OF THE MATTER
THE MAN WITHIN
MAY WE BORROW YOUR HUSBAND?
THE MINISTRY OF FEAR
ORIENT EXPRESS
OUR MAN IN HAVANA
THE POWER AND THE GLORY
THE QUIET AMERICAN
THE SHIPWRECKED
THE THIRD MAN
THIS GUN FOR HIRE
TRAVELS WITH MY AUNT
TWENTY-ONE STORIES

TRAVELS WITH MY AUNT

A NOVEL BY

GRAHAM GREENE

A NATIONAL GENERAL COMPANY

*This low-priced Bantam Book
has been completely reset in a type face
designed for easy reading, and was printed
from new plates. It contains the complete
text of the original hard-cover edition.*
NOT ONE WORD HAS BEEN OMITTED.

TRAVELS WITH MY AUNT

*A Bantam Book / published by arrangement with
The Viking Press, Inc.*

PRINTING HISTORY

A portion of this book originally appeared in PLAYBOY *magazine
October and November 1969*

Viking edition published January 1970
2nd printing ..... January 1970
3rd printing .... February 1970
4th printing .... February 1970

Book-of-the-Month-Club edition published January 1970
Bantam edition published February 1971

*Bantam Books are published by Bantam Books, Inc., a National
General company. Its trade-mark, consisting of the words "Bantam
Books" and the portrayal of a bantam, is registered in the United
States Patent Office and in other countries. Marca Registrada.
Bantam Books, Inc., 666 Fifth Avenue, New York, N.Y. 10019.*

PRINTED IN THE UNITED STATES OF AMERICA

For H. H. K.
who helped me more
than I can tell

TRAVELS WITH MY AUNT

PART I

CHAPTER 1

I met my Aunt Augusta for the first time in more than half a century at my mother's funeral. My mother was approaching eighty-six when she died, and my aunt was some eleven or twelve years younger. I had retired from the bank two years before with an adequate pension and a silver handshake. There had been a take-over by the Westminster and my branch was considered redundant. Everyone thought me lucky, but I found it difficult to occupy my time. I have never married, I have always lived quietly, and, apart from my interest in dahlias, I have no hobby. For those reasons I found myself agreeably excited by my mother's funeral.

My father had been dead for more than forty years. He was a building contractor of a lethargic disposition who used to take afternoon naps in all sorts of curious places. This irritated my mother, who was an energetic woman, and she used to seek him out to disturb him. As a child I remember going to the bathroom—we lived in Highgate then—and finding my father asleep in the bath in his clothes. I am rather short-sighted and I thought that my mother had been cleaning an overcoat, until I heard my father whisper, "Bolt the door on the inside when you go out." He was too lazy to get out of the bath and too sleepy, I suppose, to realize that his order was quite impossible to carry out. At another time, when he was responsible for a new block of flats in Lewisham, he would take his catnap in the cabin of the giant crane, and construction would be halted until he woke. My mother, who had a good head for heights, would climb ladders to the highest scaffolding in the hope of discovering him, when as like as not he would have found a corner in what was to be the underground garage. I had always thought of them as reasonably happy together: their twin roles of the hunter and the hunted probably suited them, for my mother by the time I first remembered her had developed an alert poise of the head and a wary trotting pace which reminded me of a gun-dog. I must be forgiven these memories of the past: at a funeral they are apt to come unbidden, there is so much waiting about.

Not many people attended the service, which took place at a famous crematorium, but there was that slight stirring of excited expectation which is never experienced at a graveside. Will the oven doors open? Will the coffin stick on the way to the flames? I heard a voice behind me saying in very clear old accents, "I was present once at a premature cremation."

It was, as I recognized, with some difficulty, from a photograph in the family album, my Aunt Augusta, who had arrived late, dressed rather as the late Queen Mary of beloved memory might have dressed if she had still been with us and had adapted herself a little bit towards the present mode. I was surprised by her brilliant red hair, monumentally piled, and her two big front teeth which gave her a vital Neanderthal air. Somebody said, "Hush," and a clergyman began a prayer which I believe he must have composed himself. I had never heard it at any other funeral service, and I have attended a great number in my time. A bank manager is expected to pay his last respects to every old client who is not as we say "in the red," and in any case I have a weakness for funerals. People are generally seen at their best on these occasions, serious and sober, and optimistic on the subject of personal immortality.

The funeral of my mother went without a hitch. The flowers were removed economically from the coffin, which at the touch of a button slid away from us out of sight. Afterwards in the troubled sunlight I shook hands with a number of nephews and nieces and cousins whom I hadn't seen for years and could not identify. It was understood that I had to wait for the ashes and wait I did, while the chimney of the crematorium gently smoked overhead.

"You must be Henry," Aunt Augusta said, gazing reflectively at me with her sea-deep blue eyes.

"Yes," I said, "and you must be Aunt Augusta."

"It's a very long time since I saw anything of your mother," Aunt Augusta told me. "I hope that her death was an easy one."

"Oh yes, you know, at her time of life—her heart just stopped. She died of old age."

"Old age? She was only twelve years older than I am," Aunt Augusta said accusingly.

We took a little walk together in the garden of the crematorium. A crematorium garden resembles a real garden about as much as a golf links resembles a genuine landscape. The lawns are too well cultivated and the trees too stiffly on parade: the urns resemble the little boxes containing sand where one tees up. "Tell me," Aunt Augusta said, "are you still at the bank?"

"No, I retired two years ago."

"Retired? A young man like you! For heaven's sake, what do you do with your time?"

"I cultivate dahlias, Aunt Augusta." She gave a regal right-about swing of a phantom bustle.

"Dahlias! Whatever would your father have said!"

"He took no interest in flowers, I know that. He always thought a garden was a waste of good building space. He would calculate how many bedrooms one above the other he could have fitted in. He was a very sleepy man."

"He needed bedrooms for more than sleep," my aunt said with a coarseness which surprised me.

"He slept in the oddest places. I remember once in the bathroom . . ."

"In a bedroom he did other things than sleep," she said. "You are the proof."

I began to understand why my parents had seen so little of Aunt Augusta. She had a temperament my mother would not have liked. My mother was far from being a puritan, but she wanted everything to be done or said at a suitable time. At meals we would talk about meals. Perhaps the price of food. If we went to the theatre we talked in the interval about the play—or other plays. At breakfast we spoke of the news. She was adept at guiding conversation back into the right channel if it strayed. She had a phrase, "My dear, this isn't the moment . . ." Perhaps in the bedroom, I found myself thinking, with something of Aunt Augusta's directness, she talked about love. That was why she couldn't bear my father sleeping in odd places, and, when I developed an interest in dahlias, she often warned me to forget about them during banking hours.

By the time we had finished our walk the ashes were ready for me. I had chosen a very classical urn in black steel, and I would have liked to assure myself that there had been no error, but they presented me with a package very neatly done up in brown paper with red paper seals which reminded me of a Christmas gift. "What are you going to do with it?" Aunt Augusta said.

"I thought of making a little throne for it among my dahlias."

"It will look a little bleak in winter."

"I hadn't considered that. I could always bring it indoors at that season."

"Backwards and forwards. My sister seems hardly likely to rest in peace."

"I'll think over it again."

"You are not married, are you?"

"No."

"Any children?"

"Of course not."

"There is always the question to whom you will bequeath my sister. I am likely to predecease you."

"One cannot think of everything at once."

"You could have left it here," Aunt Augusta said.

"I thought it would look well among the dahlias," I replied obstinately, for I had spent all the previous evening designing a simple plinth in good taste.

"*A chacun son goût,* " my aunt said with a surprisingly good French accent. I had never considered our family very cosmopolitan.

"Well, Aunt Augusta," I said at the gates of the crematorium (I was preparing to leave, for my garden called), "it's been many years since we saw each other . . . I hope . . ." I had left the lawn-mower outside, uncovered, and there was a hint of rain in the quick grey clouds overhead. "I would like it very much if one day you would take a cup of tea with me in Southwood."

"At the moment I would prefer something stronger and more tranquillizing. It is not every day one sees a sister consigned to the flames. Like La Pucelle."

"I don't quite . . ."

"Joan of Arc."

"I have some sherry at home, but it's rather a long ride and perhaps . . ."

"My apartment is at any rate north of the river," Aunt Augusta said firmly, "and I have everything we require." Without asking my assent she hailed a taxi. It was the first and perhaps, when I think back on it now, the most memorable of the journeys we were to take together.

I was quite right in my weather forecast. The grey clouds began to rain and I found myself preoccupied with my private worries. All along the shiny streets people were putting up umbrellas and taking shelter in the doorways of Burton's, the United Dairies, Mac Fisheries or the ABC. For some reason rain in the suburbs reminds me of a Sunday.

"What's on your mind?" Aunt Augusta said.

"It was so stupid of me. I left my lawn-mower out, on the lawn, uncovered."

My aunt showed me no sympathy. She said, "Forget your lawn-mower. It's odd how we seem to meet only at religious ceremonies. The last time I saw you was at your baptism. I was not asked but I came." She gave a croak of a laugh. "Like the wicked fairy."

"Why didn't they ask you?"

"I knew too much. About both of them. I remember you were far too quiet. You didn't yell the devil out. I wonder if he is still there?" She called to the driver, "Don't confuse the Place with the Square, the Crescent or the Gardens. I am the Place."

"I didn't know there was any breach. Your photograph was there in the family album."

9

"For appearances only." She gave a little sigh which drove out a puff of scented powder. "Your mother was a very saintly woman. She should by rights have had a white funeral. La Pucelle," she added again.

"I don't quite see ... La Pucelle means—well, to put it bluntly, *I* am here, Aunt Augusta."

"Yes. But you were your father's child. Not your mother's."

That morning I had been very excited, even exhilarated, by the thought of the funeral. Indeed, if it had not been my mother's, I would have found it a wholly desirable break in the daily routine of retirement, and I was pleasurably reminded of the old banking days, when I had paid the final adieu to so many admirable clients. But I had never contemplated such a break as this one which my aunt announced so casually. Hiccups are said to be cured by sudden shock and they can equally be caused by one. I hiccupped an incoherent question.

"I have said that your official mother was a saint. The girl, you see, refused to marry your father, who was anxious—if you can use such an energetic term in his case—to do the right thing. So my sister covered up for her by marrying him. (He was not very strongwilled.) Afterwards, she padded herself for months with progressive cushions. No one ever suspected. She even wore the cushions in bed, and she was so deeply shocked when your father tried once to make love to her—after the marriage but before your birth—that, even when you had been safely delivered, she refused him what the Church calls his rights. He was never a man in any case to stand on them."

I leant back hiccupping in the taxi. I couldn't have spoken if I had tried. I remembered all those pursuits up the scaffolding. Had they been caused then by my mother's jealousy or was it the apprehension that she might be required to pass again so many more months padded with cushions of assorted sizes?

"No," my aunt said to the taxi-driver, "these are the Gardens. I told you—I am the Place."

"Then I turn left, ma'am?"

"No. Right. On the left is the Crescent.

"This shouldn't come as a shock to you, Henry," Aunt Augusta said. "My sister—your stepmother—perhaps we should agree to call her that—was a very noble person indeed."

"And my—hic—father?"

"A bit of a hound, but so are most men. Perhaps it's their best quality. I hope you have a little bit of the hound in you too, Henry."

"I don't—huc—think so."

"We may discover it in time. You *are* your father's son. That hiccup is best cured by drinking out of the opposite rim of a glass. You can imitate a glass with your hand. Liquid is not a necessary part of the cure."

I drew a long free breath and asked, "Who was my mother, Aunt Augusta?" But she was already far away from that subject, speaking to the driver. "No, no, my man. This is the Crescent."

"You said turn *right*, lady."

"Then I apologize. It was my mistake. I am always a little uncertain about right and left. Port I can always remember because of the colour—red means left. You should have turned to port not starboard."

"I'm no bloody navigator, lady."

"Never mind. Just continue all the way round and start again. I take all the blame."

We drew up outside a public house. The driver said, "Ma'am if you had only told me it was the Crown and Anchor . . ."

"Henry," my aunt said, "if you could forget your hiccup for a moment."

"Huc?" I asked.

"It's six and six on the clock," the driver said.

"Then we will let it reach seven shillings," Aunt Augusta retorted. "Henry, I feel I ought perhaps to warn you before we go in that a white funeral in my case would have been quite out of place."

"But-you've-never-married," I said, very quickly to beat the hiccups.

"I have nearly always, during the last sixty or more years, had a friend," Aunt Augusta said. She added, perhaps because I looked incredulous, "Age, Henry, may a little modify our emotions—it does not destroy them."

Even those words did not prepare me properly for what I found next. My life in the bank had taught me, of course, to be unsurprised, even by the demand for startling overdrafts, and I had always made it a point neither to ask for nor to listen to any explanation. The overdraft was given or refused simply on the previous credit of the client. If I seem to the reader a somewhat static character he should appreciate the long conditioning of my career before retirement. My aunt, I was to discover, had never been conditioned by anything at all, and she had no intention of explaining more than she had already done.

CHAPTER 3

The Crown and Anchor was built like a bank in Georgian style. Through the windows I could see men with exaggerated moustaches in tweed coats, which were split horsily behind, gathered round a girl in jodhpurs. They were not the type to whom I would have extended much credit, and I doubted whether any of them, except the girl, had ever ridden a horse. They were all drinking bitter, and I had the impression that any spare cash they might have put aside went on tailors and hairdressers rather than equitation. A long experience with clients has made me prefer a shabby whisky-drinker to a well-dressed beer-drinker.

We went in by a side door. My aunt's apartment was on the second floor, and on the first floor there was a small sofa, which I learnt later had been bought my aunt so that she could take a little rest on the way up. It was typical of her generous nature that she had bought a sofa, which could barely be squeezed onto the landing, and not a chair for one. "I always take a little rest at this point. Come and sit down, too, Henry. The stairs are steep, though perhaps they don't seem so at your age." She looked at me critically. "You have certainly changed a lot since

13

I saw you last, though you haven't got much more hair."

"I've had it, but I've lost it," I explained.

"I have kept mine. I can still sit upon it." She added surprisingly, " 'Rapunzel, Rapunzel, let down your hair.' Not that I could have ever let it down from a second-floor flat."

"Aren't you disturbed by the noise from the bar?"

"Oh no. And the bar is very convenient if I suddenly run short. I just send Wordsworth down."

"Who is Wordsworth?"

"I call him Wordsworth because I can't bring myself to call him Zachary. All the eldest sons in his family have been called Zachary for generations—after Zachary Macaulay, who did so much for them on Clapham Common. The surname was adopted from the bishop not the poet."

"He's your valet?"

"Let us say he attends to my wants. A very gentle sweet strong person. But don't let him ask you for a CTC. He receives quite enough from me."

"What is a CTC?"

"That is what they called any tip or gift in Sierra Leone when he was a boy during the war. The initials belonged to Cape to Cairo cigarettes, which all the sailors handed out generously."

My aunt's conversation went too quickly for my understanding, so that I was not really prepared for the very large middle-aged Negro wearing a striped butcher's apron who opened the door when my aunt rang. "Why, Wordsworth," she said with a touch of coquetry, "you've been washing up breakfast without waiting for me." He stood there glaring at me, and I wondered whether he expected a CTC before he would let me pass.

"This is my nephew, Wordsworth," my aunt said.

"You be telling me whole truth, woman?"

"Of course I am. Oh, Wordsworth, Wordsworth!" she added with tender banter.

He let us in. The lights were on in the living-room, now that the day had darkened, and my eyes were dazzled for a moment by rays from the glass ornaments which flashed back from every open space. There were angels on the buffet wearing robes striped like peppermint rock; and in an alcove there was a Madonna with a gold face and a gold halo and a blue robe. On a sideboard on a gold stand stood a navy-blue goblet, large enough to hold at least four bottles of wine, with a gold trellis curled around the bowl on which pink roses grew and green ivy. There were mauve storks on the bookshelves and red swans and blue fish. Black girls in scarlet dresses held green candle sconces, and shining down on all this was a chandelier which might have been made out of sugar icing hung with pale-blue, pink, and yellow blossoms.

"Venice once meant a lot to me," my aunt said rather unnecessarily.

I don't pretend to be a judge of these things, but I thought the effect exaggerated and not in the best of taste.

"Such wonderful craftsmanship," my aunt said. "Wordsworth, be a dear and fetch us two whiskies. Augusta feels a teeny bit sad after the sad sad ceremony." She spoke to him as though he were a child—or a lover, but that relationship I was reluctant to accept.

"Everything go O.K.?" Wordsworth asked. "No bad medicine?"

"There was no contretemps," my aunt said. "Oh gracious, Henry, you haven't forgotten your parcel?"

"No, no, I have it here."

"I think perhaps Wordsworth had better put it in the refrigerator."

"Quite unnecessary, Aunt Augusta. Ashes don't deteriorate."

"No, I suppose not. How silly of me. But let Wordsworth put it in the kitchen just the same. We don't want to be reminded all the time of my poor sister. Now let me show you my room. I have more of my Venice treasures there."

She had indeed. Her dressing-table gleamed with them: mirrors and powder-jars and ash-trays and bowls for safety pins. "They brighten the darkest days," she said. There was a very large double-bed as curlicued as the glass. "I am especially attached to Venice," she explained, "because I began my real career there, and my travels. I have always been very fond of travel. It's a great grief to me that my travels now are curtailed."

"Age strikes us all before we know it," I said.

"Age? I was not referring to age. I hope I don't look all that decrepit, Henry, but I like having a companion and Wordsworth is very occupied now because he's studying to enter the London School of Economics. This is Wordsworth's snuggery," and she opened the door of an adjoining room. It was crowded with glass Disney figures and worse—all the grinning mice and cats and hares from inferior American cartoon films, blown with as much care as the chandelier.

"From Venice too," my aunt said, "clever but not so pretty. I thought them suitable, however, for a man's room."

"Does he like them?"

"He spends very little time there," my aunt said, "what with his studies and everything else . . ."

"I wouldn't like to wake up to them," I said.

"He seldom does."

My aunt led me back to the sitting-room, where Wordsworth had laid out three more Venetian glasses with gold rims and a water jug with colours mingled like marble. The bottle of Black Label looked normal and out of place, rather like the only man in a dinner-jacket at a fancy-dress party, a comparison which came at once to my mind because I have found myself several times in that uncomfortable situation, since I have rooted objection to dressing up.

Woodsworth said, "The telephone talk all the bloody time while you not here. Ar tell them you don gone to a very smart funeral."

"It's so convenient when one can tell the truth," my aunt said. "Was there no message?"

"Oh, poor old Wordsworth not understand one bloody word. Ar say to them you no talk English. They go away double quick."

My aunt poured out larger portions of whisky than I am accustomed to.

"A little more water please, Aunt Augusta."

"I can say now to both of you how relieved I am that everything went without a hitch. I once attended a very important funeral—the widow of a famous man of letters who had not been the most faithful of husbands. It was soon after the first great war had ended. I was living in Brighton, and I was very interested at that time in the Fabians. I had learnt about them from your father when I was a girl. I arrived early as a spectator and I was leaning over the Communion rail if you can call it that in a crematorium chapel—trying to make out the names on the wreaths. I was the first there, all alone with the flowers and the coffin. Wordsworth must forgive me for telling this story at such length—he has heard it before. Let me refresh your glass."

"No, no, Aunt Augusta. I have more than enough."

"Well, I suppose I was fumbling about a little too much and I must have accidentally touched a button. The coffin began to slide away, the doors opened, I could feel the hot air of the oven and hear the flap of the flames, the coffin went in and the doors closed, and at that very moment in walked the whole grand party, Mr. and Mrs. Bernard Shaw, Mr. H. G. Wells, Miss E. Nesbit (to use her maiden name), Doctor Havelock Ellis, Mr. Ramsay MacDonald, and the widower, while the clergyman (nondenominational of course) came through a door on the other side of the rail. Somebody began to play a humanist hymn by Edward Carpenter, 'Cosmos, O Cosmos, Cosmos shall we call Thee?' But there was no coffin."

"Whatever did you do, Aunt Augusta?"

"I buried my face in my handkerchief and simulated grief, but you know I don't think anyone (except, I suppose, the clergyman and he kept dumb about it) noticed that the coffin wasn't there. The widower certainly didn't, but then he hadn't noticed his wife for some years. Doctor Havelock Ellis made a very moving address (or so it seemed to me then: I hadn't finally plumped for Catholicism, though I was on the brink) about the dignity of a funeral service conducted without illusions or rhetoric. He could truthfully have said without a corpse too. Everybody was quite satisfied. You can understand why I was very careful this morning not to fumble."

I looked at my aunt surreptitiously over the whisky. I didn't know what to say. "How sad" seemed inappropriate. I wondered whether the funeral had ever really taken place, though in the months that followed I was to realize that my aunt's stories were always basically true—only minor details might sometimes be added to compose a picture. Wordsworth found the right words for me. He said, "We must allays go careful careful at a funeral." He added, "In Mendeland—ma first wife she was Mende—they go open deceased person's back an they go take out the spleen. If spleen be too big, then deceased person was a witch an everyone mock the whole family and lef the funeral double quick. That happen to ma wife's pa. He dead of malaria, but these ignorant people they don know malaria make the spleen big. So ma wife and her ma they go right away from Mendeland and come to Freetown. They don wan to be mocked by the neighbours."

"There must be a great many witches in Mendeland," my aunt said.

"Ya'as, sure thing there are. Plenty too many."

I said, "I really think I must be going now, Aunt Augusta. I can't keep my mind off the mowing-machine. It will be quite rusted in this rain."

"Will you miss your mother, Henry?"

"Oh yes ... yes," I said. I hadn't really thought about it, so occupied had I been with all the arrangements for the funeral, the interviews with her solicitor, with her bank manager, with an estate agent arranging for the sale of her little house in North London. It is difficult too for a single man to know how to dispose of all the female trappings. Furniture can be auctioned, but what can one do with all the unfashionable underclothes of an old lady, the half-empty pots of old-fashioned cream? I asked my aunt.

"I am afraid I didn't share your mother's taste in clothes, or even in cold cream. I would give them to her daily maid on condition she takes everything—everything."

"It has made me so happy meeting you, Aunt Augusta. You are my only close relative now."

"As far as you know," she said. "Your father had spells of activity."

"My poor stepmother ... I shall never be able to think of anyone else as my mother."

"Better so."

"In a new block under construction my father was always very careful about furnishing the specimen flat. I used to think that sometimes he went to sleep in it in the afternoon. I suppose it might have been in one of those I was ..." I checked the word "conceived" in deference to my aunt.

"Better not to speculate," she said.

"You will come one day and see my dahlias, won't you? They are in full bloom."

"Of course, Henry, now that I have found you again I shan't easily let you go. Do you enjoy travel?"

"I've never had the opportunity."

"With Wordsworth so occupied we might make a little trip or two together."

"Gladly, Aunt Augusta." It never occurred to me that she meant farther than the seaside.

"I will telephone you," my aunt said.

Wordsworth showed me to the door, and it was only outside, when I passed the Crown and Anchor, that I remembered I had left behind my little package. I wouldn't have remembered at all if the girl in the jodhpurs had not said angrily as I pushed past the open window, "Peter can talk about nothing but cricket. All the summer it went on. Nothing but the fucking Ashes."

I don't like to hear such adjectives on the lips of an attractive young girl, but her words reminded me sharply that I had left all that remained of my mother in Aunt Augusta's kitchen. I went back to the street door. There was a row of bells with a kind of microphone above each of them. I touched the right one and heard Wordsworth's voice. "Who be there?"

I said, "It's Henry Pulling."

"Don know anyone called that name."

"I've only just left you. I'm Aunt Augusta's nephew."

"Oh, that guy," the voice said.

"I left a parcel with you in the kitchen."

"You wan it back?"

"Please, if it's not too much trouble . . ."

Human communication, it sometimes seems to me, involves an exaggerated amount of time. How briefly and to the point people always seem to speak on the stage or on the screen, while in real life we stumble from phrase to phrase with endless repetition.

"A brown-paper parcel?" Woodsworth's voice asked.
"Yes."

"You wan me bring it down right away?"

"Yes, if it's not too much . . ."

"It's a bloody lot of trouble," Wordworth said.
"Stay there."

I was prepared to be very cold to him when he
brought the parcel, but he opened the street door
wearing a friendly grin.

"Thank you," I said, with as much coldness as I
could muster, "for the great trouble you have taken."

I noticed that the parcel was no longer sealed.
"Has somebody opened this?"

"Ar jus wan to see what you got there."

"You might have asked me."

"Why, man," he said, "you not offended at Wordsworth?"

"I didn't like the way you spoke just now."

"Man, it's jus that little mike there. Ar wan to
make it say all kind of rude things. There ar am up
there, and down there ma voice is, popping out into
the street where no one see it's only old Wordsworth.
It's a sort of power, man. Like the burning bush when
he spoke to old Moses. One day it was the parson
come from Saint George's in the square. An he says in
a dear brethren sort of voice, 'I wonder, Miss Bertram, if I could come up and have a little chat about
our bazaar.' 'Sure, man,' ar say, 'you wearing your
dog collar?' 'Why, yes,' he say, 'of course, who is that?'
'Man,' ar say, 'you better put on a muzzle too before
you come up here.' "

"What did he say?"

"He wen away and never come back. Your auntie
laugh like hell when ar told her. But ar didn't mean
him harm. It was just old Wordsworth tempted by
that little old mike."

"Are you really studying for the London School of
Economics?" I asked.

"Oh, tha's a joke your auntie makes. Ar was workin at the Grenada Palace. Ar had a uniform. Jus lak a-general. She lak ma uniform. She stop an say, 'Are you the Emperor Jones?' 'No, ma'am,' I say, 'arm only old Wordsworth.' 'Oh,' she say, 'thou child of joy, shout round me, let me hear thy shouts, thou happy shepherd boy.' 'You write that down for me,' ar say. 'It sound good. Ar like it.' Ar say it over and over. Ar know it now good lak a hymn."

I was a little confused by his garrulity. "Well, Wordsworth," I said, "thank you for all your trouble and I hope one day I shall see you again."

"This here mighty important parcel?"

"Yes. I suppose it is."

"Then ar think you owe a dash to old Wordsworth," he said.

"A dash?"

"A CTC."

Remembering what my aunt had told me, I went quickly away.

Just as I had expected, my new lawn-mower was wet all over: I dried it carefully and oiled the blades before I did anything else. Then I boiled myself two eggs and made a cup of tea for lunch. I had much to think about. Could I accept my aunt's story and in that case who was my mother? I tried to remember the friends my mother had of her own age, but what was the good of that? The friendship would have been broken before my birth. If indeed she had been only a stepmother to me, did I still want to place her ashes among my dahlias? While I washed up my lunch I was sorely tempted to wash out the urn as well into the sink. It would serve very well for the home-made jam which I was promising myself to make next year—a man in retirement must have his hobbies if he is not to age too fast—and the urn would have looked quite handsome on the tea table. It was a little sombre, but a sombre jar was well suited for damson jelly or for blackberry-and-apple jam. I was seriously tempted, but I remembered how kind my stepmother had been to me in her rather stern way when I was a child, and how could I tell that my aunt was speaking the truth? So I went out into the garden and chose a spot among the dahlias where the plinth could be built.

CHAPTER 4

I was weeding the dahlias, the Polar Beauties and the Golden Leaders and the Requiems, when my telephone began to ring. Being unused to the sound which shattered all the peace of my little garden, I assumed that it was a wrong number. I had very few friends, although before my retirement I boasted a great many acquaintances. There were clients who had stayed with me for twenty years, who had known me in the same branch as clerk, cashier and manager, and yet they remained acquaintances. It is rare for a manager to be promoted from the staff of a branch in which he will have to exercise authority, but there were special circumstances in my case. I had been acting manager for nearly a year owing to my predecessor's illness, and one of my clients was a very important depositor who had taken a fancy to me. He threatened to remove his custom if I did not remain in charge. His name was Sir Alfred Keene: he had made a fortune in cement, and my father having been a builder gave us an interest in common. He would invite me to dinner at least three times a year and he always consulted me on his investments, though he never took my advice. He said it helped him to make up his mind. He had an unmarried daughter called Barbara, who was interested in tatting, which I think she must have given to the church bazaar. She was always very kind to me, and my mother suggested I might pay her attentions, for she would certainly inherit Sir Alfred's money, but the motive seemed to me a dishonest one and in my case I have never been greatly interested in women. The bank was then my whole life, and now there were my dahlias.

Unfortunately Sir Alfred died a little before my retirement, and Miss Keene went to South Africa to live. I was intimately concerned, of course, with all her currency difficulties: it was I who wrote to the Bank of England for this permit or that and reminded them constantly that I had received no reply to my letters of the 9th ult.; and on her last night in England, before she caught her boat at Southampton, she asked me to dinner. It was a sad occasion without Sir Alfred, who had been a very jovial man, laughing immoderately even at his own jokes. Miss Keene asked me to look after the drinks and I chose an Amontillado, and for dinner Sir Alfred's favourite Chambertin. The house was one of those big Southwood mansions surrounded by rhododendron bushes which dripped that night with the steady slow November rain. There was an oil painting of a fishing boat in a storm after Van de Velde over Sir Alfred's place at the dining-room table, and I expressed the hope that Miss Keene's voyage would be less turbulent.

"I have sold the house as it stands with all the furniture," she told me. "I shall live with second cousins."

"Do you know them well?" I asked.

"I have never seen them," she said. "They are once removed. We have only exchanged letters. The stamps are like foreign stamps. With no portrait of the Queen."

"You will have the sun," I encouraged her.

"Do you know South Africa?"

"I have seldom been out of England," I said. "Once when I was a young man I went with a school friend to Spain, but my stomach was upset by the shell-fish—or perhaps it was the oil."

"My father was a very overpowering personality," she said. "I never had friends—except you, of course, Mr. Pulling."

It is astonishing to me now how nearly I came to proposing marriage that night and yet I refrained. Our interests were different, of course—tatting and dahlias have nothing in common, unless perhaps they are both the interests of rather lonely people. Rumours of the great bank merger had already reached me. My retirement was imminent, and I was well aware that the friendships I had made with my other clients would not long survive it. If I had spoken would she have accepted me?—it was quite possible. Our ages were suitable, she was approaching forty and I would soon be half way through the fifth decade, and I knew my mother would have approved. How different everything might have been if I had spoken then. I would never have heard the disturbing story of my birth, for she would have accompanied me to the funeral and my aunt would not have spoken in her presence. I would never have travelled with my aunt. I would have been saved from much, though I suppose I would have missed much too. Miss Keene said, "I shall be living near Koffiefontein."

"Where is that?"

"I don't really know. Listen. It's raining cats and dogs."

We got up and moved into the drawing-room for coffee. There was a Venetian scene copied from Canaletto on the wall. All the pictures in the house seemed to represent foreign parts, and she was leaving for Koffiefontein. I would never travel so far, I thought then, and I wished that she was staying here, in Southwood.

"It seems a very long way to go," I said.

"If there was anything to keep me here . . . Will you take one lump or two?"

"No sugar, thank you." Was it an invitation for me to speak? I have always asked myself since. I didn't love her, and she certainly didn't love me, but perhaps in a way we could have made a life together. I heard from her a year later; she wrote, "Dear Mr. Pulling, I wonder how Southwood is and whether it's raining. We are having a beautiful sunny winter. My cousins have a small (!) farm of ten thousand acres and they think nothing of driving seven hundred miles to buy a ram. I am not quite used to things yet and I think often of Southwood. How are the dahlias? I have given up tatting. We lead a very open-air existence."

I replied and gave her what news I could, but I had retired by then and was no longer at the centre of Southwood life. I told her of my mother's failing health and how the dahlias were doing. There was a rather gloomy variety in royal purple called Deuil du Roy Albert which had not been a success. I was not sorry. It was an odd name to give a flower. My Ben Hurs were flourishing.

I had neglected the telephone, feeling so sure that it was a wrong number, but when the ringing persisted, I left my dahlias and went in.

The telephone stood on the filing cabinet where I keep my accounts and all the correspondence which my mother's death caused. I had not received as many letters as I was receiving now since I ceased to be manager: the solicitor's letters, letters from the undertaker, from the Inland Revenue, the crematorium fees, the doctor's bills, National Health forms, even a few letters of condolence. I could almost believe myself a business-man again.

My aunt's voice said, "You are very slow to answer."

"I was busy in the garden."

"How was the mowing-machine, by the way?"

"Very wet, but no irreparable damage."

"I have an extraordinary story to tell you," my aunt said. "I have been raided by the police."

"*Raided* . . . by the police?"

"Yes, you must listen carefully for they may call on *you*."

"What on earth for?"

"You still have your mother's ashes?"

"Of course."

"Because they want to see them. They may even want to analyse them."

"But Aunt Augusta . . . you must tell me exactly what happened."

"I am trying to, but you continually interrupt with unhelpful exclamations. It was midnight and Wordsworth and I had gone to bed. Luckily I was wearing my best nightdress. They rang the bell down below and told us through the microphone that they were police officers and had a warrant to search the flat. 'What for?' I asked. Do you know, for a moment I thought it might be something racial. There are so many rules now for races and against races that you don't know where you stand."

"Are you sure they were police officers?"

"Of course, I asked to see their warrant, but do you know what a warrant looks like? For all I know it might have been a reader's ticket to the British Museum library. I let them in, though, because they were polite, and one of them, the one in uniform, was tall and good-looking. They were rather surprised by Wordsworth—or perhaps it was the colour of his pyjamas. They said, 'Is this your husband, ma'am?' I said, 'No, this is Wordsworth.' The name seemed to ring a bell with one of them—the young man in uniform—who kept on glancing at him surreptitiously, as though he were trying to remember."

"But what were they looking for?"

"They said they had reliable information that drugs were kept on the premises."

"Oh, Aunt Augusta, you don't think Wordsworth . . ."

"Of course not. They took away all the fluff from the seams of his pockets, and then the truth came out. They asked him what was in the brown-paper package which he was seen handing to a man who had been loitering in the street. Poor Wordsworth said he didn't know, so I chipped in and said it was my sister's ashes. I don't know why, but they became suspicious of me at once. The elder, who was in plain clothes, said, 'Please don't be flippant, ma'am. It doesn't exactly help.' I said, 'As far as my sense of humour goes, there is nothing whatever flippant in my dead sister's ashes.' 'A sort of powder, ma'am?' the younger policeman asked—he was the sharper of the two, the one who thought he knew the name of Wordsworth. 'You can call it that if you like,' I said, 'grey powder, human powder,' and they looked as though they had won a point. 'And who was the man who received this powder?' the man in plain clothes asked. 'My nephew,' I said. 'My sister's son.' I saw no reason to go into that old story which I told you yesterday with members of the Metropolitan Police. Then they asked for your address and I gave it to them. The sharp one said, 'Was the powder for his private use?' 'He wants to put it amongst his dahlias,' I said. They made a very thorough search, especially in Wordsworth's room, and they took away samples of all the cigarettes they could find, and some aspirins I had left in a cachet box. Then they said, 'Good night, ma'am,' very politely and left. Wordsworth had to go downstairs and open the door for them, and just before he left the sharp one said to him, 'What's your first name?' 'Zachary,' Wordsworth told him and he went out looking puzzled."

"What a very strange thing to have happened," I said.

"They even read some letters and asked who Abdul was."

"Who was he?"

"Someone I knew a very long time ago. Luckily I had kept the envelope and it was marked Tunis, February, 1924. Otherwise they would have read all sorts of things into it about the present."

"I am sorry, Aunt Augusta. It must have been a terrifying experience."

"It was amusing in a way. But it did give me a guilty feeling . . ."

There was a ring from the front door and I said, "Hold on a moment, Aunt Augusta." I looked through the dining-room window and saw a policeman's helmet. I returned and said, "Your friends are here."

"Already?"

"I'll ring you back when they've gone."

It was the first time I had ever been called on by the police. There was a short middle-aged man in a soft hat with a rough but kindly face and a broken nose and the tall good-looking young man in uniform. "Mr. Pulling?" the detective asked.

"Yes."

"May we come in for a few moments?"

"Have you a warrant?" I asked.

"Oh no, no, it hasn't come to that. We just want to have a word or two with you." I wanted to say something about the Gestapo, but I thought it wiser not. I led them into the dining-room, but I didn't ask them to sit down. The detective showed me an identity card and I read on it that he was Detective-Sergeant Sparrow, John.

"You know a man called Wordsworth, Mr. Pulling?"

"Yes, he's a friend of my aunt's."

"Did you receive a package from him in the street yesterday?"

"I certainly did."

"Would you have any objection to our examining the package, Mr. Pulling?"

"I most certainly would."

"You know, sir, we could easily have obtained a search warrant, but we want to do things delicately. Have you known this man Wordsworth a long time?"

"I met him for the first time yesterday."

"Perhaps, sir, he asked you as a favour to deliver that package and you, seeing no harm at all in that and him being an employee of your aunt . . ."

"I don't know what you are talking about. The package is mine. I had accidentally left it in the kitchen."

"The package is yours, sir? You admit that."

"You know very well what's in the package. My aunt told you. It's an urn with my mother's ashes."

"Your aunt has been in communication with you, has she?"

"Yes, she has. What do you expect? Waking up an old lady in the middle of the night."

"It had only just gone twelve, sir. And so those ashes . . . They are Mrs. Pulling's?"

"There they are. You can see for yourself. On the bookcase."

I had put the urn there temporarily, until I was ready to bed it, above a complete set of Sir Walter Scott which I had inherited from my father. In his lazy way my father was a great reader, though not an adventurous one. He was satisfied with possessing a very few favourite authors. By the time he had read

the set of Scott through he had forgotten the earlier
volumes and was content to begin again with *Guy
Mannering*. He had a complete set too of Marion
Crawford, and he had a love of nineteenth-century
poetry which I have inherited—Tennyson and Wordsworth and Browning and Palgrave's *Golden Treasury*.

"Do you mind if I take a look?" the detective
asked, but naturally he couldn't open the urn. "It's
sealed," he said. "With Scotch tape."

"Naturally. Even a tin of biscuits . . ."

"I would like to take a sample for analysis."

I was becoming rather cross by this time. I said, "If
you think I am going to let you play around with my
poor mother in a police laboratory . . ."

"I can understand how you feel, sir," he said, "but
we have rather serious evidence to go on. We took
some fluff from the man Wordsworth's pockets and
when analysed it contained pot."

"Pot?"

"Marijuana to you, sir. Likewise Cannabis."

"Wordsworth's fluff has got nothing to do with my
mother."

"We could get a warrant, sir, easily enough, but
seeing how you may be an innocent dupe, I would
rather take the urn away temporarily with your permission. It would sound much better that way in
court."

"You can check with the crematorium. The funeral
was only yesterday."

"We have already, sir, but you see it's quite possible—don't think I'm presuming to suggest your line
of defence, that's a matter entirely for your counsel—
that the man Wordsworth took out the ashes and
substituted pot. He may have known he was being
watched. Now wouldn't it be much better, sir, from
all points of view to know for certain that these are
your mother's ashes? Your aunt told us you planned

to keep it in your garden—you wouldn't want to see that urn every day and wonder, Are those really the ashes of the dear departed or are they an illegal supply of marijuana?"

He had a very sympathetic manner, and I really began to see his point.

"We'd only take out a tiny pinch, sir, less than a teaspoonful. We'd treat the rest with all due reverence."

"All right," I said, "Take your pinch. I suppose you are only doing your duty." The young policeman had been making notes all the time. The detective said, "take a note that Mr. Pulling behaved most helpfully and that he voluntarily surrendered the urn. That will sound well in court, sir, if the worst happens."

"When will I get the urn back?"

"Not later than tomorrow—if all is as it should be." He shook hands quite cordially as if he believed in my innocence, but perhaps that was just his professional manner.

Of course I hastened to telephone to my aunt. "They've taken away the urn," I said. "They think my mother's ashes are marijuana. Where's Wordsworth?"

"He went out after breakfast and hasn't come back."

"They found marijuana dust in the fluff of his suit."

"Oh dear, how careless of the poor boy. I thought he was a little disturbed. And he asked for a CTC before he went out."

"Did you give him one?"

"Well, you know, I'm really very fond of him, and he said it was his birthday. He never had a birthday last year, so I gave him twenty pounds."

"Twenty pounds! I never keep as much as that in the house."

"It will get him as far as Paris. He left in time for the Golden Arrow, now I come to think of it, and he always carries his passport to prove he's not an illegal immigrant. Do you know, Henry, I've a great desire for a little sea air myself."

"You'll never find him in Paris."

"I wasn't thinking of Paris. I was thinking of Istanbul."

"Istanbul is not on the sea."

"I think you are wrong. There's something called the Sea of Marmara."

"Why Istanbul?"

"I was reminded of it by that letter from Abdul the police found. A strange coincidence. First that letter and then this morning in the post another—the first for a very long time."

"From Abdul?"

"Yes."

It was weak of me, but I did not then realize the depth of my aunt's passion for travel. If I had I would have hesitated before I made the first fatal proposal: "I have nothing particular to do today. If you would like to go to Brighton . . ."

CHAPTER 5

Brighton was the first real journey I undertook in my aunt's company and proved a bizarre foretaste of much that was to follow.

We arrived in the early evening, for we had decided to spend the night. I was surprised by the smallness of her luggage, which consisted only of a little white leather cosmetics case which she called her *baise en ville*. I find it difficult myself to go away for a night without a rather heavy suitcase, for I am uneasy if I have not at least one change of suit and that entails also a change of shoes. A change of shirt, a change of underclothes and of socks are almost an essential to me, and taking into consideration the vagaries of the English climate, I like to take some woollens just in case. My aunt looked askance at my suitcase and said, "We must take a cab. I had hoped we could walk."

I had booked our rooms at the Royal Albion because my aunt wished to be near the Palace Pier and the Old Steine. She told me, incorrectly I think, that this was named after the wicked marquess of *Vanity Fair*. "I like to be at the centre of all the devilry," she said, "with the buses going off to all those places." She spoke as though their destinations were Sodom and Gomorrah rather than Lewes and Patcham and Littlehampton and Shoreham. Apparently she had come first to Brighton when she was quite a young woman, full of expectations which I am afraid were partly fulfilled.

I thought I would have a bath and a glass of sherry, a quiet dinner in the grill, and an early bedtime, so that we would both be rested for a strenuous morning on the front and in the Lanes, but my aunt disagreed. "We don't want dinner for another two hours," she said, "and first I want you to meet Hatty if Hatty's still alive."

"Who is Hatty?"

"We worked together once with a gentleman called Mr. Curran."

"How long ago was that?"

"Forty years or more."

"Then it seems unlikely . . ."

"*I* am here," Aunt Augusta said firmly, "and I got a card from her the Christmas before last."

It was a grey leaden evening with an east wind blowing on our backs from Kemp Town. The sea was rising and the pebbles turned and ground under the receding waves. Ex-President Nkrumah looked out at us from the window of the waxworks, wearing a grey suit with a Chinese collar. My aunt paused and regarded him, I thought a little sadly. "I wonder where Wordsworth is now," she said.

"I expect you'll hear from him soon."

"I very much doubt it," she said. "My dear Henry," she added, "at my age one has ceased to expect a relationship to last. Think how complicated life would be if I had kept in touch with all the men I have known intimately. Some died, some I left, a few have left me. If they were all with me now we would have to take over a whole wing of the Royal Albion. I was very fond of Wordsworth while he lasted, but my emotions are not as strong as they once were. I can support his absence, though I may regret him for a while tonight. His knackers were superb." The wind took my hat and tossed it against a lamp-post. I was too surprised by her vulgarity to catch it, and my aunt laughed like a young woman. I returned, brushing it down, but Aunt Augusta still lingered at the waxworks.

"It's a kind of immortality," she said.

"What is?"

"I don't mean the waxworks here in Brighton, they are rather a job lot, but in Madame Tussaud's. With Crippen and the Queen."

"I'd rather have my portrait painted."

"But you can't see all round a portrait, and at Tussaud's they take some of your own clothes to dress you in, or so I've read. There's a blue dress of mine I could easily spare. . . . Oh well," she said with a sigh, "it's unlikely I'll ever be famous like that. Idle dreams . . ." She walked on, I thought a little cast down. "Criminals," she said, "and queens and politicians. Love is not highly regarded, except for Nell Gwynn and the Brides in the Bath."

We came to the saloon doors of the Star and Garter and my aunt suggested that we take a drink. The walls were covered with inscriptions of a philosophic character: *Life is a one-way street and there's no coming back; Marriage is a great Institution for those who like Institutions; You will never persuade a mouse that a black cat is lucky*. There were old programmes too and photographs. I ordered a sherry and my aunt said she would like a port and brandy. When I turned round from the bar I saw her examining a yellowed photograph. There was an elephant and two performing dogs drawn up in front of the Palace Pier behind a stout man in a tail-coat wearing a top hat and a watch chain, and a shapely young woman in tights stood beside him carrying a carriage whip. "There's Curran," my aunt said. "That's how it all began." She pointed at the young woman. "And there's Hatty. Those were the days."

"Surely you never worked in a circus, Aunt Augusta?"

"Oh no, but I happened to be there when the elephant trod on Curran's toe, and we became very close friends. Poor man, he had to go to hospital, and when he came out, the circus had gone on without him to Weymouth. Hatty too, though she came back later when we were established."

"Established at what?"

"I'll tell you one day, but now we have to find Hatty." She drained her port and brandy, and out we went into the cold blow of the wind. Just opposite was a stationer's which sold comic postcards and she stopped there to inquire: the metal stands for the cards rattled and strained and turned like a windmill. I noticed a card with a bottle of Guinness on it, and a fat woman in a snorkel floating face down. The legend read *Bottoms Up!* I was looking at another of a man in hospital saying to a surgeon, *"But I said circumcision, doctor,"* when my aunt came out. "It's just here," she said. "I knew I wasn't far wrong," and in the window of the very next house a card in front of some net curtains read HATTY'S TEAPOT. BY APPOINTMENT ONLY. There were photographs by the door of Marilyn Monroe and Frank Sinatra and the Duke of Edinburgh which seemed to have been signed by their subjects, although it seemed unlikely in the case of the Duke.

We rang the bell and an old lady answered it. She was wearing a black evening dress and a lot of jet objects jangled when she moved. "You're too late," she said sharply.

"Hatty," said my aunt.

"I close at six-thirty sharp except by special appointment."

"Hatty, it's Augusta."

"Augusta!"

"Hatty! You haven't changed a bit."

But remembering the young girl in tights carrying the whip and looking sideways at Curran, I thought there had been greater changes than my aunt made out.

"This is my nephew Henry, Hatty. You remember about *him*." They exchanged a look which I found disturbing. Why should I have been discussed all those years ago? Had she let Hatty into the secret of my birth?

"Come on in, the two of you. I was just going to have a cup of tea—an unprofessional cup of tea," Hatty added and giggled.

"In here?" my aunt asked, opening a door.

"No dear, that's the waiting-room." I just had time to see an engraving by Sir Alma-Tadema of a lot of tall naked ladies in a Roman bathhouse.

"Here's my den, dear," Hatty said, opening another door. It was a small overcrowded room, and everything seemed to be covered with fringed mauve shawls, the table, the backs of chairs, the mantel—there was even a shawl dangling from a studio portrait of a stout man whom I recognized as Mr. Curran.

"The Revered," Aunt Augusta said, looking at it.

"The Revered," Hatty repeated, and then they both laughed at some secret joke of their own.

"The Rev. for short," Aunt Augusta said, "but that, of course, was only a coincidence. You remember how we explained it to the police. They've still got a photo of him, Hatty, stuck up in the Star and Garter."

"I haven't been there for years," Hatty said. "I'm off the hard liquor."

"You are there and the elephant too," Aunt Augusta said. "Can you remember the elephant's name?"

Hatty was putting out two more cups from a china

cabinet. There was a fringed shawl over that too. She said, "It wasn't a common name like Jumbo. Something classical. How one forgets things, Augusta, at our age."

"Was it Caesar?"

"No, it wasn't Caesar. Do you take sugar, Mr.—?"

"Call him Henry, Hatty."

"One lump," I said.

"Oh dear, oh dear, I had such a good memory once."

"The water's boiling, dear."

The kettle was on a spirit ring close to a big brown teapot. She began to pour out.

"Oh, I quite forgot the strainer," she said.

"Never mind, Hatty."

"It's because of my clients. I never strain theirs, so I forget when I'm alone."

There was a plate of ginger-snaps and I accepted one for politeness' sake. "From the Old Steine," Aunt Augusta told me. "Ye Olde Bunne Shoppe. You don't get ginger-snaps like that anywhere else in the world."

"And now they have turned it into a betting shop," Hatty said. "Pluto, dear? Was it Pluto?"

"No, I'm sure it wasn't Pluto. I think it began with a T."

"I can't think of anything classical beginning with T."

"There was a point to his name."

"There certainly was."

"Historical."

"Yes."

"You remember the dogs, dear. They are in the photo too."

"It was them gave Curran the idea."

"The Revered," Aunt Augusta repeated again, and they laughed in unison at their private memory. I felt very much alone, so I took another ginger-snap.

"The boy has a sweet tooth," Hatty remarked.

"To think that little shop in the Old Steine survived two great wars."

"We've survived," Hatty replied, "but they aren't turning us into betting shops."

"Oh, it will need an atom bomb to destroy *us*," Aunt Augusta said.

I thought it was time to speak. "The situation in the Middle East is pretty serious," I said, "judging from today's *Guardian*."

"You can never tell," Hatty said, and they were both for a while buried in thought. Then my aunt picked out a tealeaf, put it on the back of her hand and slapped it with the other; it clung obstinately to a vein which was surrounded by what my mother used to call grave-marks.

"Can't get rid of the fellow," Aunt Augusta said. "I hope he's tall and handsome."

"That isn't a stranger," Hatty corrected her. "That's the thought of a departed you can't get out of your mind."

"Living or dead?"

"It could be either. How stiff does he feel?"

"If he's living I suppose it could be poor Wordsworth."

"Wordsworth is dead, dear," Hatty said, "a very long time ago."

"Not my Wordsworth. It's stiff as wood. I wonder who a dead one could be."

"Poor Curran perhaps."

"I have thought a lot about him since I came to Brighton."

"Would you like me to do a professional cup, dear, for you and your friend?"

"Nephew," Aunt Augusta corrected Hatty in her turn. "It would be fun, dear."

"I'll make another pot. The leaves have to be fresh and I use Lapsang Souchong professionally, though I drink Ceylon—Lapsang give big leaves and good results."

When she came back after washing the pot and our cups my aunt said, "You must let us pay."

"I wouldn't dream of it, dear, not after all we've been through together."

"With the Revered." They giggled again.

Hatty poured in the boiling water. She said, "I don't let the pot draw. The leaves speak better fresh." She filled our cups. "Now toss the tea away, dear, in this basin."

"I've got it," my aunt said. "Hannibal."

"Who's Hannibal?"

"The elephant that trod on Curran's toe."

"I do believe you're right, dear."

"I was watching the tea and it came to me suddenly in a flash."

"I often notice that with the leaves. Things come back. You are watching the leaves and things come back."

"I suppose Hannibal's dead too."

"You can't tell, dear, with elephants."

She picked up my aunt's cup and studied it closely. "It's interesting," she said, "very interesting."

"Bad or good?"

"A bit of both."

"Just tell me the good."

"You are going to do a lot of travelling. With another person. You are going to cross the ocean. You are going to have many adventures."

"With men?"

"That the leaves don't say, dear, but knowing you as I do, it wouldn't surprise me. You will be in danger of your life and liberty on more than one occasion."

"But I'll come through?"

"I see a knife—or it might be a syringe."

"Or it could be something else, Hatty—you know what I mean?"

"There is some mystery in your life."

"That's nothing new."

"I see a lot of confusion—a lot of running about this way and that. I'm sorry, Augusta, but I can't see any peace at the close. There's a cross. Perhaps you find religion. Or it could be a doublecross."

"I've always been interested in religion," my aunt said, "ever since Curran."

"Or it could be a bird, of course—a vulture perhaps. Keep away from deserts." Hatty gave a sigh. "Things don't come to me so easily as they once did. I exhaust myself with strangers."

"But you'll take one look at Henry's cup too, dear, won't you? Just one look."

She poured my tea away and looked in the cup. "Men are difficult," she said. "They have so many occupations beyond a woman's knowledge and that affects the interpretation. I had a client once who said he was a bevel-edger. I don't know what he meant. Are you an undertaker?"

"No."

"There's something that looks like an urn. Do you see it there? On the left of the handle. That's the recent past."

"It might be an urn," I said, looking.

"You will do a lot of travelling."

"That's not very likely. I've always been rather stay-at-home. It's quite an adventure for me coming as far as Brighton."

"It's in the future you're going to travel. Across the ocean. With a lady friend."

"Perhaps he's coming with me," Aunt Augusta said.

"It's possible. The leaves don't lie. There's a round thing like a target. There's a mystery in your life too."

"I've only just discovered that," I said.

"I see a lot of confusion too and running about. Just like in Augusta's cup."

"That's most unlikely," I said. "I lead a very regular life. A game of bridge once a week at the Conservative Club. And my garden, of course. My dahlias."

"The target might be a flower," Hatty admitted. "Forgive me. I'm tired. I'm afraid it was not a very good reading."

"It was most interesting," I told her for politeness' sake. "But of course, I'm no believer."

"Have another ginger-snap," Hatty said.

CHAPTER 6

We had dinner that night at the Cricketers', a small public house nearly opposite a second-hand bookseller, where I saw a complete set of Thackeray for sale at a very reasonable price. I thought it would go well on my shelves below my father's edition of the Waverley novels. Perhaps tomorrow I would come back and buy it. The thought gave me a warm feeling towards my father, a sense of something in common. I too would start at Volume I and continue to the end, and by the time that last volume was finished it would be time to begin again. Too many books by too many authors can be confusing, like too many shirts and suits. I like to change my clothes as little as possible. I suppose some people would say the same of my ideas, but the bank had taught me to be wary of whims. Whims so often end in bankruptcy.

When I wrote that we had dinner at the Cricketers', it would have been more correct to say we ate a substantial snack. There were baskets of warm sausages on the bar, and we helped ourselves and washed the sausages down with draught Guinness. I was surprised by the number of glasses my aunt could put down and feared a little for her blood pressure.

After her second pint she said, "It was odd about that cross. In the leaves I mean. I've always been interested in religion—ever since I knew Curran."

"What church do you attend?" I asked. "Didn't you tell me you were a Roman Catholic?"

"I call myself that for convenience," she said. "It belongs to my French and Italian periods. After I left Curran. I suppose he had influenced me, and then all the girls I knew were Catholic and I didn't like to look superior. I expect you'd be surprised to hear that we ran a church once ourselves—me and Curran, here in Brighton."

" 'Ran'? I don't understand."

"It was the performing dogs that gave us the idea. Two of them came to see Curran in hospital before the circus moved on. It was visiting day and there were a lot of women around to see their husbands. At first the dogs weren't allowed into the ward. There was quite a fuss, but Curran got round matron, telling her they weren't ordinary dogs, they were human dogs. Bathed in disinfectant they were, he told her, every dog, before they were allowed to give a performance. It wasn't true, of course, but he was very convincing. They came up to the bed, wearing their pointed hats and pierrot collars, and each gave Curran a paw to shake and touched his face with its nose like an Eskimo. Then they were taken quickly away in case the doctor might appear. You should have heard those women. 'The darlings, the sweet little doggies.' It was lucky neither of them had raised a leg. 'Just like humans.' One woman said, 'You can't tell me that dogs haven't got souls.' Another one asked, 'Are they gentleman doggies or lady doggies?' as though she had been too refined to look. 'One of each,' Curran said, and just out of devilry he added, 'They are married as a matter of fact.' 'Oh, isn't that too sweet? Oh, the darlings. And have any little doggies come yet?' 'Not yet,' Curran said. 'You see, they have only been married a month. At the doggies' church in Potters Bar.' 'Married in church?' they squealed and I really thought he'd gone too far, but how they swallowed it down! They all gathered round Curran's bed and left their husbands abandoned. Not that the husbands minded. Visiting day is always a horrible reminder of home to a man."

My aunt took another sausage and ordered another Guinness. "They all wanted to know about the church in Potters Bar. 'And to think,' one said, 'we have to leave our doggies at home when we go to Saint Ethelburga's. My dog is as good a Christian as the vicar is with his raffles and his tea-fights.' 'Once a year,' Curran said, 'they have a collection of dog biscuits. To help the poor strays.' When at last they left us alone and went back to their husbands I said, 'You've started something,' and 'Why not?' Curran said."

My aunt put down her glass and asked the woman behind the bar, "Did you ever hear of the doggies' church?"

"I seem to remember hearing something, but it was donkey's years ago, wasn't it? Long before my time. Somewhere in Hove, wasn't it?"

"No, dear. Not a hundred yards from where you are standing now. We used to come to the Cricketers' after the service. The Rev. Curran and me."

"Didn't the police interfere or something?"

"They tried to make out that he had no right to the title of Rev. But we pointed out that it stood for Revered and not Reverend in *our* church, and we didn't belong to the established. They couldn't touch us, we were breakaways like Wesley, and we had all the dog-owners of Brighton and Hove behind us –they even came over from as far as Hastings. The police tried to get us once under the Blasphemy Act, but nobody could find any blasphemy in our services. They were very very solemn. Curran wanted to start

the churching of bitches after the puppies came, but
I said that was going too far—even the Church of
England had abandoned churching. Then there was
the question of marrying divorced couples—I thought
it would treble our income, but there it was Curran
who stood firm. 'We don't recognize divorce,' he said,
and he was quite right—it would have sullied the
sentiment."

"Did the police win in the end?" I asked.

"They always do. They had him up for speaking to
girls on the front, and a lot was said in court that
wasn't apropos. I was young and angry and uncom-
prehending, and I wouldn't help him any more. No
wonder he abandoned me and went to look for Hannibal. No one can stand not being forgiven. That's
God's privilege."

We left the Cricketers' and my aunt took a turning
this way and a turning that until we came to a
shuttered hall and a sign which read: TEXT FOR THE
WEEK. *"If thou hast run with the footmen, and they
have wearied thee, Then how canst thou contend
with horses? Jeremiah. 12."* I can't say that I understood the meaning very well, unless it was a warning
against Brighton races, but perhaps the ambiguity
was the attraction. The sect, I noticed, was called
The Children of Jeremiah.

"This was where we held our services," Aunt Augusta said. "Sometimes you could hardly hear the
words for the barking. 'It's their form of prayer,'
Curran would say, 'let each pray after his own fashion,' and sometimes they lay there quite peacefully
licking their parts. 'Cleansing themselves for the
House of the Lord,' Curran would say. It makes me a
little sad to see strangers here now. And I never much
cared for the prophet Jeremiah."

"I know little about Jeremiah."

"They sank him in the mud," Aunt Augusta said.
"I studied the Bible very carefully in those days, but

there was little that was favourable to dogs in the Old Testament. Tobias took his dog with him on his journey with the angel, but it played no part in the story at all, not even when a fish tried to eat Tobias. A dog was an unclean beast, of course, in those times. He only came into his own with Christianity. It was the Christians who began to carve dogs in stone in the cathedrals, and even while they were still doubtful about women's souls they were beginning to think that maybe a dog had one, though they couldn't get the Pope to pronounce one way or the other, nor even the Archbishop of Canterbury. It was left to Curran."

"A big responsibility," I said. I couldn't make out whether she was serious about Curran or not.

"It was Curran who set me reading theology," Aunt Augusta said. "He wanted references to dogs. It wasn't easy to find any—even in Saint Francis de Sales. I found lots about fleas and butterflies and stags and elephants and spiders and crocodiles in Saint Francis but a strange neglect of dogs. Once I had a terrible shock. I said to Curran, 'It's no good. We can't go on. Look what I've just found in the Apocalypse. Jesus is saying who can enter the city of God. Just listen to this—"Without are dogs and sorcerers and whoremongers and murderers and idolaters, and whosoever loveth or maketh a lie." You see the company dogs are supposed to keep?'

" 'It proves our point,' Curran said. 'Whoremongers and murderers and the rest—they all have souls, don't they? They only have to repent, and it's the same with dogs. The dogs who come to our church have repented. They don't consort any more with whoremongers and sorcerers. They live with respectable people in Brunswick Square or Royal Crescent.' Do you know that Curran was so little put off by the Apocalypse he actually preached a sermon on that very text, telling people that it was their responsibility to see that their dogs didn't backslide? 'Loose the lead and spoil the dog,' he said. 'There are only too many murderers in Brighton and whoremongers at the Metropole all ready to pick up what you loose. And as for sorcerers—' Luckily Hatty, who was with us by that time, had not yet become a fortune-teller. It would have spoilt the image."

"He was a good preacher?"

"It was music to hear him," she said with happy regret, and we began to walk back towards the front; we could hear the shingle turning over from a long way away. "He was not exclusive," my aunt said. "For him dogs were like the House of Israel, but he was an apostle also to the Gentiles—and the Gentiles, to Curran, included sparrows and parrots and white mice— not cats, cats he always regarded as Pharisees. Of course no cat dared come into the church with all those dogs around, but there was one who used to sit in the window of a house opposite and sneer when the congregation came out. Curran excluded fish too—it would be too shocking to eat something with a soul, he said. Elephants he had a very great feeling for, which was generous of him considering Hannibal had trodden on his toe. Let's sit down here, Henry. I always find Guinness a little tiring."

We sat down in a shelter. The lights ran out to sea along the Palace Pier and the edge of the water was white with phosphorescence. The waves were continually pulled up along the beach and pulled back as though someone were making a bed and couldn't get the sheet to lie properly. A bit of pop music came from the dance hall standing there like a blockade ship a hundred yards out. This trip was quite an adventure, I thought to myself, little knowing how small a one it would seem in retrospect.

"I found a lovely piece about elephants once in Saint Francis de Sales," Aunt Augusta said, "and Curran used it in his last sermon—after all that business with the girls had upset me. I really think what he wanted was to tell me it was me he loved, but I was a hard young woman in those days and I wouldn't listen. I've always kept the piece though in my purse and, when I read it, it's not the elephant that I see now, it's Curran. He was a fine big fellow—not as big as Wordsworth but a good deal more sensitive."

She fumbled in her bag and found her purse. "You read it to me, dear, I can't see properly in this light."

I held the rather yellowed creased paper at an angle to catch one of the lights of the front. It wasn't easy to read, though my aunt's handwriting was young and bold, because of the creases. " 'The elephant,' " I read, " 'is only a huge animal, but he is the most worthy of beasts that lives on the earth, and the most intelligent. I will give you an example of his excellence; he ...' " The writing ran along a crease and I couldn't read it, but my aunt chimed gently in. " 'He never changes his mate and he tenderly loves the one of his choice.' Go on, dear."

" 'With whom,' " I read, " 'nevertheless he mates but every third year, and then for five days only and so secretly that he has never been seen to do so.' "

"He was trying to explain," my aunt said, "I am sure of it now, that if he had been a little slack in his attentions, it was only because of the girls—he didn't love me less."

" 'But he is to be seen again on the sixth day, on which day, before doing anything else, he goes straight to some river wherein he bathes his whole body, for he has no desire to return to the herd until he has purified himself.' "

"Curran was always a clean man," my aunt said. "Thank you, dear, you read it very well."

"It doesn't seem very applicable to dogs," I said.

"He turned it so beautifully that no one noticed, and it was really directed at me. I remember he had a special dogs' shampoo which had been blessed at the altar on sale outside the church door that Sunday."

"What became of Curran?"

"I've no idea," Aunt Augusta said. "He must have left his church, for he couldn't have carried on without me. Hatty hadn't the right touch for a deaconess. I dream of him sometimes—but he would be ninety years old now, and I find it hard to picture him as an old man. Well, Henry, I think it is time for us both to sleep."

All the same, I found sleep difficult to attain, even in my comfortable bed at the Royal Albion. The lights of the Palace Pier sparkled on the ceiling, and round and round in my head went the figures of Wordsworth and Curran, the elephant and the dogs of Hove, the mystery of my birth, the ashes of my mother who was not my mother, and my father asleep in the bath. This was not the simple life which I had known at the bank, where I could judge a client's character by his credits and debits. I had a sense of fear and exhilaration too, as the music pounded from the Pier and the phosphorescence rolled up the beach.

CHAPTER 7

The affair of my mother's ashes was not settled so easily as I had anticipated (I call her my mother still, because at this period I had no real evidence that my aunt was telling me the truth). No urn was awaiting me in the house when I returned from Brighton, and so I rang up Scotland Yard and asked for Detective-Sergeant Sparrow. I was put on without delay to a voice which was distinctly not Sparrow's. It sounded very similar to that of a rear-admiral whom I had once had as a client. (I was very glad when he changed his account to the National Provincial Bank, for he treated my clerks like ordinary seamen and myself like a sub-lieutenant who had been court-martialled for keeping the mess books improperly.)

"Can I speak to Detective-Sergeant Sparrow?" I asked.

"On what business?" whoever it was rapped back.

"I have not yet received my mother's ashes," I said.

"This is Scotland Yard, Assistant Commissioner's Office, and not a crematorium," the voice replied and rang off.

It took me a long while (because of engaged lines) to get the same gritty voice on the line again.

"I want Detective-Sergeant Sparrow," I said.

"On what business?"

I was ready this time and prepared to be ruder than the voice could be.

"Police business of course," I said. "What other business do you deal in?" It was almost as though my aunt were speaking through me.

"Detective-Sergeant Sparrow is out. You had better leave a message."

"Ask him to ring Mr. Pulling, Mr. Henry Pulling."

"What address? What telephone number?" he snapped as though he suspected me to be some unsavoury police informer.

"He knows them both. I am not going to repeat them unnecessarily. Tell him I am disappointed at his failure to keep a solemn promise." I rang off before the other had time for a word in reply. Going out to the dahlias, I gave myself the rare award of a satisfied smile. I had never spoken to the rear-admiral like that.

My new cactus dahlias were doing well, and after my trip to Brighton their names gave me some of the pleasure of travel: Rotterdam, a deeper red than a pillar-box, and Dentelle de Venise, with spikes sparkling like hoar-frost. I thought that next year I would plant some Pride of Berlin to make a trio of cities. The telephone disturbed my happy ruminations. It was Sparrow.

I said to him firmly, "I hope you have a good excuse for failing to return the ashes."

"I certainly have, sir. There's more Cannabis than ashes in your urn."

"I don't believe you. How could my mother possibly . . . ?"

"We can hardly suspect your mother, sir, can we? As I told you, I think the man Wordsworth took advantage of your call. Luckily for your story there *are* some human ashes in the urn, though Wordsworth must have dumped most of them down the sink to make room. Did you hear any sound of running water?"

"We were drinking whisky. He certainly filled a jug of water."

"That must have been the moment, sir."

"In any case, I would like to have back the ashes that remain."

"It isn't practicable, sir. Human ashes have a kind of sticky quality. They adhere very closely to any substance, which in this case is pot. I am sending you back the urn by registered post. I suggest, sir, that you place it just where you intended and forget the unfortunate circumstances."

"But the urn will be empty."

"Memorials are often detached from the remains of the deceased. War memorials are an example."

"Well," I said, "I suppose there's nothing to be done. It won't feel the same at all. I hope you don't suspect my aunt had any hand in this?"

"An old lady like that? Oh no, sir. She was obviously deceived by her valet."

"What valet?"

"Why, Wordsworth, sir—who else?" I thought it best not to enlighten him about their relationship.

"My aunt thinks Wordsworth may be in Paris."

"Very likely, sir."

"What will you do about it?"

"There's nothing we *can* do. He hasn't committed an extraditable offence. Of course, if he ever returns ... He has a British passport." There was a note of malicious longing in Detective-Sergeant Sparrow's voice that made me feel, for a moment, a partisan of Wordsworth. I said, "I sincerely hope he won't."

"You surprise and disappoint me, sir."

"Why?"

"I hadn't taken you for one of that kind."

"What kind?"

"People who talk about there being no harm in pot."

"Is there?"

"From our experience, sir, nearly all the cases hooked on hard drugs began with pot."

"And from my experience, Sparrow, all or nearly all the alcoholics I know have started with a small whisky or a glass of wine. I even had a client who was first hooked, as you call it, on mild and bitter. In the end, because of his frequent absences on a cure, he had to give his wife a power of attorney." I rang off. It occurred to me with a certain pleasure that I had sowed a little confusion in Detective-Sergeant Sparrow's mind—not so much confusion on the subject of Cannabis but confusion about my character, the character of a retired bank manager. I discovered for the first time in myself a streak of anarchy. Had it been perhaps the result of my visit to Brighton or was it possibly my aunt's influence (and yet I was not a man easily influenced), or some bacteria in the Pulling blood? I found a buried affection for my father reviving in me. He had been a very patient as well as a very sleepy man, and yet there was about his patience something unaccountable: it might well have been absence of mind rather than patience—or even indifference. He might have been all the time, without our knowing it, elsewhere. I remembered the ambiguous reproaches launched against him by my mother. They seemed to confirm my aunt's story, for they possessed the nagging qualities of an unsatisfied woman. Imprisoned by ambitions which she had never realized, my mother had never known freedom. Freedom, I thought, comes only to the successful, and in his trade my father was a success. If a client didn't like my father's manner or his estimates, he could go elsewhere. My father wouldn't have cared. Perhaps it is freedom, of speech and conduct, which is really envied by the unsuccessful, not money or even power.

It was with these muddled and unaccustomed ideas in my mind that I awaited the arrival of my aunt for dinner. We had arranged the rendezvous before leaving the Brighton Belle at Victoria the day before. As soon as she arrived I told her about Sergeant Sparrow, but she treated my story with surprising indifference, saying only that Wordsworth should have been "more careful." Then I took her out and showed her my dahlias.

"I have always preferred cut flowers," she said, and I had a sudden vision of strange continental gentlemen offering her bouquets of roses and maidenhair fern bound up in tissue paper.

I pointed out to her the site where I had thought to put the urn in memory of my mother.

"Poor Angelica," she said, "she never understood men," and that was all. It was as though she had read my thoughts and commented on them.

I had dialled CHICKEN and the dinner arrived exactly as ordered, the main course only needing to be put into the oven for a few minutes while we ate the smoked salmon. Living alone, I had been a regular customer whenever there was a client to entertain or my mother on her weekly visit. Now for months I had neglected Chicken, for there were no longer any clients and my mother, during her last illness, had been too ill to make the journey from Golders Green.

We drank sherry with the smoked salmon, and as some small return for my aunt's generosity to me in Brighton I had bought a bottle of burgundy, Chambertin 1959, Sir Arthur Keene's favourite, to go with the chicken à la king. When the wine had spread a pleasant glow through both our minds my aunt reverted to my conversation with Sergeant Sparrow.

"He is determined," she said, "that Wordsworth is the guilty party, yet it might equally well be one of us. I don't think the sergeant is a racialist, but he is class-conscious, and though the smoking of pot depends on no class barrier, he prefers to think otherwise and to put the blame on poor Wordsworth."

"You and I can give each other an alibi," I said, "and Wordsworth did run away."

"We could have been in collusion, and Wordsworth might be taking his annual holiday. No," she went on, "the mind of a policeman is set firmly in a groove. I remember once when I was in Tunis a travelling company was there who were playing *Hamlet* in Arabic. Someone saw to it that in the Interlude the Player King was really killed—or rather not quite killed but severely damaged in the right ear—by molten lead. And who do you suppose the police at once suspected? Not the man who poured the lead in, although he must have been aware that the ladle wasn't empty and was hot to the touch. Oh no, they knew Shakespeare's play too well for that, and so they arrested Hamlet's uncle."

"What a lot of travelling you have done in your day, Aunt Augusta."

"I haven't reached nightfall yet," she said. "If I had a companion I would be off tomorrow, but I can no longer lift a heavy suitcase, and there is a distressing lack of porters nowadays. As you noticed at Victoria."

"We might one day," I said, "continue our seaside excursions. I remember many years ago visiting Weymouth. There was a very pleasant green statue of George III on the front."

"I have booked two couchettes a week from today on the Orient Express."

I looked at her in amazement. "Where to?" I asked.

"Istanbul of course."

"But it takes days . . ."

"Three nights to be exact."

"If you want to go to Istanbul surely it would be easier and less expensive to fly?"

"I only take a plane," my aunt said, "when there is no alternative means of travel."

"It's really quite safe."

"It's a matter of choice, not nerves," Aunt Augusta said. "I knew Wilbur Wright very well indeed at one time. He took me for several trips. I always felt quite secure in his contraptions. But I cannot bear being spoken to all the time by irrelevant loud-speakers. One is not badgered at a railway station. An airport always reminds me of a Butlin's Camp."

"If you are thinking of me as a companion . . ."

"Of course I am, Henry."

"I'm sorry, Aunt Augusta, but a bank manager's pension is not a generous one."

"I shall naturally pay all expenses. Give me another glass of wine, Henry. It's excellent."

"I'm not really accustomed to foreign travel. You'd find me . . ."

"You will take to it quickly enough in my company. The Pullings have all been great traveller's. I think I must have caught the infection through your father."

"Surely not my father . . . He never travelled further than Central London."

"He travelled from one woman to another, Henry, all through his life. That comes to much the same thing. New landscapes, new customs. The accumulation of memories. A long life is not a question of years. A man without memories might reach the age of a hundred and feel that his life had been a very brief one. Your father once said to me, 'The first girl I ever slept with was called Rose. Oddly enough she worked in a flower shop. It really seems a century ago.' And then there was your uncle . . ."

"I didn't know I had an uncle."

"He was fifteen years older than your father and he died when you were very young."

"He was a great traveller?"

"It took an odd form," my aunt said, "in the end."
I wish I could reproduce more clearly the tones of
her voice. She enjoyed talking, she enjoyed telling a
story. She formed her sentences carefully like a slow
writer who foresees ahead of him the next sentence
and guides his pen towards it. Not for her the broken
phrase, the lapse of continuity. There was something
classically precise, or perhaps it would be more accu-
rate to say old-world, in her diction. The bizarre
phrase, and occasionally, it must be agreed, a shocking one, gleamed all the more brightly from the old
setting. As I grew to know her better, I began to
regard her as bronze rather than brazen, a bronze
which has been smoothed and polished by touch, like
the horse's knee in the lounge of the Hôtel de Paris
in Monte Carlo, which she once described to me,
caressed by generations of gamblers.

"Your uncle was a bookmaker known as Jo," Aunt
Augusta said. "A very fat man. I don't know why I
say that, but I have always liked fat men. They have
given up all unnecessary effort, for they have had the
sense to realize that women do not, as men do, fall in
love with physical beauty. Curran was stout and so
was your father. It's easier to feel at home with a fat
man. Perhaps travelling with me, you will put on a
little weight yourself. You had the misfortune to
choose a nervous profession."

"I have certainly never banted for the sake of a
woman," I said jokingly.

"You must tell me all about your women one day.
In the Orient Express we shall have plenty of time
for talk. But now I am speaking to you of your Uncle
Jo. His was a very curious case. He made a substantial fortune as a bookmaker, yet more and more his
only real desire was to travel. Perhaps the horses
continually running by, while he had to remain stationary on a little platform with a signboard HONEST
JO PULLING, made him restless. He used to say that

one race meeting merged into another and life went by as rapidly as a yearling out of Indian Queen. He wanted to slow life up and he quite rightly felt that by travelling he would make time move with less rapidity. You have noticed it yourself, I expect, on a holiday. If you stay in one place, the holiday passes like a flash, but if you go to three places, the holiday seems to last at least three times as long."

"Is that why you have travelled so much, Aunt Augusta?"

"At first I travelled for my living," Aunt Augusta replied. "That was in Italy. After Paris, after Brighton. I had left home before you were born. Your father and mother wished to be alone, and in any case I never got on very well with Angelica. The two A's we were always called. People used to say my name fitted me because I seemed proud as a young girl, but no one said my sister's name fitted her. A saint she may well have been, but a very severe saint. She was certainly not angelic."

One of the few marks of age which I noticed in my aunt was her readiness to abandon one anecdote while it was yet unfinished for another. Her conversation was rather like an American magazine where you have to pursue a story, skipping from page twenty to page ninety-eight and turning over all kinds of subjects in between; childhood delinquency, some novel cocktail recipes, the love life of a film star, and even quite a different fiction from the one so abruptly interrupted.

"The question of names," my aunt said, "is an interesting one. Your own Christian name is safe and colourless. It is better than being given a name like Ernest, which has to be lived up to. I once knew a girl called Comfort and her life was a very sad one. Unhappy men were constantly attracted to her simply by reason of her name, when all the time, poor dear, it was really she who needed the comfort from them.

She fell unhappily in love with a man called Courage, who was desperately afraid of mice, but in the end she married a man called Payne and killed herself—in what Americans call a comfort station. I would have thought it a funny story if I hadn't known her."

"You were telling me about my Uncle Jo," I said.

"I know that. I was saying that he wanted to make life last longer. So he decided on a tour round the world (there were no currency restrictions in those days), and he began his tour curiously enough with the Simplon Orient, the train we are travelling by next week. From Turkey he planned to go to Persia, Russia, India, Malaya, Hong Kong, China, Japan, Hawaii, Tahiti, U.S.A., South America, Australia, New Zealand perhaps—somewhere he intended to take a boat home. Unfortunately he was carried off the train at Venice right at the start, on a stretcher, after a stroke."

"How very sad."

"It didn't alter at all his desire for a long life. I was working in Venice at the time, and I went to see him. He had decided that if he couldn't travel physically, he would travel mentally. He asked me if I could find him a house of three hundred and sixty-five rooms so that he could live for a day and a night in each. In that way he thought life would seem almost interminable. The fact that he had probably not long to live had only heightened his passion to extend what was left of it. I told him that, short of the Royal Palace at Naples, I doubted whether such a house existed. Even the Palace in Rome probably contained fewer rooms."

"He could have changed rooms less frequently in a smaller house."

"He said that then he would notice the pattern. It would be no more than he was already accustomed to, travelling between Newmarket, Epsom, Goodwood and Brighton. He wanted time to forget the room which he had left before he returned to it again, and there must be opportunity too to redecorate it in a few essentials. You know there was a brothel in Paris in the Rue de Provence between the last two wars. (Oh, I forgot. There have been many wars since, haven't there, but they don't seem to belong to us like those two do.) This brothel had rooms decorated in various styles—the far West, China, India, that kind of thing. Your uncle had much the same idea for his house."

"But surely he never found one," I exclaimed.

"In the end he was forced to compromise. I was afraid for a time that the best we could do would be twelve bedrooms—one room a month—but a short while afterwards, through one of my clients in Milan . . ."

"I thought you were working in Venice," I interrupted with some suspicion.

"The business I was in," my aunt said, "was peripatetic. We moved around—a fortnight's season in Venice, the same in Milan, Florence and Rome, then back to Venice. It was known as *la quindicina*."

"You were in a theatre company?" I asked.

"The description will serve," my aunt said with that recurring ambiguity of hers. "You must remember I was very young in those days."

"Acting needs no excuse."

"I wasn't excusing myself," Aunt Augusta said sharply, "I was explaining. In a profession like that, age is a handicap. I was lucky enough to leave in good time. Thanks to Mr. Visconti."

"Who was Visconti?"

"We were talking about your Uncle Jo. I found an old house in the country which had once been a *palazzo* or a *castello* or something of the kind. It was almost in ruins and there were gypsies camping in some of the lower rooms and in the cellar—an enormous cellar which ran under the whole ground floor. It had been used for wine, and there was a great empty tun abandoned there because it had cracked with age. Once there had been vineyards around the house, but an *autostrada* had been built right across the estate not a hundred yards from the house, and the cars ran by all day between Milan and Rome and at night the big lorries passed. A few knotted worn-out roots of old vines were all that remained. There was only one bathroom in the whole house (the water had been cut off long ago by the failure of the electric pump), and only one lavatory, on the top floor in a sort of tower, but of course there was no water there either. You can imagine it wasn't the sort of house anyone could sell easily—it had been on the market for twenty years and the owner was a mongoloid orphan in an asylum. The lawyers talked about historic values, but Mr. Visconti knew all about history as you could guess from his name. Of course he advised strongly against the purchase, but after all poor Jo was unlikely to live long and he might as well be made happy. I had counted up the rooms, and if you divided the cellar into four with partitions and included the lavatory and bathroom and kitchen, you could bring the total up to fifty-two. When I told Jo he was delighted. A room for every week in the year, he said. I had to put a bed in every one, even in the bathroom and kitchen. There wasn't room for a bed in the lavatory, but I bought a particularly comfortable chair with a footstool, and I thought we could always leave that room to the last—I didn't think Jo would survive long enough to reach it. He had a nurse who was to follow him from room to room, sleeping one week behind him, as it were. I was afraid he would insist on a different nurse at every stopping place, but he liked her well enough to keep her as a travelling companion."

"What an extraordinary arrangement."

"It worked very well. When Jo was in his fifteenth room he told me—I was back that week in Milan on my tour and I came out to see him with Mr. Visconti on my day off—that it really seemed at least a year since he had moved in. He was going on next day to the sixteenth room on the floor above with a different view and his suitcases were all packed and ready (he insisted on everything being moved by suitcase, and I had found a second-hand one which was already decorated with labels from all kinds of famous hotels— the George V in Paris, the Quisisana in Capri, the Excelsior in Rome, Raffles in Singapore, Shepheard's in Cairo, the Pera Palace in Istanbul).

"Poor Jo! I've seldom seen a happier man. He was certain that death would not catch him before he reached the fifty-second room, and if fifteen rooms had seemed like a year, then he had several years of travel still before him. The nurse told me that about the fourth day in each room he would get a little restless with the wanderlust, and the first day in the new room he would spend more than his usual time in sleep, tired after the journey. He began in the cellar and worked his way upwards until at last he reached the top floor, and he was already beginning to talk of revisiting his old haunts. 'We'll take them in a different order this time,' he said, 'and come at them from a different direction.' He was content to leave the lavatory to the last. 'After all these luxury rooms,' he said, 'it would be fun to rough it a bit. Roughing it keeps one young. I don't want to be like one of those old codgers one sees in the Cunard travelling first-class and complaining of the caviar.' Then it was that in the fifty-first room he had his second stroke. It paralysed him down one side and made speech difficult. I was in Venice at the time, but I got permission to leave the company for a couple of days and Mr. Visconti drove me to Jo's *palazzo*. They were having a lot of difficulty with him. He had spent seven days in the fifty-first room before the stroke knocked him out, but the doctor was insisting that he remain in the same bed without a move for at least another ten days. 'Any ordinary man,' the doctor said to me, 'would be content to lie still for a while.'

" 'He wants to live as long as possible,' I told him.

" 'In that case he should stay where he is till the end. With any luck he'll have two or three more years.'

"I told Jo what the doctor said, and he mouthed a reply. I thought I made out, 'Not enough.'

"He stayed quiet that night and all the next morning, and the nurse believed that he had resigned himself to staying where he was. She left him sleeping and came down to my room for a cup of tea. Mr. Visconti had bought some cream cakes in Milan at the good pastry-cook's near the cathedral. Suddenly from up the stairs there came a strange grating noise. 'Mamma mia,' the nurse said, 'what's that?' It sounded as though someone were shifting the furniture. We ran upstairs, and what do you think? Jo Pulling was out of bed. He had fixed an old club tie of his, the Froth-blowers or the Mustard Club or something of the kind, to the handle of the suitcase because he had no strength in his legs, and he was crawling down the passage towards the lavatory tower pulling the suitcase after him. I shouted to him to stop, but he paid me no attention. It was painful to look at him, he was going so slowly, with such an effort. It was a tiled passage and every tile he crossed cost him enormous exertion. He collapsed before we reached him and lay there panting, and the saddest thing of all to me was that he made a little pool of wee-wee on the tiles. We were afraid to move him before the doctor came. We brought a pillow and put it under his head and the nurse gave him one of his pills. 'Cattivo,' she said in Italian, which means, 'You bad old man,' and he grinned at the two of us and brought out the last sentence which he ever spoke, deformed a bit but I could understand it very well. 'Seemed like a whole lifetime,' he said and he died before the doctor came. He was right in his way to make that last trip against the doctor's orders. The doctor had only promised him a few years."

"He died in the passage?" I asked.

"He died on his travels," my aunt said in a tone of reproof. "As he would have wished."

" 'Here he lies where he longed to be,' " I quoted in order to please my aunt, though I couldn't help remembering that Uncle Jo had not succeeded in reaching the lavatory door.

"Home is the hunter, home from sea," my aunt finished the quotation in her own fashion, "and the sailor home from the hill."

We were silent for quite a while after that as we finished the chicken à la king. It was a little like the two minutes' silence on Armistice Day. I remembered that, when I was a boy, I used to wonder whether there was really a corpse buried there at the Ceno-taph, for governments are usually economical with sentiment and try to arouse it in the cheapest possible way. A brilliant advertising slogan doesn't need a body, a box of earth would do just as well, and now I began to wonder too about Uncle Jo. Was my aunt a little imaginative? Perhaps the stories of Jo, of my father and of my mother were not entirely true.

Without breaking the silence I took a reverent glass of Chambertin to Uncle Jo's memory, whether he existed or not. The unaccustomed wine sang irresponsibly in my head. What did the truth matter? All characters once dead, if they continue to exist in memory at all, tend to become fictions. Hamlet is no less real now than Winston Churchill, and Jo Pulling no less historical than Don Quixote. I betrayed myself with a hiccup while I changed our plates, and with the blue cheese the sense of material problems returned.

"Uncle Jo," I said, "was lucky to have no currency restrictions. He couldn't have afforded to die like that on a tourist allowance."

"They were great days," Aunt Augusta said.

"How are we going to manage on ours?" I asked. "With fifty pounds each we shall not be able to stay very long in Istanbul."

"Currency restrictions have never seriously bothered me," my aunt said. "There are ways and means."

"I hope you don't plan anything illegal."

"I have never planned anything illegal in my life," Aunt Augusta said. "How could I plan anything of the kind when I have never read any of the laws and have no idea what they are?"

It was my aunt herself who suggested that we should fly as far as Paris. I was a little surprised after what she had just said, for there was certainly in this case an alternative means of travel. I pointed out the inconsistency. "There are reasons," Aunt Augusta said. "Cogent reasons. I know the ropes at Heathrow."

I was puzzled too at her insistence that we must go to the Kensington air terminal and take the airport bus. "It's so easy for me," I said, "to pick you up by car and drive you to Heathrow. You would find it much less tiring, Aunt Augusta."

"You would have to pay an exorbitant garage fee," she replied, and I found her sudden sense of economy unconvincing.

I arranged next day for the dahlias to be watered by my next-door neighbour, a brusque man called Major Charge. He had seen Detective-Sergeant Sparrow come to the door with the policeman, and he was bitten by curiosity. I told him it was about a motoring offence and he became sympathetic immediately. "A child murdered every week," he said, "and all they can do is to pursue motorists." I don't like lies and I felt in my conscience that I ought to defend

Sergeant Sparrow, who had been as good as his word and posted back the urn, registered and express.

"Sergeant Sparrow is not in homicide," I replied, "and motorists kill more people in a year than murderers."

"Only a lot of jaywalkers," Major Charge said. "Cannon fodder." However, he agreed to water the dahlias.

I picked my aunt up in the bar of the Crown and Anchor, where she was having a stirrup-cup, and we drove by taxi to the Kensington terminal. I noticed that she had brought two suitcases, one very large, although, when I had asked her how long we were to stay in Istanbul, she had replied, "Twenty-four hours."

"It seems a short stay after such a long journey."

"The point is the journey," my aunt had replied. "I enjoy the travelling not the sitting still."

Even Uncle Jo, I argued, had put up with each room in his house for a whole week.

"Jo was a sick man," she said, "while I am in the best of health."

Since we were travelling first-class (which seemed again an unnecessary luxury between London and Paris) we had no overweight, although the larger of her suitcases was unusually heavy. While we were sitting in the bus I suggested to my aunt that the garage fee for my car would probably have been cheaper than the difference between first and tourist fares. "The difference," she said, "is nearly wiped out by the caviar and the smoked salmon, and surely between us we can probably put away half a bottle of vodka. Not to speak of the champagne and cognac. In any case, I have more important reasons for travelling by bus."

As we approached Heathrow she put her mouth close to my ear. "The luggage," she said, "is in a trailer behind."

"I know."

"I have a green suitcase and a red suitcase. Here are the tickets."

I took them, not understanding.

"When the bus stops, please get out quickly and see whether the trailer is still attached. If it is still there let me know at once and I'll give you further instructions."

Something in my aunt's manner made me nervous. I said, "Of course it will be there."

"I sincerely hope not," she said. "Otherwise we shall not leave today."

I jumped out as soon as we arrived, and sure enough the trailer wasn't there. "What do I do now?" I asked her.

"Nothing at all. Everything is quite in order. You may give me back the tickets and relax."

As we sat over two gins and tonics in the departure lounge a loudspeaker announced, "Passengers on Flight three-seven-eight to Nice will proceed to customs for customs inspection."

We were alone at our table and my aunt did not bother to lower her voice amid the din of passengers, glasses and loud-speakers. "That is what I wished to avoid," she said. "They have now taken to spot-checks on passengers leaving the country. They whittle away our liberties one by one. When I was a girl you could travel anywhere on the continent except Russia without a passport and you took what you liked in the way of money. Until recently they only *asked* what money you had, or at the very worst they wanted to see your wallet. If there's one thing I hate in any human being it is mistrust."

"The way you speak," I said jokingly, "I suspect we are lucky that it is not your bags which are being searched."

I could well imagine my aunt stuffing a dozen five-pound notes into the toe of her bedroom slippers.

Having been a bank manager, I am perhaps overscrupulous, though I must confess that I had brought an extra five-pound note folded up in my ticket pocket, but that was something I might genuinely have overlooked.

"Luck doesn't enter into my calculations," my aunt said. "Only a fool would trust to luck, and there is probably a fool now on the Nice flight who is regretting his folly. Whenever new restrictions are made, I make a very careful study of the arrangements for carrying them out." She gave a little sigh. "In the case of Heathrow I owe a great deal to Wordsworth. For a time he acted as a loader here. He left when there was some trouble about a gold consignment. Nothing was ever proved against him, but the whole affair had been too impromptu and disgusted him. He told me the story. A very large ingot was abstracted by a loader, and the loss was discovered too soon, before the men went off duty. They knew as a result that they would be searched by the police on leaving, all taxis too, and they had no idea what to do with the thing until Wordsworth suggested rolling it in tar and using it as a doorstop in the customs shed. So there it stayed for months. Every time they brought crates along to the shed, they could see their ingot propping open the door. Wordsworth said he got so maddened by the sight of it that he threw up the job. That was when he became a doorman at the Grenada Palace."

"What happened to the ingot?"

"I suppose the authorities lost interest when the diamond robberies started. Diamonds are money for jam, Henry. You see, they have special sealed sacks for valuable freight and these sacks are put into ordinary sacks, the idea being that the loaders can't spot them. The official mind is remarkably innocent. By the time you've been loading sacks a week or two, you can feel which sack contains another inside it.

Then all you've got to do is to slit both coverings open and take pot luck. Like a children's bran tub at Christmas. Nobody is going to discover the slit until the plane arrives at the other end. Wordsworth knew a man who struck lucky the first time and pulled out a box with fifty gem stones."

"Surely somebody's watching?"

"Only the other loaders and they take a share. Of course, occasionally a man has bad luck. Once a friend of Wordsworth's fished out a fat packet of notes, but they proved to be Pakistani. Worth about a thousand pounds if you happened to live in Karachi, but who was going to change them for him here? The poor fellow used to haunt the tarmac whenever a plane was taking off to Karachi, but he never found a safe customer. Wordsworth said he got quite embittered."

"I had no idea such things went on at Heathrow."

"My dear Henry," Aunt Augusta said, "if you had been a young man I would have advised you to become a loader. A loader's life is one of adventure with far more chance of a fortune than you ever have in a branch bank. I can imagine nothing better for a young man with ambition except perhaps illicit diamond digging. That is best practised in Sierra Leone, where Wordsworth comes from. The security guards are less sophisticated and less ruthless than in South Africa."

"Sometimes you shock me, Aunt Augusta," I said, but the statement had already almost ceased to be true. "I have never had anything stolen from my suitcase and I don't even lock it."

"That is probably your safeguard. No one is going to bother about an unlocked suitcase. Wordsworth knew a loader who had keys to every kind of suitcase. There are not many varieties, though he was baffled once by a Russian one."

The loud-speaker announced our flight and we were told to proceed at once to Gate 14 for immediate embarkation.

"For someone who doesn't like airports," I said, "you seem to know a great deal about Heathrow."

"I've always been interested in human nature," Aunt Augusta said. "Especially the more imaginative sides of it."

She ordered another two gins and tonics immediately we arrived on the plane. "There goes ten shillings towards the first-class fare," she said. "A friend of mine calculated once that on a long flight to Tahiti—it took in those days more than sixty-four hours—he recuperated nearly twenty pounds, but of course he was a hard drinker."

Again I had the impression that I was turning the pages in an American magazine in search of a contribution which I had temporarily lost. "I still don't understand," I said, "about the luggage-trailer and the suitcase. Why were you so anxious that the trailer should disappear?"

"I have an impression," my aunt said, "that you are really a little shocked by trivial illegalities. When you reach my age you will be more tolerant. Years ago Paris was regarded as the vice centre of the world, as Buenos Aires was before that, but Madame de Gaulle altered things there. Rome, Milan, Venice and Naples survived a decade longer, but then the only cities left were Macao and Havana. Macao has been cleaned up by the Chinese Chamber of Commerce and Havana by Fidel Castro. For a moment Heathrow is the Havana of the West. It won't last very long, of course, but one must admit that at the present time London Airport has a glamour which certainly puts Britain first. Have you got a little vodka for the caviar?" she asked the hostess who brought our trays. "I prefer it to champagne."

"But, Aunt Augusta, you have still not told me about the trailer."

"It's very simple," my aunt said. "If the luggage is to be loaded direct on to the aircraft, the trailer is detached outside the Queen Elizabeth building—there are always traffic hold-ups at this point and nothing is noticed by the passengers. If when the bus arrives at the BEA or Air France entrance you find the trailer is still attached, this means that the luggage is going to be sent to the customs. Personally I have a rooted objection to unknown hands, which have fiddled about in all kinds of strange luggage, some not over-clean, fiddling about in mine."

"What do you do then?"

"I reclaim my bags, saying that after all I don't require them on the voyage and wish to leave them in the cloak-room. Or I cancel my flight and try again another day." She finished her smoked salmon and went on to the caviar. "There is no such convenient system as that at Dover, or I would prefer to go by boat."

"Aunt Augusta," I said, "what are you carrying in your suitcases?"

"Only one is a little dangerous," she said, "the red. I always use red for that purpose. Red for danger," she added with a smile.

"But what have you got in the red one?"

"A trifle," Aunt Augusta said, "something to help us in our travels. I can't really endure any longer these absurd travel allowances. Allowances! For grown people! When I was a child I received a shilling a week pocket money. If you consider the value of the pound today, that is rather more than what we are allowed to travel with annually. You haven't eaten your portion of *foie gras*."

"It doesn't agree with me," I said.

"Then I will take it. Steward, another glass of champagne and another vodka."

"We are just descending, ma'am."

"The more reason for you to hurry, young man."
She fastened her seat-belt. "I'm glad that Wordsworth
left Heathrow before I came to know him. He was in
danger of being corrupted. Oh, I don't mean the
thieving. A little honest thieving hurts no one, especially when it is a question of gold. Gold needs free
circulation. The Spanish Empire would have decayed
far more quickly if Sir Francis Drake had not kept a
proportion of the Spanish gold in circulation. But
there are other things. I have mentioned Havana,
and you mustn't think me strait-laced. I am all for a
little professional sex. You have probably read about
the activities of Superman. And I am sure that the
sight of him cured many a frigidity. Thank you,
steward." She drained her vodka. "We have not done
badly. I would say we have almost covered the difference between first-class and tourist, if you take into
account a little overweight with my red suitcase.
There was a brothel in Havana where the Emperor's
Crown was admirably performed by three nice girls.
These establishments save many a marriage from
boredom. And then there was the Shanghai Theatre
in the Chinese quarter of Havana with three blue
films which were shown in the intervals of a nude
review, all for the price of one dollar with a pornographic bookshop in the foyer thrown in. I was there
once with a Mr. Fernandez who had a cattle farm in
Camagüey. (I met him in Rome after Mr. Visconti
had temporarily disappeared and he invited me to
Cuba for a month's holiday.) The place was ruined,
though, long before the revolution. I am told that to
compete with television they put in a large screen.
The films, of course, had all been shot on sixteen
millimetre, and when they were enlarged practically
to Cinerama size, it really needed an act of faith to
distinguish any feature of the human body."

The plane banked steeply over Le Bourget.

"It was all very harmless," my aunt said, "and gave employment to a great many people. But the things which go on around Heathrow . . ."

The steward brought another vodka and my aunt tossed it down. She had a strong head—I had noticed that already—but her mind under the influence of alcohol ranged to and fro.

"We were talking of Heathrow," I reminded her, for my curiosity had been aroused. In my aunt's company, I found myself oddly ignorant about my own country.

"There are a number of big firms around Heathrow," my aunt said. "Electronics, engineering, film manufacturers. Glaxo, as one would expect, is quite untouched by the Heathrow influence. After office hours some of the technicians give private parties: air crews are always welcome, so long as stewardesses are included in the party. Even loaders. Wordsworth was always invited, but only on condition he brought a girl and was willing to exchange her at the party for another. Pornographic films are shown first as an encouragement. Wordsworth was genuinely attached to his girl, but he had to surrender her in exchange for a technician's wife who was a homely woman of fifty called Ada. It seems to me that the old professional brothel system was far healthier than these exaggerated amateur distractions. But then an amateur always goes too far. An amateur is never in proper control of his art. There was a discipline in the old-time brothels. The madame in many ways played a role similar to that of the headmistress of Roedean. A brothel after all is a kind of school, and not least a school of manners. I have known several madames of real distinction who would have been just as at home in Roedean and have lent distinction to any school."

"How on earth did you get to know them?" I asked, but the plane was bumping on to the Le

Bourget field, and my aunt began to fuss about her luggage. "I think it better," she said, "if we pass through customs and immigration separately. My red case is rather a heavy one and I would be glad if you would take that with you. Employ a porter. It is always easier to obtain a taxi with a porter's help. And show in your manner that the tip will be a good one before you arrive at the customs. There is often an understanding between a porter and a *douanier*. I will meet you outside. Here is the ticket for the red case."

CHAPTER 9

I had no clear idea what my aunt intended by her elaborate precautions. There was obviously little danger from the *douanier,* who waved me through with the careless courtesy which I find so lacking in the supercilious young men in England. My aunt had booked rooms in the Saint James and Albany, an old-fashioned double hotel, of which one half, the Albany, faces the Rue de Rivoli and the other, the Saint James, the Rue Saint-Honoré. Between the two hotels lies the shared territory of a small garden, and on the garden front of the Saint James I noticed a plaque which tells a visitor that here La Fayette signed some treaty or celebrated his return from the American Revolution, I forget which.

Our rooms in the Albany looked out on the Tuileries gardens, and my aunt had taken a whole suite, which seemed rather unnecessary as we were only spending one night before we caught the Orient Express. When I mentioned this, however, she rebuked me quite sharply. "This is the second time today," she said, "that you have mentioned the subject of economy. You retain the spirit of a bank manager, even in retirement. Understand once and for all that I am not interested in economy. I am over seventy-five, so that it is unlikely I will live longer than another twenty-five years. My money is my own and I do not intend to save for the sake of an heir. I made many economies in my youth and they were fairly painless because the young do not particularly care for luxury. They have other interests than spending and can make love satisfactorily on a Coca-Cola, a drink which is nauseating in age. They have little idea of real pleasure: even their love-making is apt to be hurried and incomplete. Luckily in middle age pleasure begins, pleasure in love, in wine, in food. Only the taste for poetry flags a little, but I would have always gladly lost my taste for the sonnets of Wordsworth (the other Wordsworth I mean of course) if I could have bettered my palate for wine. Love-making too provides as a rule a more prolonged and varied pleasure after forty-five. Aretino is not a writer for the young."

"Perhaps it's not too late for me to begin," I said facetiously in an effort to close that page of her conversation, which I found a little embarrassing.

"You must surrender yourself first to extravagance," my aunt replied. "Poverty is apt to strike suddenly like influenza, it is well to have a few memories of extravagance in store for bad times. In any case, this suite is not wasted. I have to receive some visitors in private, and I don't suppose you would want me to receive them in my bedroom. One of them, by the way, is a bank manager. Did *you* visit lady clients in their bedrooms?"

"Of course not. Nor in their drawing-rooms either. I did all business at the bank."

"Perhaps in Southwood you didn't have any very distinguished clients."

"You are quite wrong," I said and I told her about the unbearable rear-admiral and my friend Sir Alfred Keene.

"Or any really confidential business."

"Nothing certainly which could not be discussed in my office at the bank."

"You were not bugged, I suppose, in the suburbs."

The man who came to see her was not my idea of a banker at all. He was tall and elegant with black sideburns and he would have fitted very well into a matador's uniform. My aunt asked me to bring her the red suitcase, and I then left them alone, but looking back from the doorway I saw that the lid was already open and the case seemed to be stacked with ten pound notes.

I sat down in my bedroom and read a copy of *Punch* to reassure myself. The sight of all the smuggled money had been a shock, and the suitcase was one of those fibre ones which are as vulnerable as cardboard. It is true that no experienced loader at Heathrow would have expected it to contain a small fortune, but surely it was the height of rashness to trust in a bluff which depended for its success on the experience of a thief. She might easily have tumbled on a novice.

My aunt had obviously spent many years abroad and this had affected her character as well as her morality. I couldn't really judge her as I would an ordinary Englishwoman, and I comforted myself, as I read *Punch,* that the English character was unchangeable. True, *Punch* once passed through a distressing period, when even Winston Churchill was a subject of mockery, but the good sense of the proprietors and of the advertisers drew it safely back into the old paths. Even the admiral had begun to subscribe again, and the editor had, quite correctly in my opinion, been relegated to television, which is at its best a vulgar medium. If the ten-pound notes, I thought, were tied in bundles of twenty, there could easily be as much as three thousand pounds in the suitcase, or even six, for surely bundles of forty would not be too thick ... Then I remembered the case was a Revela-

tion. Twelve thousand was not an impossible total. I
felt a little comforted by that idea. Smuggling on such
a large scale seemed more like a business coup than a
crime.

The telephone rang. It was my aunt. "Which
would you advise?" she asked. "Union Carbide,
Genesco, Deutsche Texaco? Or even General Electric?"

"I wouldn't like to advise you at all," I said. "I am
not competent. My clients never went in for American bonds. The dollar premium is too high."

"There's no question of a dollar premium in
France," Aunt Augusta said with impatience. "Your
customers seem to have been singularly unimagina-
tive." The line went dead. Did she expect the admiral to smuggle notes?

I went restlessly out and crossed the little garden
where an American couple (from the Saint James or
the Albany) were having tea. One of them was raising a little bag, like a drowned animal, from his cup
at the end of a cord. At that distressing sight I felt
very far away from England, and it was with a pang
that I realized how much I was likely to miss Southwood and the dahlias in the company of Aunt Augusta. I walked up to the Place Vendôme and then by
the Rue Daunou to the Boulevard des Capucines.
Outside a bar on the corner two women spoke to me,
and suddenly I saw, bearing down on me with a
happy grin of welcome, a man whom I recognized
with apprehension.

"Mr. Pullen?" he exclaimed. "Praise to the Holiest
in the height."

"Wordsworth!"

"In all His works most wonderful. You wan those
two gels?"

"I was just taking a stroll," I said.

"Women lak that they humbug you," Wordsworth
said. "They just short-timers. They do jig-jig, one two

three, out you go. If you wan a gel you come along with Wordsworth."

"But I don't want a girl, Wordsworth. I am here with my aunt. I am taking a little walk by myself because she has business to transact."

"Your auntie here?"

"Yes."

"Where you live?"

I didn't want to give our address without my aunt's permission. I had a vision of Wordsworth moving in, to the room next door. Suppose Wordsworth began to smoke marijuana in the Saint James and Albany . . . I was uncertain of French laws on the subject.

"We are staying with friends," I said vaguely.

"With a man?" Wordsworth asked with instant savagery. It seemed incredible that anyone could be jealous of a woman of seventy-five, but jealous Wordsworth undoubtedly was, and now I saw the banker with sideburns in a different light.

"My dear Wordsworth," I said, "you are imagining things," and I allowed myself a white lie. "We are staying with an elderly married couple." I felt it was hardly suitable to discuss my aunt like this at a street corner, and I began to move down the boulevard, but Wordsworth kept pace with me. "You got CTC for Wordsworth?" he asked. "Ar find you lovely gel, schoolteacher."

"I don't *want* a girl, Wordsworth," I repeated, but I gave him a ten-franc note to keep him quiet.

"Then you have one drink with old Wordsworth. Ar know A-one first-class joint right here."

I agreed to a drink, and he led the way into the entrance of what seemed to be a theatre, the Comédie des Capucines. A gramophone was howling below, as we descended under the theatre.

"I'd rather go somewhere more quiet," I said.

"You jus wait. This A-one racket." It was very hot in the cellar. A number of unaccompanied young women were sitting at the bar, and turning towards the music, I saw an almost naked woman passing between the tables, where a number of men, wearing shabby macintoshes like uniforms, sat before untasted drinks.

"Wordsworth," I said crossly, "if this is what you call jig-jig I don't want it."

"No jig-jig here," Wordsworth said. "If you wan jig-jig you take her to hotel."

"Take who?"

"These gels—you wan one?"

Two of the girls at the bar came and sat down, one on either side of me. I felt imprisoned. Wordsworth, I noticed, had already ordered four whiskies, which he obviously couldn't pay for with the ten francs I had given him.

"Zach, *chéri*," one of the girls said, "present your friend please."

"Mr. Pullen, you meet Rita. Lovely gel. School-teacher."

"Where does she teach?"

Wordsworth laughed. I realized I had made a fool of myself, and I watched Wordsworth with dismay as he entered into what seemed a long business negotiation with the girls.

"Wordsworth," I said, "what are you doing?"

"They wan two hunded francs. I say no. I tell em we got British passports."

"What on earth has that got to do with it?"

"They know British people very poor, can't afford good dash." He began to talk to them again in a kind of French which I couldn't follow at all, though they seemed to understand him well enough.

"What are you talking Wordsworth?"

"French."

"I don't understand a word."

"Good Coast French. This lady she know Dakar

well. Ar tell her ar work in Conakry one time. They
say hunded and fifty francs."

"You can thank them very much, Wordsworth, but
say that I'm not interested. I have to return to my
aunt."

One of the women laughed. I suppose she recognized the word "aunt," though I couldn't for the life
of me see why a rendezvous with an aunt should be
funnier than a rendezvous with a cousin, an uncle or
even one's mother. The girl repeated *"tante"* and
both laughed.

"Tomorrow?" Wordsworth asked.

"I am going with my aunt to Versailles and in the
evening we take the Orient Express to Istanbul."

"Istanbul," Wordsworth exclaimed. "What she do
there? Who she go for see?"

"I imagine we shall see the Blue Mosque, Santa
Sophia, the Golden Horn, the Topkapi museum."

"You be careful, Mr. Pullen."

"Please call me by my right name: 'Pulling.' " I
tried to temper my rebuke with humour. "You would
not like it if I continually called you Coleridge."

"Coleridge?"

"Coleridge was a poet and a friend of Wordsworth."

"Ar never met that man. If he say ar did he humbug you."

I said firmly, "Now I really must be off, Wordsworth. Get the bill or I shall leave you to pay."

"You waste good White Horse?"

"You can drink it yourself or share it with these
ladies." I paid the bill—it seemed an exorbitant one,
but I suppose the floor show was thrown in. A naked
black girl was dancing with a white feather boa. I
wondered what all the men here did for a living. It
seemed extraordinary that one could watch such a
scene during banking hours.

Wordsworth said, "You give three hunded francs to these ladies for private show."

"The price seems to be going up."

"Maybe ar make them say two hunded francs. You lef it to Wordsworth. O.K.?"

It was no use appealing to Wordsworth's sense of morality. I said, "As you have a British passport, you should know that an Englishman is allowed to take only fifteen pounds in currency out of the country. Two hundred francs would exhaust the whole amount."

This was a reason Wordsworth could understand. He looked down at me from his great height with melancholy and commiseration. "Governments all the same no good," he said.

"One must make sacrifices. The cost of defence and the social services is very high."

"Travellers' cheques," Wordsworth suggested quickly.

"They can only be exchanged at a bank, an official exchange or a registered hotel. In any case, I shall need them in Istanbul."

"Your auntie got plenty."

"She has only a travel allowance too," I said.

I felt the weakness of this last argument, for Wordsworth cannot have lived for very long with my aunt before learning that she resorted to ways and means. I changed the subject by attacking him. "What on earth did you mean, Wordsworth, by sending me away with Cannabis in my mother's urn?"

His mind was elsewhere, brooding perhaps on the travel allowance.

"No cannibals," he said, "in England. No cannibals in Sierra Leone."

"I'm talking about the ashes."

"Cannibals in Liberia, not Sierra Leone."

"I didn't say 'cannibals.' "

"Leopard Society in Sierra Leone. They kill plenty people but not chop them."

"Pot, Wordsworth, pot." I hated the vulgar word which reminded me of childhood. "You mixed pot with my mother's ashes."

At last I had embarrassed him. He drank the whisky quickly. "You come away," he said, "ar show you much better damned place. Rue de Douai."

I harried him all the way up the stairs. "You had no business to do such a thing, Wordsworth. The police came and took the urn."

"They give it you back?" he asked.

"Only the urn. The ashes were inextricably mixed with pot."

"Old Wordsworth meant no harm, man," he said, halting on the pavement. "Those bloody police."

I was glad to see there was a taxi rank close by. I was afraid he might try to follow me and discover the whereabouts of Aunt Augusta.

"In Mendeland," he said, "you bury food with your ma. You bury pot. All the same thing."

"My mother didn't even smoke cigarettes."

"With your pa you bury best hatchet."

"Why not food with him too?"

"He go hunt food with hatchet. He kill bush chicken."

I got into the taxi and drove away. Looking through the rear window, I could see Wordsworth standing bewildered on the pavement edge, like a man on a river bank waiting for a ferry. He raised his hand tentatively, as though he were uncertain of my response, whether I had left him in friendship or anger, as the traffic swept between us. I wished then that I had given him a bigger CTC. After all he meant no harm. Even in his size he exhibited a clumsy innocence.

CHAPTER 10

I found Aunt Augusta sitting alone in the centre of
the large and shabby salon filled with green velvet
chairs and marble mantelpieces. She had not bothered to remove the suitcase, which lay open and
empty on the floor. There were traces of tears in her
eyes. I turned on the dim lights of the dusty chandelier, and my aunt gave me an uncertain smile.

"Has something happened, Aunt Augusta?" I
asked. It occurred to me that she might have been
robbed by the man with sideburns and I regretted
having left her alone with such a large amount of
cash.

"Nothing, Henry," she said in a voice surprisingly
gentle and wavery. "I decided after all on a deposit
account in Berne. What banalities they drive us to
with their rules and regulations." At this moment she
had all the weary manner I would have expected of
an old lady of seventy-five.

"You are upset."

"Only by memories," Aunt Augusta said, "For me
this hotel has many memories, and very old ones at
that. You would have been only a boy . . ."

Suddenly I felt a real affection for my aunt. Perhaps a hint of weakness is required to waken our

affections, and I remembered Miss Keene's fingers
faltering over her tatting as she spoke of unknown
South Africa—it had been then that I came nearest to
a proposal.

"What kind of memories, Aunt Augusta?"

"Of a love affair, Henry. A very happy one while it
lasted."

"Tell me."

I was moved, as I had sometimes been at the theatre, at the sight of old age remembering. The faded
luxury of the room seemed like a stage set at the
Haymarket. It brought to my mind photographs of
Doris Keene in *Romance,* and who was it in *Mile-
stones?* Having very few memories of my own to linger
over, I appreciate sentiment all the more in others.

She dabbed at her eyes. "You'd be bored, Henry.
An unfinished bottle of champagne found in an old
cupboard with all the sparkle gone ..." The jaded
phrase was worthy of a Haymarket author.

I drew up a chair and took her small hand in
mine, it was creamy to the touch and I was much
moved by a small brown grave-mark which she had
failed to cover with powder. "Tell me," I repeated.
We were both silent, thinking of very different things.
I felt as though I were on the stage taking part in a
revival of *The Second Mrs. Tanqueray.* My aunt had
led a very mixed-up life—that was certain—but she
had loved deeply in her time, in the Hotel Saint
James and Albany, and who knew what excuses in
her past there might be for her relations with poor
Wordsworth? This sitting-room of the hotel reminded
me of that other Albany in London where Captain
Tanqueray had lived.

"Dear Aunt Augusta," I said and put my arm
around her shoulder. "It helps sometimes to speak to
another person. I know I belong to a different generation—perhaps a more conventional generation ..."

"It's a rather disgraceful story," my aunt said and she looked down in her lap with an air of modesty which I had never seen before.

I found myself kneeling uncomfortably beside her, one knee in the empty suitcase, holding her hand. "Trust me," I said.

"It's your sense of humour, Henry, that I don't fully trust. I don't think we find the same things funny."

"I was expecting a sad story," I said rather sharply, climbing out of the suitcase.

"It *is* a very sad story in its special way," my aunt said, "but it's rather funny too." I had let go her hand and now she turned it this way and that like a glove in a bargain basement. "I must really have a manicure tomorrow," she said.

I felt some irritation at her quick change of mood. I had been betrayed into a feeling of sentiment which was not natural to me. I said, "I saw Wordsworth just now," thinking to embarrass her.

"What? Here?" she exclaimed.

"I am sorry to disappoint you, no. Not here in the hotel. In the street."

"Where is he living?"

"I didn't ask. Nor did I give him your address. I hadn't realized that you would be so anxious to see him again."

"You are a hard man, Henry."

"Not hard, Aunt Augusta. Prudent."

"I don't know from which side of the family you inherited prudence. Your father was lazy but never, never prudent."

"And my mother?" I asked in the hope of trapping her.

"If she had been prudent you would not be here now." She went to the window and looked across the Rue de Rivoli into the Tuileries gardens. "So many nursemaids and perambulators," she said and sighed.

Against the hard afternoon light she looked old and vulnerable.

"Would you have liked a child, Aunt Augusta?"

"At most times it would have been inconvenient," she said. "Curran was not to be trusted as a father, and by the time I knew Mr. Visconti the hour was really getting late—not too late, of course, but a child belongs to the dawn hours, and with Mr. Visconti one was already past the blaze of noon. In any case, I would have made a very unsatisfactory mother. God knows where I would have dragged the poor child after me, and suppose he had turned out completely respectable . . ."

"Like myself," I said.

"I don't yet despair of you," my aunt said. "You were reasonably kind about poor Wordsworth. And you were quite right not to give him my address. He wouldn't fit in with the Saint James and Albany. What a pity that the days of slavery are passed, for then I could have pretended that he served some utilitarian purpose. I might have lodged him in the Saint James across the garden." She gave a reminiscent smile. "I really think I ought to tell you about Monsieur Dambreuse. I loved him a lot, and if we didn't have a child together, it was purely owing to the fact that it was a late love. I took no precautions, none at all."

"Were you thinking about him when I came in?"

"I was. They were six of the happiest months of my life, those which we shared, and they were all spent here in the Albany. I met him first one Monday evening outside Fouquet's. He asked me to join him in a coffee, and by Thursday we were installed here, a genuine couple on good terms with the porter and the maid. The fact that he was a married man didn't worry me at all, for I am not in the least a jealous woman, and anyway I had far the larger slice of him, or so I thought. He told me he had a house in the country, where his wife lived with his six children, happy and occupied and requiring very little attention, somewhere near Toulouse. He would leave me on a Saturday morning after *petit déjeuner* and return in time for bed on Monday evening. Perhaps as a sign of his fidelity, he was always very loving on a Monday night, so much so that the middle of the week would often pass very quietly. That suited my temperament well—I have always preferred an occasional orgy to a nightly routine. I really loved Monsieur Dambreuse—perhaps not with the tenderness I felt for Curran but with more freedom from care than I had ever experienced with Mr. Visconti. The deepest love is not the most carefree. How Monsieur Danbreuse and I used to laugh. Of course I realized later that he had a very good reason for laughter."

Why should I have been haunted at that moment by the thought of Miss Keene? "Have you ever been to Koffiefontein?" I asked.

"No," my aunt said. "Why? Where is it?"

"A very long way away," I said.

"The really awful thing that I discovered," my aunt said, "was that Monsieur Dambreuse never went very far away. Not even as far as Toulouse. He was in fact a real Parisian. The truth, when it came out, was that he had a wife and *four* children (one was already employed in the PTT) no further away than the Rue de Miromesnil—ten minutes' walk, taking the back way by the Hotel Saint James into the Rue Saint-Honoré, and he had another mistress installed in a first-floor suite exactly the same as ours (he was a very just man) in the Saint James. The week-ends he spent with his wife and family in the Rue de Miromesnil and the afternoons of Tuesday, Wednesday, Thursday, Friday, when I thought he was at work, he spent with this girl, who was called Louise Dupont, in the Saint James across the garden. I must say it was an achievement for a man who was well over fifty and

had retired from full-time work (he was a director of
a metallurgical company) for reasons of ill-health."

"Was he older than I am?" I remarked before I
realized what I was saying.

"Certainly he was. He had told the other woman
exactly what he had told me. She knew about the
wife in Toulouse, but she had no idea at all that
there was another woman more or less in the same
hotel. He was a man of great fantasy and he liked
women of a certain age. It was a very happy time,
and sometimes he reminded me a little of your father—
there were periods of lethargy punctuated by bursts
of energy. He told me later, when everything was
known, that he thought of me always as his lady of
the night. I looked so well, he said, by full electric
light. The other woman he knew as the afternoon
girl—although she was only a year or two younger
than me. He was a very lecherous man, quite out of
place, I would have thought, in a metallurgical company."

"How did you discover?"

"He traded too much on his luck. Everything had
gone so easily for six months. When I went shopping
I always went out by the Rue de Rivoli. When I had
shopped enough I would take tea at W. H. Smith's
bookshop. And Louise was, of course, usually occupied in the afternoons. She shopped in the morning
when I was engaged, for Monsieur Dambreuse never
rose before eleven, and she always left the hotel by
the Rue Saint-Honoré. Then one day the spirit of
devilry took him. It was a week-end and he had led
his wife and two younger children to the Louvre to
look at the Poussins. Afterwards his family wanted tea
and his wife suggested the Ritz. 'It's too noisy,' he
told her, 'it's like a parrot cage of dowagers. Now I
know a quiet little garden where nobody ever comes
...' The trouble that afternoon was that both of us
came—I and Louise.

"I had never had tea in the garden between the Saint James and Albany before, nor had Louise, but some impulse—I sometimes believe in a Higher Power, even though I am a Catholic—led the two of us that afternoon into the garden. We were the only people there, and you know how sociable French women are. A polite bow and *"Bonjour, madame,"* an exchange of words between our tables about the balmy weather, and within a few minutes we were seated together, offering each other the sugar and the sandwiches, and only too glad perhaps of a little female conversation after six months in a hotel room with one man.

"We introduced ourselves, and both of us spoke of our so-called husbands. It seemed no more than a curious coincidence when we found that the two of them worked for the same metallurgical firm. One of the things about Monsieur Dambreuse that I particularly like in memory is the fact that he always preferred to tell the truth when it was practicable— indeed he was more trustworthy than most men, who often lie uselessly from vanity. 'I wonder whether they know each other,' Louise was saying when into the garden walked Monsieur Dambreuse, followed by his rather stout wife and two overgrown children, the female one squinting a little and suffering from hay fever. Louise cried, "Achille,' and when I think of his expression as he turned and saw the two of us sitting at tea together, I cannot help smiling even today." My aunt dabbed her eyes with her handkerchief. "And crying a little too," she added, "for it was the end of an idyll. A man cannot forgive being made to look foolish."

I said with some indignation, "Surely it was for you to forgive?"

"Oh no, dear, I was quite ready to continue as we were. Louise too would have agreed to share him, and I don't think Madame Dambreuse ever quite realized the situation. His name really was Achille and he introduced us to her as the wives of two fellow directors of the metallurgical firm. But Monsieur Dambreuse never quite recovered his self-esteem. Now when he was rather tranquil in midweek he knew I realized the cause and it embarrassed him. He was not a promiscuous man. He had loved his little secret. He felt naked, poor man, and exposed to ridicule."

"But surely, Aunt Augusta," I exclaimed, "you couldn't bear the man after you had discovered how he had deceived you all those months?"

She got up and strode towards me with her small hands clenched. I thought she was going to hit me. "You young fool," she said as if I were no more than a schoolboy. "Monsieur Dambreuse was a *man*, and I only wish you had been given a chance of growing up like him."

Suddenly she smiled and put her hand comfortingly against my cheek. "I am sorry, Henry, it is not your fault. You were brought up by Angelica. Sometimes I have an awful feeling that I am the only one left anywhere who finds any fun in life. That was why I was crying a little when you came in. I said to Monsieur Dambreuse, 'Achille, I love the things we do just as much as before. I don't mind knowing where you go in the afternoons. It doesn't make any difference.' But of course it did to him, because he had no secret any more. His fun had been in the secret, and he left us both only so that somewhere he could find a new secret. Not love. Just a secret. The saddest thing he ever said to me was, 'There's no other Saint James and Albany in all Paris.' I said, 'Couldn't you take two rooms at the Ritz on different floors?' He said, 'The lift man would know. It wouldn't be really secret.' "

I had listened to her with amazement and some perturbation. I realized for the first time the perils that lay ahead of me. I felt as though I were being dragged at her heels on an absurd knight errantry, like Sancho Panza at the heels of Don Quixote, but in the cause of what she called fun instead of chivalry. "Why are you going to Istanbul, Aunt Augusta?" I asked.

"Time will show," she said.

A far-fetched idea came to me. "You are not looking for Monsieur Dambreuse?"

"No, no, Henry. Achille is probably dead just like Curran—he would be nearly ninety years old by now anyway. And Mr. Visconti—poor foolish Mr. Visconti. He too will be getting on—eighty-five at least, an age when you need a woman's company. There was a story that he came back to Venice after the war and was drowned in the Grand Canal after a fight with a gondolier about a woman, but I never really believed that. He wasn't the kind who fought about a woman, he was up to so many tricks, he always survived. What a long life I have had—just like your Uncle Jo."

She was touched again by melancholy, and for the first time I thought that perhaps dahlias were not a sufficient occupation for a man's retirement. "I'm glad to have found you, Aunt Augusta," I said on an impulse.

She replied in a slang expression quite out of character, "Oh, there's life in the old girl yet," with a smile so speculative, so carefree and youthful, that I was no longer surprised by Wordsworth's jealousy.

CHAPTER 11

The Orient Express left the Gare de Lyon just after
midnight. The two of us had spent an exhausting
day—first at Versailles, which my aunt curiously
enough was seeing for the first time (she found the
palace a little vulgar). "I didn't get very far afield,"
she told me, "in the days of Monsieur Dambreuse,
and in earlier times when I lived in Paris I was much
too occupied."

I had become very curious about my aunt's history,
and I was interested to arrange her various periods in
some kind of chronological sequence. "Would that
earlier time have been before or after you went on
the stage?" I asked her. We were standing on the
terrace looking down towards the lake, and I had
been thinking how much more pretty and homely
Hampton Court was than Versailles. But then Henry
VIII was a more homely man than Louis XIV; an
Englishman could identify more easily with a man of
his married respectability than with the luxurious
lover of Madame de Montespan. I remembered the
old music-hall song, " 'Enery the Eighth I am."

> I married the widder next door,
> She 'ad 'ad seven 'Eneries before.
> 'Enery the Eighth I am.

97

Nobody could have written a music-hall song about the Sun King.

"On the stage, did you say?" my aunt asked rather absentmindedly.

"Yes. In Italy."

She seemed to be trying hard to recollect, and I was aware as never before of her great age. "Oh," she said, "yes, yes, now I remember. You mean the touring company. That came after my Paris days. It was in Paris that I was spotted by Mr. Visconti."

"Was Mr. Visconti a theatrical manager?"

"No, but he was a great amateur of what you insist on calling the stage. We met one afternoon in the Rue de Provence and he said I had a fine talent, and he persuaded me to leave the company I was with. And so we travelled together to Milan, where my career really started. It was fortunate for me; if I had stayed in France I would never have been able to help your Uncle Jo, and Jo, having quarrelled with your father, left me most of his money. Poor dear man, I can see him still, crawling, crawling, down the corridor toward the lavatory. Let us go back to Paris and visit the Musée Grévin. I need to be cheered up." And cheered up she certainly was by the waxworks. I remembered how at Brighton she had told me that her idea of fame was to be represented at Tussaud's, dressed in one of her own costumes, and I really believe she would have opted for the Chamber of Horrors rather than have had no image made of her at all. A bizarre thought, for my aunt was not of a criminal temperament, even though some of her activities were not strictly legal. I think that the childish saying, "Finding's keeping," was one of her ten commandments.

I would myself have preferred to visit the Louvre and see the Venus of Melos and the Winged Victory, but my aunt would have none of it. "All those naked

women with bits missing," she said. "It's morbid. I
once knew a girl who was chopped up that way
between the Gare du Nord and Calais Maritime. She
had met a man in the place where I worked who
travelled in ladies' underwear—or so he said, and he
certainly had an attaché case with him full of rather
fanciful brassières which he persuaded her to try on.
There was one shaped like two clutching black hands
that greatly amused her. He invited her to go to
England with him, and she broke her contract with
our *patronne* and decamped. It was quite a *cause
célèbre*. He was called the Monster of the Chemins de
Fer by the newspapers, and he was guillotined, after
making his confession and receiving the sacrament, in
an odour of sanctity. It was said by his counsel that
he had a misplaced devotion to virginity owing to his
education by the Jesuits, and he therefore tried to
remove all girls who led loose lives like poor Anne-
Marie Callot. The brassières were a kind of test. You
were condemned if you chose the wrong one, like
those poor men in *The Merchant of Venice*. He was
certainly not an ordinary criminal, and a young woman who was praying for him in a chapel in the Rue
du Bac had a vision of the Virgin, who said to her,
'The crooked ways shall be made straight,' which she
took as proclaiming his salvation. There was a popu-
lar Dominican preacher, on the other hand, who
believed it to be a critical reference to his Jesuit
education. Anyway quite a cult started for what they
called 'the good murderer.' Go and see your Venus if
you want, but let me go to the waxworks. Our manager had to identify the body and he said it was just a
torso, and that gave me a turn against all old stat-
ues."

In the evening we had a quiet dinner at Maxim's, in
the smaller room where Aunt Augusta thought to
escape the tourists. There was one, however, whom

we could not escape; she wore a suit and a tie, and she had a voice like a man's. She not only dominated her companion, a little mousy blond woman of uncertain age, she dominated the whole room. Like so many English abroad she seemed to ignore the presence of foreigners around her and spoke in a loud voice as though she were alone with her companion. Her voice had a peculiar ventriloquial quality, and when I first became aware of it I thought it came from the mouth of an old gentleman with a rosette of the Legion of Honour in his buttonhole who sat at the table opposite ours, and who had obviously been taught to chew every morsel of his meat thirty-two times. "Four-legged animals, my dear, always remind me of tables. So much more solid and sensible than two legs. One could sleep standing up." Everyone who could understand English turned to look at him. His mouth closed with a startled snap when he saw himself the centre of attention. "One could even serve dinner on a man with a broad enough back," the voice said, and the mousy woman giggled and said, "Oh, Edith," and so identified the speaker. I am sure the woman had no idea of what she was doing—she was an unconscious ventriloquist, and surrounded as she believed by ignorant foreigners and perhaps excited a little by unaccustomed wine, she really let herself go.

It was a deep, cultured, professorial voice. I could imagine it lecturing on English literature at one of the older universities, and for the first time my attention strayed from Aunt Augusta. "Darwin—the other Darwin—wrote a poem on the Loves of the Plants. I can well imagine a poem on the Loves of the Tables. Cramping it might be, but how deliciously so, when you think of a nest of tables, each fitting so blissfully, my dear, into one another."

"Why is everyone staring at you?" Aunt Augusta

asked. It was an embarrassing moment, all the more
so as the woman had suddenly stopped speaking and
had plunged into her *carré d'agneau*. The trouble is
that I have an unconscious habit of moving my lips
when I am thinking, so that to all except my immediate neighbours I seemed to be the author of her
ambiguous remark.

"I have no idea, Aunt Augusta," I said.

"You must have been doing *something* very odd,
Henry."

"I was only thinking."

How I wish I could conquer the habit. It must
have been established first when I was a cashier and
silently counted bundles of notes. The habit betrayed
me very badly once with a woman called Mrs. Blen-
nerhasset, who was stone deaf and a lip-reader. She
was a very beautiful woman who was married to the
mayor of Southwood. She came to my private office
once about some question of investments, and while
I turned over her file my thoughts couldn't help
dwelling a little wistfully on her loveliness. One is
more free in thought than in speech and when I
looked up I saw that she was blushing. She finished
her business very quickly and left. Later, to my surprise, she dropped in to see me again. She made some
small alteration to the decision we had reached about
her War Loan and then said, "Did you really mean
what you told me?" I thought she was referring to my
advice about National Savings Certificates.

"Of course," I said. "That is my honest opinion."

"Thank you," she said. "You mustn't think I am at
all offended. No woman could be when you put it so
poetically, but, Mr. Pulling, I must tell you that I
truly love my husband." The awful thing, of course,
was that she couldn't in her deafness distinguish between the lip movements made by spoken words and
the movements which expressed my unspoken

thoughts. She was always kind to me after that day, but she never came to my private office again.

That night at the Gare de Lyon I saw my aunt into her couchette and ordered her *petit déjeuner* from the conductor for eight a.m. Then I waited on the platform for the train from London to come in from the Gare du Nord. It was five minutes late, but the Orient Express had to wait for it.

As the train moved slowly in, drowning the platform with steam, I saw Wordsworth come striding through the smoke. He recognized me at the same moment and cried, "Hi, fellah." He must have learnt the Americanism during the war when the convoys for the Middle East gathered in Freetown Harbour. I went reluctantly towards him. "What are you doing here?" I asked. I have always disliked the unexpected, whether an event or an encounter, but I was growing accustomed to it in my aunt's company.

"Mr. Pullen, Mr. Pullen," Wordsworth said, "you an honest man, Mr. Pullen." He reached my side and grasped my hand. "Ar allays was your friend, Mr. Pullen." He spoke as if he had known me for years and I had been a long time in his debt. "You no humbug me, Mr. Pullen?" He gazed wildly up and down the train. "Where's that gel?"

"My aunt," I said, "if that's whom you mean, is fast asleep by now in her couchette."

"Then please go double quick tell her Wordsworth here."

"I have no intention of waking her up. She's an old lady and has a long journey ahead of her. If it's money you want, you can take this." I held out to him a fifty-franc note.

"I no wan CTC," Wordsworth said, waving one hand hard for emphasis, while at the same time he took the note with the other. "I wan my bebi gel."

Such an expression used in connection with Aunt Augusta offended me and I turned away to climb the steep steps into the coach, but he put his hand on my arm and held me back on the platform. He was a very strong man. "You jig-jig with my bebi gel," he accused me.

"You're preposterous, Wordsworth. She is my aunt. My mother's sister."

"No humbug?"

"No humbug," I said, though I hated the expression. "Even if she were not my aunt, can't you understand that she is a very old lady?"

"No one too old for jig-jig," Wordsworth said. "You tell her she come back here to Paris. Wordsworth wait long long time for her. You speak her sweet. You tell her she still my bebi gel. Wordsworth no slip good when she gone."

The conductor asked me to get onto the train, for we were about to leave, and Wordsworth unwillingly released me. I stood on the top of the steps as the train began to move out from the Gare de Lyon in short jerks, and Wordsworth followed it down the platform, wading through the steam. He was crying, and I was reminded of a suicide walking out fully dressed into the surf. Suddenly, staring at a window beyond me, he began to sing:

> "'Slip gud-o, bebi gel:
> An luk me wan minit
> Befo yu slip."

The train gathered momentum and with a final jerk and strain it had left him behind.

I squeezed down the corridor to my aunt's couchette which was number 72. The bed was made up, but there was a strange girl in a mini-skirt sitting on it, while my aunt leant out of the window waving and blowing kisses. The girl and I looked at each other with embarrassment. We could hardly speak and interrupt this ceremony of separation. She was very young, perhaps eighteen, and she was elaborately made up with a chalk-white face, dark-shadowed eyes and long auburn hair falling over her shoulders. With the strokes of a pencil she had continued her eyelashes below and above the lids, so that the real eyelashes, standing out, had a false effect like a stereoscopic photograph. Her shirt had two buttons missing at the top as though they had popped off with the tension of her puppy fat and her eyes bulged like a Pekinese dog's, but they were pretty nonetheless. They had in them what used to be called by my generation a sexy look, but this might have been caused by short sight or constipation. Her smile, when she realized that I was not a stranger intruding into my aunt's compartment, was oddly timid for someone who looked so flagrant. It was as though someone else had dolled her up to attract. She was like a kid tethered to a tree to draw a tiger out of the jungle.

My aunt pulled in her head; her face was smeared with smuts and tears. "Dear man," she said. "I had to take a last look. At my age one never knows."

I said with disapproval, "I thought that chapter was closed," and added for the sake of the girl, "Aunt Augusta."

"One can never be quite sure," my aunt said. "This is Seventy-one," she added, indicating the girl.

"Seventy-one?"

"The next-door couchette. What's your name, dear?"

"Tooley," the girl replied. It might have been a pet name or a family name—one couldn't be sure.

"Tooley is going to Istanbul too. Aren't you, dear?"

"En passant," she said with an American accent.

"She's going to Katmandu," my aunt explained.

"I thought that was in Nepal."

"I guess that's where it is," the girl said. "Something like that."

"She and I got talking," my aunt told me, "because—what's your name again, dear?"

"Tooley," the girl said.

"Tooley has brought a sack of provisions with her. Do you realize, Henry, that the Orient Express has no restaurant car? How times have changed. No restaurant car till after the Turkish frontier. We face two days of starvation."

"I've got a lot of milk chocolate," the girl said, "and a little sliced ham."

"And thirst," Aunt Augusta said.

"I've got a dozen bottles of Coke, but it's getting pretty warm now."

"When I think of the party I once had on this very train," Aunt Augusta said, "with Mr. Visconti and General Abdul. Caviar and champagne. We practically lived in the dining-car. One meal ran into another and night into day."

"You are very welcome to share my Coke," Tooley said. "And the milk chocolate. The ham too, of course, but there's not much of that."

"At least the conductor has promised us coffee and *croissants*," I said, in the morning."

"I shall sleep as late as I can," my aunt said, "and we shall be able to get a bite at Milan station. With Mario," she added.

"Who's Mario?" I asked.

"We stop at Lausanne and Saint Maurice," said the well-informed girl.

"Switzerland is only bearable covered with snow," Aunt Augusta said, "like some people are only bearable under a sheet. Now I shall go to bed. You two young people are old enough to be left alone."

Tooley looked at me askance as though after all I might be the tiger type. "Oh, I'll sleep too," she said,

"I love sleep." She looked at a huge wrist-watch on a strap an inch wide with only four numerals, coloured scarlet. "It's not one yet," she said doubtfully. "I'd better take a pill."

"You'll sleep," my aunt said in a tone not to be denied.

Chapter 12

We were just pulling out of Lausanne when I awoke. I could see the lake between two tall grey apartment buildings and there was a tasteful advertisement for chocolates and then another for watches. It was the conductor who had woken me, bringing me coffee and *brioches* (I had asked for *croissants*). "Is the lady in Seventy-two awake?" I asked.

"She did not wish to be disturbed before Milan," he replied

"Is it true that there's no restaurant car?"

"Yes, monsieur."

"At least you will give us breakfast tomorrow?"

"No, monsieur, I leave the train at Milan. There is another conductor."

"Italian?"

"Yugoslav, monsieur."

"Does he speak English or French?"

"It is not likely."

I felt hopelessly abroad.

I drank my coffee, and then from the corridor I watched the small Swiss towns roll smoothly by: the Montreux Palace in baroque Edwardian like the home of a Ruritanian king, and rising behind it, out of a bank of morning mist, pale mountains like an

underexposed negative: Aigle, Bex, Visp . . . We
stopped at nearly every station, but it was seldom that
anyone either got in or out. Like my aunt, foreign
passengers were not interested in Switzerland without
snow, and yet it was here that I was seriously tempted
to leave her. I had fifty pounds of travellers' cheques
and I had no interest at all in Turkey. I caught
glimpses of meadows running down to water, of old
castles on hills spiked with vines and of girls on
bicycles; everything seemed clean and arranged and
safe, as my life had been before my mother's funeral.
I thought of my garden. I missed my dahlias, and at
some small station where a postman was delivering
letters from a bicycle, there was a bed of mauve and
red flowers. I think I might really have got off if the
girl called Tooley hadn't at that moment touched my
arm. Was there anything so wrong with the love of
peace that I had to be forcibly drawn away from it by
Aunt Augusta?

"Did you sleep well?" Tooley asked.

"Oh yes, and you?"

"I hardly slept a wink." Her Pekinese eyes stared
up at me, as though she were waiting for something
from my plate. I offered her a *brioche*, but she refused it.

"Oh no, thanks a lot. I've had a chocolate bar."

"Why couldn't you sleep?"

"I'm sort of worried."

I remembered, from my cashier days, faces just as
timid as hers, peering through a hygienic barrier
where a notice directed them to speak through a slot
placed inconveniently low. I almost asked her whether she had an overdraft.

"Anything I can do?"

"I just want to talk," she said.

"What could I do but invite her in? My bed had
been made into a sofa while I stood in the corridor,
and we sat down side by side. I offered her a ciga-

rette. It was an ordinary Senior Service, but she turned it over as though it were something special she had never seen before.

"English?" she asked.

"Yes."

"What does Senior Service mean?"

"The Navy."

"You don't mind, do you, if I smoke one of my own?" She took a tin marked EUCALYPTUS-AND-MEN-THOL LOZENGES out of her bag and picked from it an anonymous cigarette which looked as though it had been home-rolled. On second thoughts she offered me one, and I thought it would be a little unkind of me to refuse. It was a very small cigarette, and it looked rather grubby. It had an odd herbal flavour, not disagreeable.

"I've never smoked an American cigarette before," I said.

"I got these in Paris—from a friend."

"Or French ones."

"He was a terribly nice man. Groovy."

"Who was?"

"This man I met in Paris. I told him my trouble too."

"What is your trouble?"

"I had a quarrel—with my boy-friend, I mean. He wanted to go third-class to Istanbul. I said it's crazy, we couldn't sleep together in the third-class, and I've got the money, haven't I? 'Your stinking allowance,' he said. 'Sell all you have and give it to the poor'— that's a quotation, isn't it, from somewhere? I said, 'It wouldn't be any use. Father would pay me back.' 'He need never know,' he said. 'He has sources of information,' I said, 'he's very high up, I mean, in the CIA'. He said, 'You can stick your money up your arse'—that's an English expression, isn't it? He's English. We met when we were sitting down in Trafalgar Square."

"Feeding the pigeons?" I asked.

She gave a bubble of a laugh and choked on the smoke. "You are ironic," she said. "I like men who are ironic. My father's ironic too. You are a bit like him when I come to think of it. Irony is a very valuable literary quality too, isn't it, like passion?"

"You mustn't ask me about literature, Miss Tooley," I said. "I'm very ignorant."

"Don't call me *Miss* Tooley. Tooley's what my friends call me."

At Saint Maurice a gang of schoolgirls passed down the platform. They were nice-looking schoolgirls; not one of them wore a mini-skirt or visible make-up and they carried neat little satchels.

"How can such a beautiful country be so dull?" Tooley thought aloud.

"Why dull?"

"They aren't turned on here," she said. "None of them will ever be turned on. Would you like another cigarette?"

"Thank you. They are very mild. Agreeable flavour too. They don't rasp the throat."

"I do like the expressions you use. They really are groovy."

I felt more awake than I usually do at that hour of the morning, and I found Tooley's company something of a novelty. I was glad that my aunt was sleeping late and giving me an opportunity to get better acquainted. I felt protective. I would have liked a daughter, though I had never been able to imagine Miss Keene as a mother. A mother should not be in need of protection herself.

"This friend of yours in Paris," I said, "was a very good judge of cigarettes."

"He was fabulous," she said. "I mean, he's really together."

"French?"

"Oh no, he came from darkest Africa."

"A Negro?"

"We don't call them that," she said reprovingly. "We call them coloured or black—whichever they prefer."

A sudden suspicion struck me. "Was he called Wordsworth?"

"I only knew him as Zach."

"That's the man. Was it you he came to see off at the station?"

"Sure. Who else? I never expected him, but there he was at the gate to say good-bye. I bought him a platform ticket, but I think he was scared. He wouldn't come any further."

"He knows my aunt too," I said. I didn't tell her that he had used her ticket for another purpose.

"Now isn't that the wildest sort of coincidence? Like something in Thomas Hardy."

"You seem to know a lot about literature."

"I'm majoring in English literature," she said. "My father wanted me to take social science because he wanted me to serve a while in the Peace Corps, but I guess our ideas didn't coincide in that and other things."

"What does your father do?"

"I told you—he has a very secret job in the CIA."

"That must be interesting," I said.

"He travels about a terrible lot. I haven't seen him more than once since Mom divorced him last fall. I tell him he sees the world horizontally, I mean that's superficial, isn't it? I want to see the world vertically."

"In depth," I said. I was rather proud of catching up with her ideas.

"These help," she said, waving her cigarette. "I feel a bit turned on already. It's your fabulous way of talking. I feel I sort of met you in the English literature course. As a character. We did Dickens in depth."

"Vertically," I said, and we laughed together.

"What's your name?"

"Henry." She laughed again and I followed suit though I was not sure why.

"They didn't even call you Harry?" she asked.

"Harry is the diminutive. One cannot be baptized Harry. There was never a Saint Harry."

"Is that what they call Canon Law?"

"I believe so."

"Because I knew a fabulous guy once who was baptized Knock-Me-Down."

"I doubt if he was really baptized that."

"Are you a Roman Catholic?"

"No, but I believe my aunt is one. I'm not quite sure thought."

"I nearly became a Roman Catholic once. Because of the Kennedys. But then when two of them got shot—I mean I'm superstitious. Was Macbeth a Catholic?"

"It's not a question that's ever occurred to me . . . I suppose . . . well, I mean I don't really know." It seemed to me that I was picking up her phrases.

"Maybe we ought to lock the door and open the window," she said. "What country are we in now?"

"I think we must be coming near to the Italian frontier."

"Then open the window quick." I couldn't follow her reasoning, but I obeyed. I had already finished my cigarette, and she tossed away her stump and then emptied the ash-tray on to the line. Then I remembered Wordsworth.

"What have we been smoking?" I said.

"Pot, of course. Why?"

"Do you realize we could be sent to prison? I don't know the Swiss law or the Italian, but . . ."

"I wouldn't be. I'm under age."

"And me?"

"You could plead innocence," she said and began to laugh: she was laughing when the door opened and the Italian police looked in.

"Passports," they demanded, but they didn't even open them; the draught of the open window blew off one man's cap, and I could only hope the smell of Cannabis had dispersed down the corridor. They were followed closely by the customs men, who were equally considerate, except that one man wrinkled his nose. A few minutes later they were safely on the platform.

The sign read: DOMODOSSOLA.

"We're in Italy," I said.

"Then have another."

"I'll do no such thing, Tooley. I had no idea . . . For goodness' sake get rid of them before night. Yugoslavia's a Communist country, and they won't hesitate to imprison someone under age."

"I was always taught that Yugoslavs were *good* Communists. We sell them strategic material, don't we?"

"But not drugs," I said.

"Now you're being ironical again. I mean I wanted to tell you my great trouble, but how can I do it if you're ironical?"

"You said just now that irony was a valuable literary quality."

"But you aren't a novel," she said and began to cry as Italy went by outside. The Cannabis had caused the laughter and now, I suppose, it caused the tears. I felt a little unhappy myself, watching her. My head swam. I shut the window and saw through the pane a hill-village all yellow and ochre, like something grown of itself out of rain and earth, and beside the line a factory and a red housing estate and an *autostrada* and an advertisement for Perugina and all the wires and grids of a smokeless age.

"What's your trouble, Tooley?" I asked.

"I forgot the damn pill and I haven't had the curse for six weeks. I nearly talked to your mother last night . . ."

"My aunt," I corrected her. "You ought to speak to her. I don't really know about these things."

"But I want to talk to a man," Tooley said. "I mean I'm sort of shy of women. I don't get on terms with them fast the way I do with men. The trouble is men are so ignorant now. In the old days a girl never knew what to do, and now it's the men who don't know. Julian said it was my fault—he trusted me."

"Julian is the boyfriend?" I asked.

"He was angry because I forgot the pill. He wanted to hitch-hike to Istanbul. He said it might do the trick."

"I thought he wanted to go third-class."

"That was before I told him. And before he met a man with a truck going to Vienna. Then he gave me an ultimatum. We were in this café in the Place Saint Michel and he said, 'We've got to leave now or never,' and I said, 'No,' and he said, 'Find your own fucking way then.'"

"Where is he now?"

"Somewhere between here and Istanbul."

"How will you find him?"

"They'll know at the Gulhane."

"What's that?"

"It's near the Blue Mosque. Everyone knows where everyone is at the Gulhane." She began to remove carefully the traces of tears. Then she looked at her huge watch with the four numbers and said, "It's nearly lunchtime. I'm as hungry as a dog. I hope I'm not feeding two. Want some chocolate?"

"I'll wait until Milan," I said.

"Have another cigarette?"

"No, thank you."

"I will. It might do the trick." She began to smile again. "It's funny the ideas I get. I mean, I think

almost anything might do the trick. I drank brandy
and ginger ale in Paris because at school they said
ginger did the trick. And I had sauna baths too. It's
funny when all you really need is a curettage. Wordsworth said he'd find me a doctor, but he said he'd
need a few days to find him, and then I'd have to lay
up a little, and it wouldn't be much good getting to
the Gulhane and finding Julian gone. Gone where? I
ask you. I met a boy in Paris who said they were
turning us all out of Katmandu and Vientiane was
the place now. Not for Americans, of course, because
of the draft."

There were moments when she gave the impression
that all the world was travelling.

Tooley said, "I slept with a boy in Paris when
Julian walked out because I thought, well, it might
stir things up a bit. I mean the curse comes that way
sometimes right on top of the orgasm, but I didn't get
any orgasm. I guess I was worrying about Julian,
because I don't ofen have difficulty that way."

"I think you ought to go straight back home and
tell your parents."

"In the singular," she said. "I don't count Mom,
and I don't exactly know where Father is. He travels
an awful lot. Secret missions. He might be in Vientiane for all I know—they say it's lousy with CIA."

"Haven't you anywhere you call home?" I asked
her.

"Julian and me felt like home, but then he got
angry about my forgetting the pill. He's very quick-
tempered. 'If I have to remind you all the time,' he
said, 'it takes away my spontaneity, don't you understand that?' He's got a theory women want to castrate
their men, and one way is to take away their spontaneity."

"And you felt at home with him?"

"We could discuss just everything," she said with a
happy and reminiscent smile as the pot began to

work again. "Art and sex and James Joyce and psychology."

"You oughtn't to smoke that stuff," I protested.

"Pot? Why? There's no harm in pot. Acid's another thing. Julian wanted me to try acid, but I said no. I mean, I don't want to warp my chromosomes."

There were moments when I didn't understand a word she said, and yet it seemed to me that I could listen to her for a long while without wearying. There was something gentle and sweet about her which reminded me of Miss Keene. It was an absurd comparison to make, of course, and perhaps this was what she meant by being turned on.

CHAPTER 13

When a train pulls into a great city I am reminded of the closing moments of an overture. All the rural and urban themes of our long journey were picked up again: a factory was followed by a meadow, a patch of *autostrada* by a country road, a gas-works by a modern church: the houses began to tread on each other's heels, advertisements for Fiat cars swarmed closer together, the conductor who had brought breakfast passed, working intensely down the corridor to rouse some important passenger, the last fields were squeezed out and at last there were only houses, houses, houses, and MILANO flashed the signs, MILANO.

I said to Tooley, "We've arrived. We'd better get lunch. It's our last chance to get a square meal . . ."

"Your mother . . ." Tooley began.

"Aunt Augusta—she's here."

The conductor had preceded her down the corridor (I should have realized who the important passenger was) and now she stood in the doorway of our compartment wrinkling her nose. "What have you two been up to?" she asked.

"Smoking and talking," I said.

"You seem extraordinarily cheerful, Henry. It's not

quite like you." She sniffed again. "I can almost believe that poor Wordsworth is with us still."

"It's fabulous," Tooley said, "that you know Wordsworth, I mean."

"Il y a un monsieur qui vous demande, madame,"
the conductor interrupted, and I saw beyond my
aunt, between a trolley of newspapers and a trolley of
refreshments, a very tall thin man with exquisite
white hair gesticulating with an umbrella.

"Oh, it's Mario," my aunt said, without bothering
to turn. "I wrote to him that we should need lunch.
He will have ordered it. Come, my dear, come, Henry, there's no time to be lost." She preceded us down
the steps and dropped straight into the arms of the
white-haired man, who with steely strength held her
for a moment suspended. *"Madre mia, madre mia,"*
he said breathlessly and dropped his umbrella as he
put her carefully down onto the platform as though
she might break—the very idea connected with Aunt
Augusta was ridiculous.

"What on earth is he calling you that for?" I whispered. Perhaps it was the effect of the Cannabis, but I
had taken an extreme dislike to the man who was
now kissing Tooley's hand.

"I knew him since he was a baby," Aunt Augusta
said. "He is Mr. Visconti's son."

He was very good-looking in a histrionic way; he
had the appearance of an ageing actor and I didn't
like the way he was trying to dazzle Tooley with
pieces of his repertoire. After his burst of theatrical
emotion with my aunt he was conducting Tooley
ahead of us down the platform to the restaurant,
holding his umbrella by the ferrule and pointing the
crook up like a crozier. With his white hair and his
head bent towards Tooley he looked like a hypnotic
bishop instructing a neophyte on purity.

"What does he do, Aunt Augusta. Is he an actor?"

"He writes verse dramas."

"Can he live on that?"

"Mr. Visconti settled a little money on him before the war. Luckily, in Swiss francs. I suspect too that he gets money from women."

"Rather disgusting at his age," I said.

"He can make a woman laugh. Look how Tooley is laughing now. His father was the same. It's the best way, Henry, to win a woman. They are wiser than men. They think of the period that must elapse between one love-making and another. In my youth not many women smoked cigarettes. Look out for that trolley."

I could feel in my head the cunning of Cannabis. "He must have been born when you knew Mr. Visconti . . . Did you know his mother too?"

"Not very well."

"She must have been a beautiful woman."

"I am not a fair judge. I detested her and she detested me. Mario always thought of me as his real mother. Mr. Visconti called her the blond cow. She was German."

Mario Visconti had ordered a *saltimbocca Romana* for each of us and a bottle of Frascati wine. My aunt began to speak to him in Italian. "You must forgive me," my aunt said, "but Mario speaks no English, and it is many years since we have seen each other."

"Do you speak Italian?" I asked Tooley.

"Not a word."

"You seemed to be having quite a conversation."

"Oh, he was very expressive."

"What was he expressing?"

"He sort of liked me. What does *cuore* mean?"

I looked at Mario Visconti with resentment and saw that he had begun to weep. He was talking a great deal and using his hands in explanation and once he picked up his umbrella and held it above his head. In the short intervals between paragraphs he put a lot of *saltimbocca Romana* into his mouth, leaning his handsome face forward over the plate, so that the fork only had a short distance to travel and the tears only a little way to fall. It was lucky that the dish was heavily salted already. My aunt lent him a wispy lace handkerchief, which he applied to his eyes and afterwards adjusted becomingly in his breast pocket to show a frilly corner. Then he became dissatisfied with the wine, which seemed very good to me, and called to the waiter to change it. Only after he had tasted a new bottle did he resume his tears. I noticed the waiters were as indifferent to the scene as usherettes at a cinema are to a movie which has been running a week.

"I don't like a man who cries," I said to Tooley.

"Have you never cried?"

"No," I said and then added for the sake of accuracy, "not in public." The waiter brought us all ice-creams in three colours. They looked dangerous to me and I left mine untasted, but Mario's disappeared quickly and I noticed how his tears were quenched as though the ice had frozen the ducts. He gave my aunt a shy boyish smile which went strangely with his white hair, and she surreptitiously lent him her purse to pay with.

On the steps of the train I was afraid he would begin to cry again when he embraced her, but instead he gave her a small brown-paper parcel and walked silently away, holding up his crook to hide his emotion or perhaps his lack of it. "So that's that," my aunt said with cool thoughtfulness. Tooley had disappeared —I suspected into the lavatory to smoke another cigarette—and I decided to tell Aunt Augusta about her trouble.

But I found when I sat down beside her that she wanted to do the talking herself. "Mario seems rather an old man," she said, "or has he dyed his hair, I wonder? He cannot be more than forty-five. Or six. I am bad about dates."

"He certainly looks a good deal older than that. Perhaps it is the poetry."

"I have never much cared," she said, "for men with umbrellas, but he was charming as a child." She looked out of the window and I looked too: a new housing estate in red brick straggled beside the line and on the hill beyond a medieval village crumbled away behind its ramparts.

"Why was he crying?" I asked.

"He wasn't crying. He was laughing," she said. "Something about Mr. Visconti. I haven't seen Mario for more than thirty years," she said. "He was a sweet boy then—too sweet perhaps to last. The war came. We were separated."

"And his father?"

"I never associated sweetness with Mr. Visconti. Charm perhaps. He was a terrible twister. Very generous with cream buns, of course, but one can't live on cream buns. Perhaps I am being unfair. One is apt to be unfair to somebody one has loved a great deal. And after all he was kind to me from the very start —he found me my situation in Italy."

"At the theatre?"

"I can't think why you persist in calling it a theatre. 'All the world's a stage,' of course, but a metaphor as general as that loses all its meaning. Only a second-rate actor could have written such a line out of pride in his second-rate calling. There were occasions when Shakespeare was a very bad writer indeed. You can see how often in books of quotations. People who like quotations love meaningless generalizations."

I was a little shocked by her unexpected attack on Shakespeare. Perhaps it was because he wrote verse dramas like Mario. "You were talking about Mr. Visconti, I reminded her."

"I must admit he was very kind to me in Paris. I was quite heartbroken when I left Curran. I couldn't appeal to your father because I had promised Angelica to stay away, and when Curran left, after our final quarrel, he took everything except the cash in the church collecting-boxes and twelve tins of sardines. He had an unnatural passion for sardines. He said they calmed his nerves, that eating them was like pouring oil on troubled waters. There was enough in the collecting-boxes to pay my passage across the Channel and I was lucky to get this job of mine in the Rue de Provence. But I wasn't really happy there, and I was grateful to Mr. Visconti when he took me to Italy. The work, of course, was the same, but I enjoyed the travel from one city to another. And every eight weeks when I came back to Milan I enjoyed seeing Mr. Visconti. Cream buns were a great improvement on sardines. Sometimes too he would pop up unexpectedly in Venice. He was a twister, no doubt of it, but there are many worse people than twisters." She sighed, looking out at the dull scenery of the Po. "I grew to be very very fond of him. Fonder than any other man I have ever known. Except the first, but the first is always a special case."

"How did you come to retire?" I asked. I was going to say "from the stage," but I remembered her inexplicable dislike of the term. I had not forgotten Tooley's trouble, but I thought it only fair to let my aunt finish first with the memories stirred up by the sight of Visconti's son.

"Your Uncle Jo left me all his money. It was quite a shock. The house, too, of course, but there was nothing to be done about that. It's still crumbling away near the *autostrada*. I settled the house on Mario when I had to leave Italy because of the war and I think he sometimes takes a woman there to spend a week-end in the ancient family *palazzo*. He even calls it the Palazzo Visconti (he's a bit of a snob: quite unlike his father). One day they'll want to build a connecting road to the *autostrada* and then the state will have to pay him compensation if he can show that the house was inhabited."

"Why didn't you marry Mr. Visconti, Aunt Augusta?"

"There's no divorce in Italy, and Mr. Visconti was a Catholic, even though a nonpractising one. He even insisted on my being received into the Church. It was his wife who had all the money and that hampered Mr. Visconti badly until he managed to get his fingers on most of what Jo had left me. I was very careless in those days and Mr. Visconti was very plausible. It was lucky that no one would buy the house—that at least was left me for a time. He had a scheme for selling fresh vegetables—tomatoes, particularly, of course—to Saudi Arabia. At the beginning I think he really believed he would make our fortune. Even his wife lent him money. I shall always remember the conferences at the Excelsior in Rome with Arab notables in long robes who arrived with a dozen wives and a food-taster. Mr. Visconti would take a whole floor in the Excelsior—you can imagine that made quite a hole in Jo's money. But it was very romantic while it lasted. I had my fun. Mr. Visconti was never for a moment dull. He even persuaded the Vatican to put in money, so we had cardinals for cocktails at the Grand Hotel. The Grand had once been a convent, and I suppose they felt more at home there. They were greeted at the door by flunkeys with tall candles, and it was a wonderful sight when the Arabs and the cardinals met, the desert robes and the scarlet skull-caps and all the bowings and embracings and the genuflections of the management and the kissing of rings and the blessings. The Arabs, of course, only drank orange juice, and the tasters stood at the bar sampling each jug and occasionally snatching a whisky and soda on the side. Everybody enjoyed these parties, but only the Arabs could really afford their fun, as it turned out."

"Was Mr. Visconti ruined?"

"He pulled out in time with what was left of my money and what was left of his wife's, and to do him justice he had settled some of mine on Mario. Of course he disappeared for a while, but he came back after things had quieted down. The Vatican made a very profitable deal, you remember, with Mussolini, so that what they lost to Mr. Visconti seemed very small beer indeed. He had left me enough to live on in a modest way, but I have never been very keen on modesty. Life was very monotonous after Mr. Visconti disappeared. I even visited Havana, as I told you, and afterwards I went back to Paris for a while. (Mario was with the Jesuits in Milan) —that was when I met Monsieur Dambreuse. But when the affair was over I came back to Rome. I always hoped that one day Mr. Visconti would turn up again. I had a two-room apartment, and I did a little part-time work in an establishment behind the *Messaggero*. Life was very middle-class after all the Arabs and the cardinals. I had been spoilt by Curran and Mr. Visconti. No men have ever given me more amusement than those two did. Poor Wordsworth!" my aunt added. "He was not in the same league." She gave a very young laugh and laid her hand on my knee. "And then—Oh praise to the Holiest in the height, as Wordsworth is fond of saying—I was putting in a little part-time behind the *Messaggero* when who should walk into the reception room but Mr. Visconti. A pure coincidence. He wasn't looking for me. But how happy we were. How happy. Just to see each other again. The girls didn't understand when we joined hands then and there and danced between the sofas. It was one o'clock in the morning. We didn't go upstairs. We went straight out into the lane outside. There was a drinking fountain shaped like an animal's head, and he splashed my face with water before he kissed me."

"What was that half-time employment?" I suddenly broke out. "Who were the girls? What were the sofas there for?"

"What does it matter now?" my aunt said. "What did any of it matter? We were together again and he splashed me and splashed me and he kissed me and kissed me."

"But surely you must have despised the man after all he had done to you?"

We were crossing the long aqueduct through the lagoons which leads to Venice-Mestre, but there were no signs of the beautiful city, only tall chimneys with pale gas flames hardly visible in the late-afternoon sunlight. I was not expecting my aunt's outburst.

She turned on me with real fury as though I were a child who had carelessly broken some vase she had cherished over the years for its beauty and the memories it contained. "I despise no one," she said, "no one. Regret your own actions, if you like that kind of wallowing in self-pity, but never, never despise. Never presume yours is a better morality. What do you *suppose* I was doing in the house behind the *Messaggero?* I was cheating, wasn't I? So why shouldn't Mr. Visconti cheat me? But you, I suppose, never cheated in all your little provincial banker's life because there's not anything you wanted enough, not even money, not even a woman. You looked after people's money like a nanny who looks after other people's children. Can't I see you in your cage, stacking up the little fivers endlessly before you hand them over to their proper owner? Angelica certainly brought you up as she wanted you. Your poor father didn't have a chance. He was a cheat too, and I only wish you were. Then perhaps we'd have something in common."

I was astounded. I could find nothing to say in reply. I thought of leaving the train at Venice, but then there was Tooley and I felt responsible for Tooley. The squalid station wrapped us round with its dirt and its noise. I said, "I think I'd better find Tooley," and I went away, leaving the old lady glaring on her couchette. Only as I closed the door of the compartment I thought I heard her laugh.

CHAPTER 14

I felt glad that I had not lost my temper, but nonetheless I was shocked and needed a little time for reflection, so I climbed down on to the platform and began to look around me for food. It was the last chance before Belgrade next morning. I bought six ham rolls off a trolley and a bottle of Chianti and some sweet cakes—it was not so good a meal as Chicken would have provided, I thought sadly, and what a dreary station it was. Travel could be a great waste of time. This was the hour of the early evening when the sun had lost its heat and the shadows fell across my small lawn, the hour when I would take my yellow watering-can and fill it from the garden tap . . .

Tooley's voice said, "Would you mind getting me some more Coke?"

"There's nowhere on the train to keep it cold."

"I don't mind warm Coke."

Oh, the absurdity of it all, I could have cried aloud, for now the man with the trolley wouldn't take a pound note, and I had to give him two of the dollars which I was carrying in my pocket-book against emergencies, and he refused any change, though I knew the exact rate and told him the lire required.

"Julian did a fabulous picture of a Coke bottle once," Tooley said.

"Who's Julian?" I asked absent-mindedly.

"The boy-friend, of course. I told you. He painted the Coke bright yellow. *Fauve*," she added in a defiant way.

"He paints, does he?"

"That's why he thinks the East's very important to him. You know, like Tahiti was for Gauguin. He wants to experience the East before he starts on his big project. Let me take the Coke."

There was less than an hour's wait at Venice, but the dark was falling when we pulled out and I saw nothing at all—I might have been leaving Clapham for Victoria. Tooley sat with me and drank one of her Cokes. I asked her what her boy-friend's project was.

"He wants to do a series of *enormous* pictures of Heinz soups in fabulous colours, so a rich man could have a different soup in each room in his apartment —say fish soup in the bedroom, potato soup in the dining-room, leek soup in the drawing-room, like they used to have family portraits. There would be these fabulous colours, all *fauve*. And the cans would give a sort of unity—do you see what I mean? It would be kind of intimate—you wouldn't break the mood every time you changed rooms. Like you do now if you have de Staël in one room and a Rouault in another."

The memory of something I had seen in a Sunday supplement came back to me. I said, "Surely somebody once *did* paint a Heinz soup tin?"

"Not Heinz, Campbell's," Tooley said. "That was Andy Warhol. I said the same thing to Julian when he first told me of the project. 'Of course,' I said, 'Heinz and Campbell are not a bit the same shape. Heinz is sort of squat and Campbell's are long like English pillar-boxes.' I love your pillar-boxes. They are fabulous. But Julian said that wasn't the point.

He said that there are certain subjects which belong to a certain period and culture. Like the Annunciation did. Botticelli wasn't put off because Piero della Francesca had done the same thing. He wasn't an *imitator*. And think of all the Nativities. Well, Julian says, we sort of belong to the soup age—only he didn't call it that. He said it was the Art of the Techno-Structure. In a way, you see, the more people who paint soups the better. It *creates* a culture. One Nativity wouldn't have been any use at all. It wouldn't have been noticed."

I was badly out of my depth with Tooley in terms of culture and of human experience. She was closer to my aunt: she would never, I felt sure, have criticized Mr. Visconti: she would have accepted him, as she accepted Julian's project, a voyage to Istanbul, my company, her baby.

"Where does your mother live?"

"I guess she's in Bonn at the moment. She married a man on Time-Life who covers West Germany and Eastern Europe, so they move around a lot. Like Father. Do you want a cigarette?"

"Not for me. And you'd better wait till we're past the next frontier."

It was nearly nine-thirty in the evening when we arrived at Sezana. A surly passport man looked at us as though we were Imperialist spies. Old women heavily laden with small parcels came down the un-platformed track, making for the third-class. They emerged from everywhere like a migration, even from between the goods trucks which stood uncoupled all along the line looking as though they would never be linked together. No one else joined the train: no one got off. There were no lights, no waiting-room in sight, it was cold and the heating had not been turned on. On the road beyond—if there was a road —no cars passed. No railway hotel offered a welcome.

"I'm cold," Tooley said. "I'm going to bed." She

offered to leave me a cigarette, but I refused. I didn't want to be compromised on this cold frontier. Another uniformed man looked in and regarded my new suitcase on the rack with hatred.

At moments during the night I woke—in Ljubljana, in Zagreb—but there was nothing to be seen except the lines of stationary rolling-stock which looked abandoned, as though nothing was left anywhere to put in the trucks, no one had the energy any more to roll them, and it was only our train which steamed on impelled by a foolish driver who hadn't realized that the world had stopped and there was nowhere for us to go.

At Belgrade, Tooley and I had breakfast in the station hotel—dry bread and jam and bad coffee, and we bought a bottle of sweet white wine for lunch, but they had no sandwiches. I let my aunt sleep on: it was not a meal worth waking her to share.

"Why are you two going to Istanbul?" Tooley asked, taking a spoonful of jam—she had given up trying to crumble the bread.

"She likes to travel," I said.

"But why to Istanbul?"

"I haven't asked her."

In the fields horses moved slowly along, dragging harrows. We were back in the pre-industrial age. Tooley and I were both depressed, yet it wasn't the lowest point of our journey; that came as evening fell in Sofia, and we tried to buy something to eat, but no one would take any money but Bulgarian except at an exorbitant rate, and even when I agreed to that, there were only tepid sausages on sale made of some coarse unrecognizable meat and chocolate cake made of a chocolate substitute and pink fizzy wine. I hadn't seen my aunt all day except once when she looked in on us and refused Tooley's last bar of chocolate and said sadly and unexpectedly, "I loved chocolate once. I am growing old."

"So this is the great Orient Express," Tooley said.

"All that's left of it."

"Istanbul can't be much worse, can it?"

"I've never been there, but I don't imagine so."

"I guess you are going to tell me that I mustn't smoke because there'll soon be another frontier."

"There will be three frontiers," I said, looking at the time-table, "in less than four hours. The Bulgarian frontier, the Greek-Macedonian frontier, the Turkish frontier."

"Maybe it's real luxury travel," Tooley said, "for people not in a hurry. Do you think they have an abortionist on the train? It's lucky I'm not nine months gone, isn't it, or I wouldn't know whether my baby was going to be Bulgarian or Turkish or—what was the other?"

"Greek-Macedonian."

"That sounds a bit special. I'd choose that. Not a Bulgar. If he was a boy there'd be dirty jokes."

"But you wouldn't have a choice."

"I'd hang on. When they said push I wouldn't push. Not till after the Greek-Macedonian frontier. How long are we in Greece-Macedonia?"

"Only forty minutes," I said.

"My, it's complicated. I'd have to work quick." She added, "It's not funny at all. I'm scared. What's Julian going to say when the curse hasn't come? I really thought the train would do it, sort of shake it out of me, I mean."

"It's Julian's fault as much as yours."

"But it isn't any longer, not with the pill. It's all the girl's fault now. I really did forget. When I take a sleeping pill I wake up muzzy and forget, and then when I take a methedrine to wake up properly I get so excited I don't remember all the dull things—like the pill and washing the dishes. But I guess Julian won't believe all that. He'll feel trapped. He often feels trapped. He was trapped first by his family, he

says, and then he was nearly trapped by Oxford—so
he went away fast without a degree. Then he very
nearly got trapped by the Trotskyists, but he realized
just in time. He sees traps a terribly long way ahead.
But, Henry, I don't mean to be a trap. Really I don't.
I can't call you Henry. It doesn't sound like a real
name. Can I call you Smudge?"

"Why Smudge?"

"I had a dog once called Smudge. I used to talk to
him a lot. When Father and Mother got divorced I
told him all the horrid details. About the mental
cruelty I mean."

She leant against me in the carriage. I liked the
smell of her hair. I suppose if I had known more
about women I could have identified the shampoo
she must have had in Paris. Her hand was on my knee,
and the enormous wrist-watch stared up at me with
its great blank white face and its four figures in
scarlet, 12 3 6 9, as if those were the only important
ones to remember—the hours when you had to take
your medicine. I remembered Miss Keene's minute
gold wristwatch like a doll's which Sir Alfred had
given her on her twenty-first birthday. In its tiny ring
it contained all the figures of the hours as though none
were unimportant or without its special duty. Most
of the hours of my life had been eliminated from
Tooley's watch. There were no hours marked there
for sitting quietly and watching a woman tat. I felt as
though one night in Southwood I had turned my
back on any possibility of home, so that here I was
shaken up and down between two segments of Bulgarian darkness.

"What was the mental cruelty?" I had to ask her
questions: it was the only way in which I could find
my way about in this new world, but questioning was
not a habit I had ever formed. For years people had
asked me questions: "What unit trust would you rec-
ommend? Do you think I should sell my hundred

Imperial Tobacco shares before the next cancer report?" And when I retired most of the questions I might have wanted to ask were answered for me in *Everyman His Own Gardener*.

"The only mental cruelty I ever saw personally," Tooley said, "was when Father woke her up bringing her breakfast in bed. I don't think that awful Bulgarian sausage was good for my metabolism. I've got a terrible stomach-ache. I'll go and lie down. You don't think it was horse, do you?"

"I've always understood that horse has a sweetish taste."

"Oh God, Smudge," she said. "I didn't want a literal answer, not real information I mean." She dabbed her lips against my cheek and was off.

I went down the corridor rather nervously to find Aunt Augusta. I'd hardly seen her all day and the problem of Tooley was one which I felt she ought to share. I found her with a Baedeker opened and a map of Istanbul spread over her knee. She looked like a general planning a campaign.

"I'm sorry about yesterday afternoon, Aunt Augusta," I said. "I really didn't mean to say anything against Mr. Visconti. After all I don't know the circumstances. Tell me more about him."

"He was a quite impossible man," my aunt said, "but I loved him and what he did with my money was the least of his faults. For example he was what they call a collaborator. During the German occupation he acted as adviser to the German authorities on questions of art, and he had to get out of Italy very quickly after the death of Mussolini. Goering had been making a big collection of pictures, but even he couldn't easily steal pictures from places like the Uffizi where the collection was properly registered, but Mr. Visconti knew a lot about the unregistered— all sorts of treasures hidden away in *palazzos* almost as crumbling as your Uncle Jo's. Of course his part got to be known, and there'd be quite a panic in a country place when Mr. Visconti appeared taking lunch in the local *taverna*. The trouble was he wouldn't play even a crooked game straight or the Germans might have helped him to escape. He began to take money from this *marchese* and that not to tip off the Germans—this gave him liquid cash or sometimes a picture he fancied for himself, but it didn't make him friends and the Germans soon suspected what was going on. Poor old devil," she added, "he hadn't a friend he could trust. Mario was still at school with the Jesuits and I had gone back to England when the war began."

"What happened to him in the end?"

"I thought for a long time he'd been liquidated by the partisans, for I never believed that story about the gondolier. I suspect he got someone to spread it for him. Mr. Visconti, as I told you, was not a man for fighting with knives or fists. A man who fights never survives long, and Mr. Visconti was great at survival. Why, the old sod," she said with tender delight, "he survives to this moment. He must be eighty-four if he's a day. He wrote to Mario and Mario wrote to me, and that's why you and I have taken the train to Istanbul. I couldn't explain all that in London, it was too complicated, and anyway I hardly knew you. Thank goodness for the gold brick, that's all I can say."

"The gold brick?"

"Never mind. That's quite another thing."

"You told me about a gold brick at London Airport, Aunt Augusta. Surely . . . ?"

"Of course not. It's not that one. That was quite a little one. Don't interrupt. I'm telling you now about poor Mr. Visconti. It seems he's fallen on very lean times."

"Where is he? In Istanbul?"

"It's better you shouldn't know, for there are people still after him. Oh dear, he certainly escaped the hard way. Mr. Visconti was a good Catholic, but he was very very anticlerical, and yet in the end it was the priesthood which saved him. He went to a clerical store in Rome, when the Allies were coming close, and he paid a fortune to be fitted out like a monsignor even to the purple socks. He said that a friend of his had lost all his clothes in a bombing raid and they pretended to believe him. Then he went with a suitcase to the lavatory in the Grand Hotel, where we had given all those cocktail parties to the cardinals, and changed. He kept away from the reception-desk, but he was unwise enough to look in at the bar—the barman, he knew, was very old and short-sighted. Well, you know, in those days a lot of girls used to come to the bar to pick up German officers. One of these girls—I suppose it was the approach of the Allied troops that did it—was having a *crise de conscience*. She wouldn't go to her friend's bedroom, she regretted her lost purity, she would never sin again. The officer plied her with more and more cocktails, but with every drink she became more religious. Then she spied Mr. Visconti, who was having a quick whisky in a shady corner. 'Father,' she cried to him, 'hear my confession.' You can imagine the tension in the bar, the noise outside as the evacuation got under way, the crying children, people drinking up what there was in the bar, the Allied planes overhead . . .'"

"How did you hear the story, Aunt Augusta?"

"Mr. Visconti told Mario the essentials when he got to Milan, and I can imagine the rest. Especially I can picture poor Mr. Visconti in his purple socks. 'My child,' he said, 'this is no fit place for a confession.'

" 'Never mind the place. What does the place matter? We are all about to die, and I am in mortal sin. Please, please, Monsignor.' (She had noticed his socks by this time.) What worried Mr. Visconti most was the attention she was provoking.

" 'My child,' he told her, 'in this state of emergency a simple act of contrition is enough,' but oh no, she wasn't going to be fobbed off with something cheap like that—'Bargain sale owing to closing down of premises.' She came and knelt at his knees. 'Your Grace,' she exclaimed. She was used to giving officers a superior rank—it nearly always pleased a captain to be called a major.

" 'I am not a bishop,' Mr. Visconti said. 'I am only a humble monsignor.' Mario questioned his father closely about this episode, and I have really invented nothing. If anyone has invented a detail it is Mario. You have to remember that he writes verse plays.

" 'Father,' the girl implored, taking the hint, 'help me.'

" 'The secrecy of the confessional,' Mr. Visconti pleaded back—they were now, you see, pleading to each other, and she pawed Mr. Visconti's knee, while he pawed the top of her head in an ecclesiastical way. Perhaps it was the pawings which made the German officer interrupt with impatience.

" 'For God's sake,' he said, "if she wants to confess, Monsignor, let her. Here's the key of my room, just down the passage, past the lavatory.'

"So off went Mr. Visconti with the hysterical girl—he remembered just in time to put down his whisky. He had no choice, though he hadn't been to confession himself for thirty years and he had never learnt the priest's part. Luckily there was an air-conditioner in the room breathing heavily, and that obscured his whispers, and the girl was too much concerned with her role to pay much attention to his. She began right away; Mr. Visconti had hardly time to sit on the bed, pushing aside a steel helmet and a bottle of *Schnapps*, before she was getting down to details. He had wanted the whole thing finished as quickly as possible, but he told Mario that he couldn't help becoming a little interested now she had got started and wanting to know a bit more. After all, he was a novice—though not in the ecclesiastical sense.

" 'How many times, my child?' That was a phrase he remembered very well from his adolescence.

" 'How can you ask that, Father? I've been at it all the time ever since the ocupation. After all they were our allies, Father.'

" 'Yes, yes, my child.' I can just see him enjoying the chance he had of learning a thing or two, even though his life was in danger. Mr. Visconti was a very lecherous man. He said, 'Always the same thing, my child?'

"She regarded him with astonishment. 'Of course not, Father. Who on earth do you think I am?'

"He looked at her kneeling in front of him, and I am sure he longed to pinch her. Mr. Visconti was always a great pincher. 'Anything unnatural, my child?'

" 'What do you mean unnatural, Father?'

"Mr. Visconti explained.

" 'Surely that's not unnatural, Father?'

"Then they had quite a discussion about what was natural and what wasn't, with Mr. Visconti almost forgetting his danger in the excitement, until someone knocked on the door and Mr. Visconti, vaguely sketching a cross in a lop-sided way, muttered what sounded through the noise of the air-conditioner like an absolution. The German officer came in the middle of it and said, 'Hurry up, Monsignor. I've got a more important customer for you.'

"It was the general's wife, who had come down to the bar for a last dry Martini before escaping north and heard what was going on. She drained her Martini in one gulp and commanded the officer to arrange her confession. So there was Mr. Visconti caught again. There was an awful row now in the Via Veneto as the tanks drove out of Rome. The general's

wife had positively to shout at Mr. Visconti. She had a
rather masculine voice and Mr. Visconti said it was
like being on the parade ground. He nearly clicked his
feet together in his purple socks when she bellowed at
him, 'Adultery. Three times.'

" 'Are you married, my daughter?'

" 'Of course I'm married. What on earth do you
suppose? I'm Frau General'—I've forgotten what ugly
Teutonic name she had.

" 'Does your husband know of this?'

" 'Of course he doesn't know. He's not a priest.'

" 'Then you have been guilty of lies too?'

" 'Yes, yes, naturally, I suppose so, you must hurry,
Father. Our car's being loaded. We are leaving for
Florence in a few minutes.'

" 'Haven't you anything else to tell me?'

" 'Nothing of importance.'

" 'You haven't missed Mass?'

" 'Oh, occasionally, Father. This is war-time.'

" 'Meat on Fridays?'

" 'You forget. It is permitted now, Father. Those
are Allied planes overhead. We have to leave immediately.'

" 'God cannot be hurried, my child. Have you
indulged in impure thoughts?'

" 'Father, put down yes to anything you like, but
give me absolution. I have to be off.'

" 'I cannot feel that you've properly examined your
conscience.'

" 'Unless you give me absolution at once, I shall
have you arrested. For sabotage.'

"Mr. Visconti said, 'It would be better if you gave
me a seat in your car. We could finish your confession
tonight.'

" 'There isn't room in the car, Father. The driver,
my husband, myself, my dog—there simply isn't space
for another passenger.'

" 'A dog takes up no room. It can sit on your knee.'

" 'This is an Irish wolfhound, Father.'

" 'Then you must leave it behind,' Mr. Visconti said firmly, and at that moment a car back-fired and the Frau General took it for an explosion.

" 'I need Wolf for my protection, Father. War is very dangerous for women.'

" 'You will be under the protection of our Holy Mother Church,' Mr. Visconti said, 'as well as your husband's.'

" 'I cannot leave Wolf behind. He is all I have in the world to love.'

" 'I would have assumed that with three adulteries—and a husband . . .'

" 'They mean nothing to me.'

" 'Then I suggest,' Mr. Visconti said, 'that we leave the general behind.' And so it came about. The general was dressing down the hall porter because of a mislaid spectacle-case when the Frau General seated herself beside the driver and Mr. Visconti sat beside Wolf at the back. 'Drive off,' the general's wife said.

"'The driver hesitated, but he was more afraid of the wife than the husband. The general came out into the street and shouted to them as they drove off—a tank had stopped to give precedence to the staff car. Nobody paid any attention to the general's shouts except Wolf. He clambered all over Mr. Visconti, thrusting his evil-smelling parts against Mr. Visconti's face, knocking off Mr. Visconti's clerical hat, barking furiously to get out. The Frau General may have loved Wolf, but it was the general whom Wolf loved. Probably the general concerned himself with his food and his exercise. Blindly Mr. Visconti fumbled for the handle of the window. Before the window was properly open Wolf jumped right in the path of the following tank. It flattened him. Mr. Visconti, looking back, thought that he resembled one of those biscuits they make for children in the shape of animals.

"So Mr. Visconti was rid of both dog and general and was able to ride in reasonable comfort to Florence. Mental comfort was another matter, and the general's wife was hysterical with grief. I think Curran would have dealt with the situation a great deal better than Mr. Visconti. At Brighton, Curran would offer the last sacrament in the form of a ritual bone, which the poor beast of course could not possibly chew, to a dying dog. A lot of dogs were killed by cars on Brighton front, and the police were quite annoyed by owners who refused to have the bodies shifted until Curran had been summoned to give the corpse absolution. But Mr. Visconti, as I have told you, was not a religious man, and the consolations he offered, I can well imagine, were insufficient and unconvincing. Perhaps he spoke of punishment for the Frau General's sins (for Mr. Visconti had a sadistic streak), and of the purgatory which we suffer on earth. Poor Mr. Visconti, he must have had a hard time of it all the way to Florence."

"What happened to the general?"

"He was captured by the Allies, I believe, but I'm not sure whether or not he was hanged at Nuremberg."

"Mr. Visconti must have a great deal on his conscience."

"Mr. Visconti hasn't got a conscience," my aunt said with pleasure.

Chapter 15

For some reason an old restaurant car with a kind of faded elegance was attached to the express after the Turkish frontier, when it was already too late to be of much use. My aunt rose that day early, and the two of us sat down to excellent coffee, toast and jam: Aunt Augusta insisted on our drinking in addition a light red wine, though I am not accustomed to wine so early in the morning. Outside the window an ocean of long undulating grass stretched to a pale green horizon. There was the talkative cheerfulness of journey's end in the air, and the car filled with passengers whom we had never seen before: a Vietnamese in blue dungarees spoke to a rumpled girl in shorts, and two young Americans, the man with hair as long as the girl's, joined them, holding hands. They refused a second cup of coffee after carefully counting their money.

"Where's Tooley?" my aunt asked.

"She wasn't feeling well last night. I'm worried about her, Aunt Augusta. Her young man's hitch-hiking to Istanbul. He may not have arrived. He may even have gone on without her."

"Where to?"

"She's not sure. Katmandu or Vientiane."

"Istanbul is a rather unpredictable place," Aunt Augusta said. "I'm not even sure what I expect to find there myself."

"What do you think you'll find?"

"I have a little business to do with an old friend, General Abdul. I was expecting a telegram at the Saint James and Albany, but none came. I can only hope that there's a message waiting for us at the Pera Palace."

"Who's the General?"

"I knew him in the days of poor Mr. Visconti," my aunt said. "He was very useful to us in the negotiations with Saudi Arabia. He was Turkish Ambassador then in Tunis. What parties we had in those days at the Excelsior. A little different from the Crown and Anchor and a drink with poor Wordsworth."

The scenery changed as we approached Istanbul. The grassy sea was left behind and the express slowed down to the speed of a little local commuters' train. When I leant from the window I could see over a wall into the yard of a cottage; I was in talking distance of a red-skirted girl who looked up at us as we crawled by; a man mounted a bicycle and for a while kept pace with us. Birds on a red tiled roof looked down their long beaks and spoke together like village gossips.

I said, "I'm awfully afraid that Tooley's going to have a baby."

"She ought to take precautions, Henry, but in any case it's far too early for you to worry."

"Good heavens, Aunt Augusta, I didn't mean that ... how can you possibly think ... ?"

"It's a natural conclusion," my aunt said, "you have been much together. And the girl has a certain puppy charm."

"I'm too old for that sort of thing."

"You are a young man in your fifties," Aunt Augusta replied.

The door of the restaurant car clanged, and there was Tooley, but a Tooley transformed. Perhaps it was only that she had put on less shadow, but her eyes seemed to be sparkling as I had never known them to do before. "Hi," she called down the length of the car. The four young people turned and looked at her and called back "Hi," as though they had been long acquainted. "Hi," she greeted them in return, and I felt a small ache of jealousy, irrational as the irritations of early morning.

"Good morning, good morning," she said to the two of us; she seemed to be speaking a different language to the old. "Oh, Mr. Pulling, it's happened."

"What's happened?"

"The curse. I've got the curse. I was right, you see. The jolting of the train, I mean—it did do it. I've got a terrible belly-ache, but I feel fabulous. I can't wait to tell Julian. Oh, I hope he's at the Gulhane, when I get there."

"You going to the Gulhane?" the American boy called across.

"Yes, are you?"

"Sure. We can all go together."

"That's fabulous."

"Come and have a coffee if you've got the money."

"You don't mind, do you?" Tooley said to my aunt. "They're going to the Gulhane too."

"Of course we don't mind, Tooley."

"You've been so kind, Mr. Pulling," she said. "I don't know what I'd have done without you. I mean it was a bit like the dark night of the soul."

I realized then that I preferred her to call me Smudge.

"Go gently on the cigarettes, Tooley," I advised her.

"Oh," she said, "I don't need to economize now. They'll be easy to get, I mean at the Gulhane. You can get anything at the Gulhane. Even acid. I'll be seeing you both again before we go, won't I?"

But she didn't. She had become one of the young now, and I could only wave to her back as she went ahead of us through the customs. The two Americans still walked hand in hand, and the Vietnamese boy carried Tooley's sack and had his arm round her shoulder to protect her from the crowd which was squeezing to get through the barrier into the customs hall. My responsibility was over, but she stayed on in my memory like a small persistent pain which worries even in its insignificance; doesn't a sickness as serious as cancer start in just such a way?

I wondered whether Julian was waiting for her. Would they go on to Katmandu? Would she always remember to take her pill? When I shaved again more closely at the Pera Palace I found I had missed in the obscurity of my coach a small dab of lipstick upon the cheek. Perhaps that was why my aunt had jumped to so wrong a conclusion. I wiped it off and found myself wondering at once where she was now. I scowled at my own face in the glass, but I was really scowling at her mother in Bonn and her father somewhere in the CIA, and Julian afraid of castration, and at all those who ought to have been looking after her and yet felt no responsibility at all.

Aunt Augusta and I had lunch in a restaurant called Abdullah's and then she took me around the tourist sights—the Blue Mosque and Santa Sophia—but I could tell all the time that she was worried. There had been no message waiting for her at the hotel.

"Can't you telephone to the general?" I asked her.

"Even at the Tunis Embassy," she said, "he never trusted his own line."

We stood dutifully in the centre of Santa Sophia—the shape, which had been beautiful once perhaps, was obscured by ugly Arabic signs painted in pale khaki, so that it looked like the huge drab waiting-hall of a railway station out of peak traffic hours. A few people stood about looking for the times of trains, and there was a man who carried a suitcase.

"I'd forgotten how hideous it was," my aunt said. "Let's go home."

Home was an odd word to use for the Pera Palace, which had the appearance of an Eastern pavilion built for a world fair. My aunt ordered two *rakis* in the bar, which was all fretwork and mirrors—there was still no message from General Abdul, and for the first time I saw my aunt nonplussed.

"When did you last hear from him?" I asked.

"I told you I heard from him in London, the day after those policemen came. And I had a message from him in Milan through Mario. Everything was in order, he said. If there had been any change Mario would have known."

"It's nearly dinner-time."

"I don't want any food. I'm sorry, Henry. I feel a little upset. Perhaps it is the result of the train's vibration. I shall go to bed and wait for the telephone. I cannot believe that he will let me down. Mr. Visconti had a great belief in General Abdul, and there were very few people whom he trusted."

I had dinner by myself in the hotel in a vast restaurant which reminded me of Santa Sophia—not a very good dinner. I had drunk several *rakis*, to which I was unaccustomed, and perhaps the absence of my aunt made me a little light-headed. I was not ready for bed, and I wished I had Tooley with me as a companion. I went outside the hotel and found a taxi-driver there who spoke a little English. He told me he was Greek but that he knew Istanbul as well as if it were his own city. "Safe," he kept on saying, "safe with me," waving his hand as though to indicate that there were wolves lurking by the walls and alleys. I told him to show me the city. He drove down narrow street after narrow street with no vista anywhere and very little light, and then drew up at a dark and forbidding door with a bearded night watchman asleep on the step. "Safe house," he said, "safe, clean. Very safe," and I was reminded uncomfortably of something I would have gladly forgotten, the house with the sofas behind the *Messaggero*.

"No, no," I said, "drive on. I didn't mean that." I tried to explain. "Take me," I said, "somewhere quiet. Somewhere you would go yourself. With your friends. For a drink. With your friends."

We drove several miles along the Sea of Marmara and came to a stop outside a plain uninteresting building marked WEST BERLIN HOTEL. Nothing could have belonged less to the Istanbul of my imagination. It was three square stories high and might well have been built among the ruins of Berlin by a local contractor at low cost. The driver led the way into a hall which occupied the whole ground space of the hotel. A young woman stood by a small piano and sang what I supposed were sentimental songs to an audience of middle-aged men in their shirt-sleeves sitting at big tables drinking beer. Most of them, like my own driver, had big grey moustaches, and they applauded heavily and dutifully when the song was over. Glasses of beer were placed in front of us, and the driver and I drank to each other. It was good beer, I noticed, and when I poured it on top of all the *raki* and the wine I had already drunk, my spirits rose. In the young girl I saw a resemblance to Tooley, and in the heavy men around me I imagined—"Do you know General Abdul?" I asked the driver. He hushed me quickly. I looked around again and realized that there was not a single woman in the big hall except the young singer, and at this moment the piano stopped, and with a glance at the clock, which marked midnight, the girl seized her handbag and went out through a door at the back. Then, after the glasses had been refilled, the pianist struck up a more virile tune, and all the middle-aged men rose and put their arms around each other's shoulders and began to dance forming circles which they enlarged, broke and formed again.

They charged, they retreated, they stamped the ground in unison. No one spoke to his neighbour, there was no drunken jollity, I was like an outsider at some religious ceremony of which he couldn't interpret the symbols. Even my driver left me to put his arm round another man's shoulder, and I drank more beer to drown my sense of being excluded. I was drunk, I knew that, for drunken tears stood in my eyes, and I wanted to throw my beer glass on the floor and join the dancing. But I was excluded, as I had always been excluded. Tooley had joined her young friends and Miss Keene had departed to cousins in Koffiefontein, leaving her tatting on a chair under the Van de Velde. I would always be protected, as I had been when a cashier, by a hygienic plastic screen. Even the breath of the dancers didn't reach me as they circled my table. My aunt was probably talking about things which mattered to her with General Abdul. She had greeted her adopted son in Milan more freely than she had ever greeted me. She had said good-bye to Wordsworth in Paris with blown kisses and tears in her eyes. She had a world of her own to which I would never be admitted, and I would have done better, I told myself, if I had stayed with my dahlias and the ashes of my mother who was not—if my aunt were to be believed—my real one. So I sat in the West Berlin Hotel shedding beery tears of self-pity and envying the men who danced with their arms around strangers' shoulders. "Take me away," I said to the driver when he returned, "finish your beer but take me away."

"You are not pleased?" he asked as we drove uphill towards the Pera Palace.

"I'm tired, that's all. I want to go to bed."

Two police cars blocked our way outside the Pera Palace. An elderly man who carried a walking stick crooked over his left arm was reaching with a stiff right leg towards the ground as we drew up. My driver told me in a tone of awe, "That is Colonel Hakim." The colonel wore a very English suit of grey flannel with chalk stripes, and he had a small grey moustache. He looked like any veteran member of the Army and Navy alighting at his club.

"Very important man," my driver told me. "Very fair to Greeks."

I went past the colonel into the hotel. The receptionist was standing in the entrance presumably to welcome him; I was of so little importance that he wouldn't shift to let me by. I had to walk round him and he didn't answer my good night. A lift took me up to the fifth floor. When I saw a light under my aunt's door, I tapped and went in. She was sitting upright in bed wearing a bed-jacket and she was reading a paperback with a lurid cover.

"I've been seeing Istanbul," I told her.

"So have I." The curtains were drawn back and the lights of the city lay below us. She put her book down. The jacket showed a naked young woman lying in bed with a knife in her back, regarded by a man with a cruel face in a red fez. The title was *Turkish Delight*. "I have been absorbing local atmosphere," she said.

"Is the man in the fez the murderer?"

"No, he's the policeman. A very unpleasant type called Colonel Hakim."

"How very odd because . . ."

"The murder takes place in this very Pera Palace, but there are a good many details wrong, as you might expect from a novelist. The girl is loved by a British secret agent, a tough sentimental man called Amis, and they have dinner together on her last night at Abdullah's—you remember we had lunch there ourselves. They have a love scene too in Santa Sophia, and there is an attempt on Amis's life at the Blue Mosque. We might almost have been doing a literary pilgrimage."

"Hardly literary," I said.

"Oh, you're your father's son. He tried to make me read Walter Scott, especially *Rob Roy,* but I much prefer this. It moves a great deal quicker and there are fewer descriptions."

"Did Amis murder her?"

"Of course not, but he is suspected by Colonel Hakim, who has very cruel methods of interrogation," my aunt said with relish.

The telephone rang. I answered it.

"Perhaps it's General Abdul at last," she said, "though it seems a little late for him to ring."

"This is the reception speaking. Is Miss Bertram there?"

"Yes, what is it?"

"I am sorry to disturb her, but Colonel Hakim wishes to see her."

"At this hour? Quite impossible. Why?"

"He is on the way up now." He rang off.

"Colonel Hakim is on the way to see you," I said.

"Colonel Hakim?"

"The real Colonel Hakim. He's a police officer too."

"A police officer?" Aunt Augusta said. "Again? I begin to think I am back in the old days. With Mr. Visconti. Henry, will you open my suitcase? The green one. You'll find a light coat there. Fawn with a fur collar."

"Yes, Aunt Augusta, I have it here."

"Under the coat in a cardboard box you will find a candle—a decorated candle."

"Yes, I see the box."

"Take out the candle, but be careful because it's rather heavy. Put it on my bedside table and light it. Candlelight is better for my complexion."

It was extraordinarily heavy, and I nearly dropped it. It probably had some kind of lead weight at the bottom, I thought, to hold it steady. A big brick of scarlet wax which stood a foot high, it was decorated on all four sides with scrolls and coats of arms. A great deal of artistry had gone into moulding the wax, which would melt away only too quickly. I lit the wick. "Now turn out the light," my aunt said, adjusting her bed-jacket and puffing up her pillow. There was a knock on the door and Colonel Hakim came in.

He stood in the doorway and bowed. "Miss Bertram?" he asked.

"Yes. You are Colonel Hakim?"

"Yes. I am sorry to call on you so late without warning." He spoke English with only the faintest intonation. "I think we have a mutual acquaintance, General Abdul. May I sit down?"

"Of course. You'll find that chair by the dressing-table the most comfortable. This is my nephew, Henry Pulling."

"Good evening, Mr. Pulling. I hope you enjoyed the dancing at the West Berlin Hotel. A convivial spot unknown to most tourists. May I turn on the light, Miss Bertram?"

"I would rather not. I have weak eyes, and I always prefer to read by candlelight."

"A very beautiful candle."

"They make them in Venice. The coats of arms belong to their four greatest doges. Don't ask me their names. How is General Abdul? I had been hoping to meet him again."

"I am afraid General Abdul is a very sick man." Colonel Hakim hooked his walking stick over the mirror before he sat down. He leant his head forward to my aunt at a slight angle, which gave him an air of deference, but I noticed that the real reason was a small hearing aid that he carried in his right ear. "He was a great friend of you and Mr. Visconti, was he not?"

"The amount you know," my aunt said with an endearing smile.

"Oh, it's my disagreeable business," the colonel said, "to be a Nosey Harker."

"Parker."

"My English is rusty."

"You had me followed to the West Berlin Hotel?" I asked.

"Oh no, I suggested to the driver that he should take you there," Colonel Hakim said. "I thought it might interest you and hold your attention longer than it did. The fashionable night clubs here are very banal and international. You might just as well be in Paris or London, except that in those cities you would see a better show. Of course I told the driver to take you somewhere else first. One never knows."

"Tell me about General Abdul," my aunt said impatiently. "What is wrong with him?"

Colonel Hakim leant forward a little more in his chair and lowered his voice as though he were confiding a secret. "He was shot," he said, "while trying to escape."

"Escape?" my aunt exclaimed. "Escape from whom?"

"From me," Colonel Hakim said with shy modesty and he fiddled at his hearing-aid. A long silence followed his words. There seemed nothing to say. Even my aunt was at a loss. She sat back against the cushions with her mouth a little open. Colonel Hakim took a tin out of his pocket and opened it. "Excuse me," he said, "eucalyptus and menthol. I suffer from asthma." He put a lozenge into his mouth and sucked. There was silence again until my aunt spoke.

"Those lozenges can't do you much good," she said.

"I think it is only the suggestion. Asthma is a nervous disease. The lozenges *seem* to alleviate it, but only perhaps because I believe they alleviate it." He panted a little when he spoke. "I am always apt to get an attack when I am at the climax of a case."

"Mr. Visconti suffered from asthma too," Aunt Augusta said. "He was cured by hypnotism."

"I would not like to put myself so completely in someone else's hands."

"Of course Mr. Visconti had a hold on the hypnotist."

"Yes, that makes a difference," Colonel Hakim said with approval. "And where is Mr. Visconti now?"

"I've no idea."

"Nor had General Abdul. We only want the information for the Interpol files. The affair is more than thirty years old. I just ask you in passing. I have no personal interest. It is not the real subject of my interrogation."

"Am I being interrogated, Colonel?"

"Yes. In a way. I hope an agreeable way. We have found a letter from you to General Abdul which speaks about an investment he had recommended. You wrote to him that you found it essential to make the investment while in Europe and anonymously, and this presented certain difficulties."

"Surely you are not working for the Bank of England, Colonel?"

"I am not so fortunate, but General Abdul was planning a little trouble here; he was very short of funds. Certain friends with whom he had speculated in the old days came back to his mind. So he got in touch with you (perhaps he hoped through you to contact Visconti again), with a German called Weissmann of whom you probably haven't heard, and with a man called Harvey Crowder, who is a meat packer in Chicago. The CIA have had him under observation for a long while and they reported to us. Of course I mention these names only because all the men are under arrest and have talked."

"If you really have to know," my aunt said, "for the sake of your files, General Abdul recommended me to buy Deutsche Texaco Convertible Bonds—out of the question in England because of the dollar premium, and away from England, for an English resident, quite illegal. So I had to remain anonymous."

"Yes," Colonel Hakim said, "that is not bad at all as a cover story." He began to pant again and took another lozenge. "I only mentioned those names to show you that General Abdul is now a little senile. One doesn't finance an operation in Turkey with foreign money of that kind. A wise woman like yourself must have realized that if his operation had any chance of success, he could have found local support. He would not have had to offer a Chicago meat packer twenty-five per-cent interest and a share of the profits."

"Mr. Visconti would certainly have seen through that," my aunt said.

"But now you are a lady living alone. You haven't the benefit of Visconti's advice. You might be tempted a little by the quick profits . . ."

"Why? I have no children to leave them to, Colonel."

"Or perhaps by the sense of adventure."

"At my age!" My aunt beamed with pleasure.

There was a knock on the door and a policeman entered. He spoke to the colonel and the colonel translated for our benefit. "Nothing," he said, "has been found in Mr. Pulling's baggage, but if you wouldn't mind . . . My man is very careful, he will wear clean gloves, and I assure you he will leave not the smallest wrinkle . . . Would you mind if I put on the electric light while he works?"

"I would mind a great deal," my aunt said. "I left my dark glasses on the train. Unless you wish to give me a splitting headache . . ."

"Of course not, Miss Bertram. He will do without. You will forgive us if the search takes a little longer."

The policeman first went through my aunt's handbag and handed certain papers to Colonel Hakim. "Forty pounds in travellers' cheques," he noted.

"I have cashed ten," my aunt said.

"I see from your air ticket you plan to leave tomorrow—I mean today. A very short visit. Why did you come by train, Miss Bertram?"

"I wanted to see my stepson in Milan."

The colonel gave her a quizzical look. "May one ask? According to your passport you are unmarried."

"Mr. Visconti's son."

"Ah, always that Mr. Visconti."

The policeman was busy now with my aunt's suitcase. He looked in the cardboard box which had contained the candle, shook it and smelt it.

"That is the box for my candle," my aunt said. "As I told you, I think, they make these candles in Venice. One candle does for a whole journey—I believe it is guaranteed for twenty-four hours continuously. Perhaps forty-eight."

"You are burning a real work of art," the colonel said.

"Henry, hold the candle for the policeman to see better."

Again I was astonished by the weight of the candle when I lifted it.

"Don't bother, Mr. Pulling, he has finished."

I was glad to put it down again.

"Well," Colonel Hakim said with a smile, "we have found nothing compromising in your luggage." The policeman was repacking the case. "Now just as a formality we must go through the room. And the bed, Miss Bertram, if you will consent to sit in a chair."

He took part in this search himself, limping from one piece of furniture to another, sometimes feeling with his stick, under the bed, and at the back of a drawer. "And now Mr. Pulling's pockets," he said. I emptied them rather angrily on the dressing-table. He looked carefully through my notebook and drew out a cutting from the *Daily Telegraph*. He read it aloud with a puzzled frown: " 'Those that took my fancy were the ruby-red Maître Roger, light-red, white-tipped Cheerio, deep crimson Arabian Night and Black Flash, and scarlet Bacchus . . .'

"Please explain, Mr. Pulling."

"It is self-explanatory," I said stiffly.

"Then you must forgive my ignorance."

"The report of a dahlia show. In Chelsea. I am very interested in dahlias."

"Flowers?"

"Of course they are flowers."

"The names sounded so oddly like those of horses. I was puzzled by the 'deep crimson.' " He put the cutting down and limped to my aunt's side. "I will say good night now, Miss Bertram. You have made my duty tonight a most agreeable one. You cannot think how bored I get with exhibitions of injured innocence. I will send a police car to take you to your plane tomorrow."

"Please don't bother. We can take a taxi."

"We should be sorry to see you miss your plane."

"I think perhaps I ought to stop over one more day and see poor General Abdul."

"I am afraid he is not allowed visitors. What is this book you are reading? What a very ugly fellow with a red fez. Has he stabbed the girl?"

"No. He is the policeman. He is called Colonel Hakim," my aunt said with a look of satisfaction.

After the door had closed I turned with some anger on my aunt. "Aunt Augusta," I said, "what did all that mean?"

"Some little political trouble, I would imagine. Politics in Turkey are taken more seriously than they are at home. It was only quite recently that they executed a Prime Minister. We dream of it, but they act. I hadn't realized, I admit, what General Abdul was up to. Foolish of him at his age. He must be eighty if a day, but I believe in Turkey there are more centenarians than in any other European country. Yet I doubt whether poor Abdul is likely to make his century."

"Do you realize that they're deporting us? I think we should call the British Embassy."

"You exaggerate, dear. They are just lending us a police car."

"And if we refuse to take it?"

"I have no intention of refusing. We were already booked on the plane. After making my investment here, I had no intention of lingering around. I didn't expect quick profits, and twenty-five per cent always involves a risk."

"What investment, Aunt Augusta? Forty pounds in travellers' cheques?"

"Oh no, dear. I bought quite a large gold ingot in Paris. You remember the man from the bank . . ."

"So that was what they were looking for. Where on earth had you hidden it, Aunt Augusta?"

I looked at the candle, and I remembered its weight.

"Yes, dear," my aunt said, "how clever of you to guess. Colonel Hakim didn't. You can blow it out now." I lifted it up again—it must have weighed nearly twenty pounds.

"What do you propose to do with this now?"

"I shall have to take it back to England with me. It may be of use another time. It was most fortunate, when you come to think of it, that they shot poor General Abdul before I gave him the candle and not after. I wonder if he is really still alive. They would be likely to glide over any grisly detail like that with a woman. I shall have a Mass said for him in any case, because a man of that age is unlikely to survive a bullet long. The shock alone, even if it were not in a vital part . . ."

I interrupted her speculations. "You're not going to take that ingot back into England?" Ingot—England. I was irritated by the asburd jangle which sounded like a comic song. "Have you no respect at all for the law?"

"It depends, dear, to which law you refer. Like the Ten Commandments. I can't take very seriously the one about the ox and the ass."

"The English customs are not so easily fooled as the Turkish police."

"A used candle is remarkably convincing. I've tried it before."

"Not if they lift it up."

"But they won't, dear. Perhaps if the wick and the wax were intact they might think they could charge me purchase tax. Or some suspicious officer might think it a phony candle containing drugs. But a *used* candle. Oh no, I think the danger is very small. And there's always my age to protect me."

"I refuse to go back into England with that ingot." The jangle irritated me again.

"But you have no choice, dear. The colonel will certainly see us on to the plane and there is no stop before London. The great advantage of being deported is that we shall not have to pass the Turkish customs again."

"Why on earth did you do it, Aunt Augusta? Such a risk . . ."

"Mr. Visconti is in need of money."

"He stole yours."

"That was a long time ago. It will all be finished by now."

CHAPTER 16

It seemed at first another and a happier world which I had reentered: I was back home, in the late afternoon, as the long shadows were falling; a boy whistled a Beatle tune and a motor-bicycle revved far away up Norman Lane. With what relief I dialled Chicken and ordered myself cream of spinach soup, lamb cutlets and Cheddar cheese: a better meal than I had eaten in Istanbul. Then I went into the garden. Major Charge had neglected the dahlias; it was a pleasure to give them water, which the dry soil drank like a thirsty man, and I could almost imagine that the flowers were responding with a lift of the petals. The Deuil du Roy Albert was too far gone to benefit, but the colour of the Ben Hurs took on a new sheen, as though the long dry chariot race were now a memory only. Major Charge looked over the fence and asked, "Good journey?"

"Interesting, thank you," I said dryly, pouring the water in a thick stream on to the roots. I had removed the absurd nozzle which serves no useful purpose.

"I was very careful," Major Charge said, "not to give them too much water."

"The ground certainly seems very dry."

"I keep goldfish," Major Charge said. "If I go away, my damned daily always gives them too much food. When I return I find half the little buggers dead."

"Flowers are not the same as goldfish, Major. In a dry autumn like this they can do with a great deal of water."

"I hate excess," Major Charge said. "It's the same in politics. I've no use for Communist or Fascist."

"You are a Liberal?"

"Good God, man," he said, "what makes you think that?" and disappeared from sight.

The afternoon post arrived punctually at five: a circular from Littlewood's, although I never gamble, a bill from the garage, a pamphlet from the British Empire Loyalists which I threw at once into the waste-paper basket, and a letter with a South African stamp. The envelope was typewritten, so that I did not at once conclude that it had been sent by Miss Keene. I was distracted too by a package of Omo propped against the scraper. I had certainly not ordered any detergent. I looked closer and saw that it was a gift package. What a lot of money manufacturers waste by not employing the local stores to do their distribution. There they would have known that I am already a regular purchaser of Omo. I took the packet into the kitchen and noticed with pleasure that mine was almost exhausted, so I had been saved from buying another.

It was getting chilly by this time, and I turned on the electric fire before opening the letter. I saw at once that it came from Miss Keene. She had bought herself a typewriter, but it was obvious that as yet she had not had much practice. Lines were unevenly placed, and her fingers had often gone astray to the wrong keys or missed a letter altogether. She had driven in, she wrote, to Koffiefontein—three hours by road—to a matinée of *Gone with the Qind* which

had been revived at a cinema there. She wrote that
Clark Fable was not as good as she remembered him.
How typical it was of her gentleness, and perhaps
even of her sense of defeat, that she had not troubled
to correct her errors. Perhaps it would have seemed
to her like disguising a fault. "Once a week," she
wrote, "my cousin drives into the bak. She's on very
good terms with the manger, but he is not a real
friend as you always were to my father and me. I miss
very much St. John's Church and the vicar's sermons.
The only church near here is Dutch Deformed, and I
don't like it at all." She had corrected Deformed.
She may have thought that otherwise I might take
it for an unkindness.

I wondered how I was to reply. I knew that the
letter she would like best would contain news of
Southwood: the small details of every day, even to the
condition of my dahlias. How was I to deal with my
bizarre journey to Istanbul? To mention it only in
passing would seem both unnatural and pretentious,
but to describe the affair of Colonel Hakim and the
gold brick and General Abdul would cause her to feel
that my mode of life had entirely changed, and this
might increase her sense of separation and of loneliness near Koffiefontein. I asked myself whether it
would not be better to refrain from writing at all, but
then on the last page—her paper had slipped in the
machine and the print ran diagonally up into the
previous line—she had typed, "I look forward so to
your letters because they bring Southwood close to
me." I put her letter away with others of hers that I
kept in a drawer of my desk.

It was quite dark now, and yet more than an hour
would have to pass before Chicken arrived, so I went
to choose a book from my shelves. Like my father, I
rarely buy new books, though I don't confine my
reading, as he did, to almost a single author. Modern
literature has never appealed to me; to my mind it

was in the Victorian age that English poetry and
fiction reached the highest level. If I had been able to
write myself—and in my boyhood before my mother
found me the position at the bank I sometimes had
that dream—I would have modelled myself on one of
the minor Victorians (for the giants are inimitable):
perhaps R. L. Stevenson or even Charles Reade. I
have quite a collection too of Wilkie Collins, though
I prefer him when he is not writing a detective story,
for I don't share my aunt's taste in that direction. If I
could have been a poet I would have been happy in a
quite humble station, to be recognized, if at all, as an
English Mahony and to have celebrated Southwood
as he celebrated Shandon (it is one of my favourite
poems in Palgrave's *Golden Treasury*). Perhaps it was
Miss Keene's mention of St. John's Church, the bells
of which I can hear on a Sunday morning while I am
working in the garden, that made me think of him
and take down the volume.

> There's a bell in Moscow,
> While on tower and kiosk O
> In Santa Sophia
>   The Turkman gets;
> And loud in air
> Calls men to prayer
> From the tapering summit
>   Of tall minarets.
>
> Such empty phantom
> I freely grant them;
> But there is an anthem
>   More dear to me—
> 'Tis the bells of Shandon,
> That sound so grand on
> The pleasant waters
>   Of the River Lee.

The lines on Santa Sophia had never before rung
so true: that dingy mausoleum could not compare

with our St. John's and the mention of it would remind me always of Colonel Hakim.

One book leads to another, and I found myself, for
the first time in many years, taking down a volume of
Walter Scott. I remembered how my father had used
the volumes for playing the *Sortes Virgilianae*—a
game my mother considered a little blasphemous unless it was played with the Bible, in all seriousness. I
sometimes suspected my father had dog-eared various
pages so that he could hit on a suitable quotation to
tease and astound my mother. Once, when he was
suffering severely from constipation, he opened *Rob
Roy* apparently at random and read out, "Mr. Owen
entered. So regular were the motions and habits of
this worthy man ..." I tried the *Sortes* myself now
and was astonished at the apposite nature of the
quotation which I picked: "I had need of all the
spirits a good dinner could give, to resist the dejec-
tion which crept insensibly on my mind."

It was only too true that I was depressed: whether
it was due to Miss Keene's letter or to the fact that
I missed my aunt's company more than I had anticipated, or even that Tooley had left a blank behind
her, I could not tell. Now that I had no responsibility
to anyone but myself, the pleasure of finding again
my house and garden had begun to fade. Hoping to
discover a more encouraging quotation, I opened
Rob Roy again and found a snapshot lying between
the leaves: the square yellowing snapshot of a pretty
girl in an old-fashioned bathing-dress taken with an
old-fashioned Brownie. The girl was bending a little
towards the camera; she had just slipped one shoulder out of its strap, and she was laughing, as though
she had been surprised at the moment of changing. It
was some moments before I recognized Aunt Augusta
and my first thought was how attractive she had been
in those days. Was it a photograph taken by her
sister, I wondered? But it was hardly the kind of

photograph my mother would have given my father. I had to admit that it was more likely he had taken it himself and hidden it there in a volume of Scott which my mother would never read. This then was how she had looked—she could have hardly been more than eighteen—in the long ago days before she knew Curran or Monsieur Dambreuse or Mr. Visconti. She had an air of being ready for anything. A phrase about Die Vernon printed on one of the two pages between which the photograph lay caught my eye: "Be patient and quiet, and let me take my own way; for when I take the bit between my teeth, there is no bridle will stop me." Had my father deliberately chosen that page with that particular passage for concealing the picture? I felt the melancholy I sometimes used to experience at the bank when it was my duty to turn over old documents deposited there, the title-deeds of a passion long spent. I thought of my father with an added tenderness—of that lazy man lying in his overcoat in the empty bath. I had never seen his grave, for he had died on the only trip which he had ever taken out of England, and I was not even sure of where it lay.

I rang up my aunt, "Just to say good night and make sure that all is well."

"The apartment," she told me, "seems a little solitary without Wordsworth."

"I am feeling lonely too—without you and Tooley."

"No news when you came home?"

"Only a letter from a friend. She seems lonely too."

I hesitated before I spoke again. "Aunt Augusta, I have been thinking, I don't know why, of my father. It's strange how little one knows of one's own family. Do you realize I don't even know where he is buried?"

"No?"

"Do you?"

"Of course."

"I would have liked, if only once, to visit his grave."

"Cemeteries to me are rather a morbid taste. They have a sour smell like jungles. I suppose it comes from all that wet greenery."

"As one grows old, I think, one becomes more attached to family things—to houses and graves. I feel very badly that my mother had to finish like that in a police laboratory."

"Your stepmother," my aunt corrected me.

"Where *is* my father?"

"As a half-believing Catholic," Aunt Augusta said, "I cannot answer that question with any certainty, but his body, what is left of it, lies in Boulogne."

"So near? Why wasn't it brought back?"

"My sister had a very practical and unsentimental side. Your father had gone to Boulogne without her knowledge on a day excursion. He was taken ill after dinner and died almost immediately. Food poisoning. It was before the days of antibiotics. There had to be an autopsy and my sister didn't like the idea of transporting home a mutilated corpse. So she had him buried in the cemetery there."

"Were you present?"

"I was on tour in Italy. I only heard about it much later. My sister and I didn't correspond."

"So you've never seen the grave either?"

"I once suggested to Mr. Visconti that we make a trip, but his favourite Biblical quotation was, 'Let the dead bury their dead.'"

"Perhaps one day we might go together."

"I am strongly of Mr. Visconti's opinion, but I am always ready for a little travel," my aunt added with unsentimental glee.

"This time you must be my guest."

"The anniversary of his death," my aunt said, "falls on October second. I remember the date because it is the feast day of the Guardian Angel. The Angel

seems to have slipped up badly on that occasion,
unless of course he was saving your father from a
worse fate. That is quite a possibility, for what on
earth was your father doing in Boulogne out of season?"

CHAPTER 17

Strangely enough, I felt almost immediately at home in Boulogne.

As the direct boat from Folkestone no longer sailed, we took the Golden Arrow from Victoria, and I was relieved to notice that my aunt had not brought with her the red suitcase. The English side of the Channel lay bathed in a golden autumn sunlight. By the time we reached Petts Wood the buses had all turned green, and at Orpington the oast-houses began to appear with their white cowls like plumes in a medieval helmet. The hops climbing their poles were more decorative than vines, and I would gladly have given all the landscape between Milan and Venice for these twenty miles of Kent. There were comfortable skies and unspectacular streams; there were ponds with rushes and cows which seemed contentedly asleep. This was the pleasant land of which Blake wrote, and I found myself regretting that we were going abroad again. Why had my father not died in Dover or Folkestone, both equally convenient for a day's excursion?

And yet when at last we came to Boulogne, stepping out of the one coach from Calais reserved for that port on the Flèche d'Or, I felt that I was at home. The skies had turned grey and the air was cold and there were flurries of rain along the quays, but there was a photograph of the Queen over the reception desk in our hotel, and on the windows of a *brasserie* I could read GOOD CUP OF TEA. EAST KENT COACH PARTIES WELCOME HERE. The leaden gulls which hovered over the fishing boats in the leaden evening had an East Anglian air. A scarlet sign flashed over the Gare Maritime saying CAR FERRY and BRITISH RAILWAYS.

It was too late that evening to search for my father's grave (in any case, the next day was his true anniversary), and so my aunt and I walked up together to the Ville Haute and strolled around the ramparts and through the small twisted streets which reminded me of Rye. In the great crypt of the cathedral an English king had been married, there were cannon balls lying there shot by the artillery of Henry VIII, and in a little square below the walls was a statue of Edward Jenner in a brown tailed-coat and brown tasselled boots. An old film of *Treasure Island* with Robert Newton was showing at a small cinema in a side-street not far from a club called Le Lucky, where you could listen to the music of the Hearthmen. No, my father had not been buried on foreign soil. Boulogne was like a colonial town which had only recently ceased to be part of the Empire, and British Railways lingered on at the end of the quay as though it had been granted permission to stay until the evacuation was complete. Locked bathing-huts below the casino were like the last relics of the occupying troops, and the mounted statue of General San Martín on the quay might have been that of Wellington.

We had dinner in the restaurant of the Gare Maritime, after walking over the cobble-stones and across the railway lines with no one about. The pillars of the station resembled the pillars in a cathedral deserted after dark: only a train from Lyon was announced like a hymn number which no one had bothered to take down. No porter or passenger stirred on the long platforms. The British Railways office stood empty and unlighted. There was a smell everywhere of oil and weed and sea and a memory of the morning's fish. In the restaurant we proved to be the sole diners: only two men and a dog stood at the bar and they were preparing to go. My aunt ordered soles *à la Boulonnaise* for both of us.

"Perhaps my father came here the night before he died," I considered aloud. Ever since I had picked *Rob Roy* from the shelf I had thought frequently of my father, and remembering the photograph and the expression of the young girl, I believed that my aunt must have loved him too in her way. But if I were looking for sentimental memories I had come to the wrong character—a man dead was a man dead, so far as my aunt was concerned.

"Order the wine, Henry," she said. "You know you have a morbid streak. This whole expedition is a sign of it—and the urn which you so carefully preserve. If your father had been buried at Highgate I would never have come with you. I don't believe in pilgrimages to graves unless they serve another purpose."

"What other purpose does this serve?" I asked rather snappily.

"I have never before been to Boulogne," Aunt Augusta said. "I am always ready to visit a new place."

"Like Uncle Jo," I said, "you want to prolong life."

"Certainly I do," my aunt replied, "because I enjoy it."

"And how many rooms have you occupied so far?"

"A great many," my aunt said cheerfully, "but I don't think I have yet reached the lavatory floor."

"I got to go home." One of the men at the bar spoke in piercing English. He was a little tight and when he stooped to pat his dog he missed it completely.

"One more for the ferry," his companion said. From the phrase I took it that he belonged to British Railways.

"The bloody Maid of Kent. My wife was a maid of Kent once."

"But no longer, billyo, no longer."

"No longer. Tha's why I have to be home at twenty-one fucking hours."

"She's jealous, billyo."

"She's hungry."

"I've never loved a weak man," my aunt said. "Your father wasn't weak—he was lazy. Nothing in his opinion was really worth a fight. He wouldn't have fought for Cleopatra herself—but he would have found a way round. Unlike Antony. It astonishes me that he ever came as far as Boulogne."

"Perhaps it was on business."

"He would have sent his partner. Now his partner—his name was William Curlew—was a weak man if ever there was one. He envied your father his little adventures—he found it hard enough to satisfy one woman. It weighed on his mind terribly, for his wife was really without fault. She was sweet, efficient, good-tempered—the fact that she was a little demanding might have been taken by another man as a virtue. Your father, who was a much more imaginative man than people usually thought or your mother realized, suggested a plan to him, for, as William had pointed out, one can't leave a perfect woman—one has to be left. He was to write his wife anonymous letters accusing himself of infidelity. The letters would serve a fourfold purpose. They would protect his vanity, offer a reasonable explanation of his flagging attentions, crack his wife's perfection, and might even lead eventually to divorce with his honour as a man saved (for he was determined to deny nothing). Your father composed the first letter himself; William typed it badly on his own typewriter, and put it in the kind of yellow envelope he used for bills (that was a mistake). The letter read: 'Your husband, madam, is a shameful liar and an ignoble lecher. Ask him how he spends his evenings when you are at the Women's Institute, and how he gets through all the money he spends. What you save on the housekeeping enriches another woman's placket.' Your father liked obsolete words—that was the influence of Walter Scott.

"There was to be a party at the Curlews' the evening the letter arrived. Mrs. Curlew was very busy plumping cushions; she took the yellow envelope for a bill, and so she put it down on a table without looking at it. You can imagine poor William's anxiety. I knew him well in those days, indeed your parents and I were both present at the party. Your father hoped to be in at the death, but when the time came to go, and your father couldn't linger any longer, even on the excuse of talking a little business, the letter still remained unopened. He had to learn the details of what happened later from William.

"Melany—that was her silly name and it sounded even sillier when attached to Curlew—was tidying up the glasses when William found the yellow envelope under an occasional table. 'Is this yours, dear?' he asked and she said it was only a bill.

" 'Even a bill has to be opened,' William said and handed her the envelope. Then he went upstairs to shave. She never insisted on his shaving before dinner, but very early in their marriage she had indicated unmistakably that she preferred him at night with a smooth cheek—her skin was very delicate. (Foreigners always said that her complexion was typically English.) The bathroom door was open and William saw her put the yellow envelope down on the dressing-table still sealed. He nicked himself in three places under the strain of waiting and had to stick on little dabs of cotton wool to stop the bleeding."

The man trailed past our table with the dog. "Come on, you bugger," he said, hauling dispiritedly on the lead.

"Back to the maid of Kent," his friend teased him from the bar.

I had begun to recognize the gleam in my aunt's eyes. She had had it in Brighton, when she recounted the history of the dogs' church, and in Paris when she told me of the affair with Monsieur Dambreuse, and in the Orient Express when she described Mr. Visconti's escape ... She was deeply absorbed in her story. I am sure my father—the admirer of Walter Scott—would not have told the story of the Curlews nearly so dramatically; there would have been less dialogue and more description.

"William," my aunt went on, "came in from the bathroom and climbed into the enormous double bed which Melany had chosen herself at Maples. In his anxiety, William had not taken a book with him. He wanted the crisis to arrive. 'I won't be long, dear,' Melany said, busy with Pond's cold cream, which she preferred to any newer brand for the sake of her old-world complexion.

" 'Was it a bad bill,' William asked.

" 'Bill?'

" 'The one you dropped.'

" 'Oh that. I haven't opened it yet.'

" 'You'll lose it again if you're not careful.'

" 'That would be a good thing to do, wouldn't it, with a bill?' Melany said good-humouredly, but the words belied her nature—she never kept a tradesman waiting and never allowed one to extend her credit beyond a month. Now she wiped her fingers on the Kleenex and opened the yellow envelope. The first words she read, unevenly typed, were 'Your husband, madam ...'

" 'No,' she said, 'not bad. Just tiresome.' And she read the letter carefully to the end—it was signed 'A neighbour and well-wisher.' Then she tore it in little pieces and dropped them in her wastepaper basket.

" 'You shouldn't destroy a bill,'' William said.

" 'A few shillings at the newspaper shop. I paid it this morning.' She looked at William and said, 'What a good husband you've always been, William.' She came to the bed and kissed him and William could detect her intention. 'How tired a party makes me,' he said, excusing himself weakly, with a faint yawn.

" 'Of course, dear,' Melany said, lying down beside him without any complaint. 'Happy dreams,' and then she noticed all those dabs of cotton wool. 'Oh you poor dear,' she said, 'you've cut yourself. Let your Melany make them clean,' and then and there she busied herself, for ten minutes at least, washing the wounds in chemist's alcohol and fixing bits of Elastoplast, as though nothing important had happened. 'How funny you look now,' she said, 'quite gay and carefree, and William told your father there was no longer any hint of danger in the kiss she planted on the end of his nose. 'Dear funny William. I could forgive you anything. It was then William gave up all hope—she was a perfect wife, uncrackably perfect, and your father used to say that the word 'forgive' tolled on in William's ears like the bell at Newgate signalling an execution.''

"So he never escaped?" I asked.

"He died many years later in Melany's arms," Aunt Augusta said, and we finished our apple tart in silence.

CHAPTER 18

Next morning, which was just as grey as the last had been, Aunt Augusta and I climbed the long hill towards the cemetery. A shop advertised DEUIL EN 24 HEURES, and a wild boar, hung outside a butcher's shop, dripped blood, and a notice pinned on the muzzle read RETENEZ VOS MORCEAUX POUR JEUDI, but Thursday meant nothing to me, and not very much to Aunt Augusta. "The feast of the Little Flower," she said, looking the date up in her missal, which she had brought with her because it was a suitable occasion, "but a boar seems hardly suitable. Also apparently the feast of Saint Thomas of Hereford, who died in exile in Orvieto, but I doubt if even the English have heard of him."

Outside the gates of the Ville Haute there was a plaque commemorating the death of a "Hero of the Resistance." "The dead of an army," my aunt said, "become automatically heroes like the dead of the Church become martyrs. I wonder about this man Saint Thomas. I would have thought he was very lucky to die in Orvieto rather than in Hereford. A small civilized place even today with a far, far better climate and an excellent restaurant in the Via Garibaldi."

"Are you really a Roman Catholic?" I asked my aunt with interest. She replied promptly and seriously, "Yes, my dear, only I just don't believe in all the things they believe in."

To find my father's grave in the enormous grey cemetery would have been like finding an individual house without a street number in Camden Town. The noise of trains came up from below the hill and the smoke of coal fires from the high town blew across the maze of graves. A man from a little square house, which was like a tomb itself, offered to conduct us. I had brought a wreath of flowers, though my aunt thought my gesture a little exaggerated. "They will be very conspicuous," she said. "The French believe in remembering the dead once a year on the Feast of All Souls. It is tidy and convenient like Communion at Easter," and it is true that I saw few flowers, even *immortelles,* among the angels, the cherubs, the bust of a bald man like a *lycée* professor, and the huge tomb, which apparently contained La Famille Flageollet. An English inscription on one monument caught my eye: *In loving memory of my devoted son Edward Rhodes Robinson who died in Bombay where he is buried,* but there was nothing English about his pyramid. Surely my father would have preferred an English graveyard of lichened stones with worn-out inscriptions and tags of pious verse to these shiny-black made-to-last slabs which no Boulogne weather could ever erode, all with the same headlines, like copies of the same newspaper: *A la mémoire, Ici repose le corps* ... Except for a small elderly woman in black who stood with bowed head at the end of a long aisle like the solitary visitor in a provincial museum, there seemed no one but ourselves in the whole heartless place.

"*Je me suis trompé,*" our conductor said, turning sharply on his heel, and he led us back towards the grave where the old woman stood, apparently in prayer.

"How odd! There seems to be another mourner," Aunt Augusta said, and sure enough, on the slab of marble lay a wreath twice as large as mine made of flowers twice as expensive from the hot-houses of the south. I laid my own beside it. The headlines were hidden: there was only part of my father's name sticking out like an exclamation: ... *chard Pulling,* and a date, *October 2, 1923.*

The little woman looked at us with astonishment. *"Qui êtes-vous?"* she asked us.

Her accent was not quite French and my aunt replied as bluntly in English, "Who are you?"

"Miss Paterson," the little woman replied with a hint of frightened defiance.

"And what has this grave to do with you?" my aunt demanded.

"I have come here on this day for more than forty years, and I have never seen either of you here before."

"Have you any rights over this grave?" my aunt asked.

Something in the woman's manner had riled her— perhaps it was her air of timid belligerence, for my aunt had little patience with weakness even when it was concealed.

The woman was cornered and showed fight. "I've never heard there are rights in a grave," she said.

"A grave—like a house—has been paid for by someone."

"And if a house is left abandoned for forty years, hasn't even a stranger the right ... ?"

"Who are you?" my aunt repeated.

"I told you. I am Miss Paterson."

"Did you know my brother-in-law?"

"Your brother-in-law!" the old lady exclaimed. She

looked at my wreath, she looked at me, she looked at my aunt.

"And this, my good woman, is Richard Pulling's son."

She said with dismay, "The family," as though the word meant, "the enemy."

"So you see," my aunt said, "we at any rate do have certain rights."

I couldn't understand my aunt's harshness and I intervened. "I think it is very kind of you," I said, "to lay flowers on my father's grave. It may seem strange to you that I have never been here before . . ."

"It is quite typical of you all," Miss Paterson said, "of you all. Your mother never even came to the funeral. I was the only one. I and the concierge of the hotel. A kind man." She added with tears in her eyes, "It was a wet wet day, and he brought his big umbrella . . ."

"Then you knew my father . . . You were here . . . ?"

"He died gently gently in my arms," Miss Paterson said. She had a way of repeating words as though she were used to reading children's books aloud.

"It is very cold," my aunt interrupted. "Henry, you have laid your wreath, I shall go back to the hotel. This is not a place for prolonged conversation." She began to walk away: it was almost like an admission of defeat, and she tried to carry it off with disdain, like a Great Dane which turns its back on some small defenceless dog defiant in a corner and pretends it unworthy of its teeth.

I said to Miss Paterson, "I must see my aunt home. Couldn't you come and take a cup of tea with us this evening? I was only a small boy when my father died. I hardly knew him. I should have come here before, but, you know, I thought nobody cared any more about such things . . ."

"I know I am old-fashioned," Miss Paterson said, "so very old-fashioned."

"But you will at least have tea with us? At the Meurice?"

"I will come," Miss Paterson said with frightened dignity. "You must tell your aunt, however—she is your aunt?—that she mustn't take offence at me. He has been dead a long time. It is unfair to her to be jealous of me because I care so much, so much still."

I repeated the message to my aunt exactly, and she was astonished. "Did she really believe me to be jealous? The only time I can remember being jealous was over Curran, and that experience taught me better. You know how little jealous I was even of Monsieur Dambreuse . . ."

"You don't have to defend yourself to me, Aunt Augusta," I said.

"Defend myself? I certainly have not fallen as low as that. I am trying to explain my feelings, that is all. The woman seemed to me totally inadequate to her grief. You can't pour a glass of wine into an after-dinner cup of coffee. She irritated me. To think that she was with your father when he died."

"Presumably there was a doctor too."

"He wouldn't have died if she had not been so feeble. I am convinced of that. Your father had to be shaken into action. The trouble with Richard was his appearance. He was strikingly good-looking. He never had to make an effort with a woman. And finally he was too lazy to struggle. If I had been with him I would have seen that he was alive today."

"Today?"

"He would not have been much older than Mr. Visconti."

"Be kind to her all the same, Aunt Augusta."

"I shall be as sweet as sugar," my aunt promised.

And that afternoon I could tell that she was really trying to hide her irritation at Miss Paterson's mannerisms, of which there were many besides her habit of repeating words. She had, for example, a twitch in her right foot (the first time it happened I really thought that Aunt Augusta had kicked her), and, when she had been silent a little while and her mind wandered, her teeth began to click as though she were manipulating a pair of false dentures. We had tea in my aunt's room, for there was no proper lounge in the square miniature skyscraper which sat between two identical others on the quay.

"You must forgive us," my aunt said, "they have only Lipton's Indian."

"Oh, but I like Lipton's," Miss Paterson said, "with one little little lump."

"Did you come via Calais?" my aunt asked, making polite conversation. "We came that way yesterday. Or by the ferry?"

"Oh no," Miss Paterson said, "you see, I live here. I have always lived here, that is to say since Richard died." She gave a scared glance at me and said, "Mr. Pulling, I mean."

"Even during the war?" my aunt asked with a touch of suspicion. She would have been glad, I think, to have found a chink in Miss Paterson's integrity, if only a small error of fact.

"It was a time of some privation," Miss Paterson said. "Perhaps the bombardments seemed less terrible to me because I had my children to think of."

"Your children?" my aunt exclaimed. "Surely Richard . . ."

"Oh, no, no, no," Miss Paterson said, "I refer only to the children whom I taught. I taught English in the *lycée*."

"Didn't the Germans intern you?"

"The people here were very good to me. I was protected. The mayor provided me with an identity card." Miss Paterson's leg jumped. "After the war they even gave me a medal."

"A medal for teaching English?" my aunt asked incredulously.

"And other things," Miss Paterson said. She leant back in her chair and her teeth began to click. Her thoughts were far away.

"Tell me about my father," I told her. "What brought him to Boulogne?"

"He wanted to give me a holiday," Miss Paterson said. "He was worried about my health. He said I needed sea air." My aunt rattled her spoon and I feared for her patience. "Just a day trip you know. We took the boat like you to Calais, for he wanted to show me where the burghers came from, and then we took a bus here to see the Napoleon column—he had just read his biography by Sir Walter Scott—and we found there was no boat back from Boulogne."

"That came as a surprise to him, I suppose?" my aunt asked with an irony which was obvious to me but not to Miss Paterson.

"Yes," Miss Paterson said. "He was very apologetic for his lack of forethought. However, we found two clean rooms in a little little inn up in the high town in the square by the *mairie*."

"Adjoining rooms, I assume," my aunt said. I couldn't understand why she was so severe.

"Yes," Miss Paterson said, "because I was frightened."

"Of what?"

"I had never been abroad before, nor had Mr. Pulling. I had to translate for both of us."

"You knew French,"

"I had taken a course at the Berlitz."

"You mustn't mind our interest, Miss Paterson," I said. "You see, I have never heard any details of my father's death—my mother never spoke of it. She always shut me up when I asked questions. She told me he had died on a business trip, and somehow I always assumed that he had died at Wolverhampton—he often went to Wolverhampton."

"When did you meet my brother-in-law," Aunt Augusta asked. "May I pour you another cup of tea?"

"Yes, please. A little bit weaker if it would not be a trouble to you. We met on the top of a forty-nine bus."

My aunt paused with a lump of sugar in mid-air. "A forty-nine bus?" she repeated.

"Yes, you see, I had heard him ask for his ticket, and when his destination came he was fast asleep, so I woke him up, but it was too late. It was a request stop. He was very grateful and came all the way to Chelsea Town Hall with me. I had a basement room then in Oakley Street and he walked back to the house with me. I remember it all so clearly, so clearly," Miss Paterson said, "as thought it were only yesterday. We found many things in common." Her foot gave a kick again.

"That surprises me," my aunt said.

"Oh, how we talked that day!"

"What about?"

"Mainly I think about Sir Walter Scott. I knew *Marmion* and little else, but he knew everything that Sir Walter had ever written. He could quote ... He had a wonderful memory for poetry." She whispered as though to herself:

> "Where shall the traitor rest,
>   He the deceiver,
> Who could win maiden's breast,
>   Ruin and leave her?
> In the last battle ..."

"And so it all began," my aunt interrupted in a tone of impatience. "And the traitor rests in Boulogne."

Miss Paterson coiled up in her chair and kicked her foot vigorously.

"Nothing began—in the way you mean," she said. "In the night I heard him knock on the door and call 'Dolly!'"

"Dolly!" my aunt repeated with distaste as though "Dolly" were an unmentionable word.

"Yes. That was what he called me. My name is Dorothy."

"You had locked your door, of course."

"I had done no such thing. He was a man I trusted absolutely. I told him to come in. I knew he wouldn't have woken me for any trivial reason."

"Certainly I would not describe his reason as trivial," my aunt said, "go on," but Miss Paterson was far away again and her teeth clicked and clicked. She was gazing at something we could not see, and there were the beginnings of tears in her eyes. I put my hand on her arm and said, "Miss Paterson, don't talk about it any more if it hurts you." I was angry with my aunt: her face looked as hard as a face stamped on a coin.

Miss Paterson looked at me and I could watch her beginning to return from that long time ago. "He came in," she said, "and he whispered, 'Dolly, my darling,' and he fell down on the floor. I got down beside him and put his poor poor head in my lap and he never spoke again. I never knew why he came or what he meant to say to me."

"I can guess," Aunt Augusta said.

Again Miss Paterson coiled herself back in her chair and struck back. It was a sad sight to see these two old women at loggerheads over something that had happened so many years ago. "I hope you are right," Miss Paterson said. "I know well what you are thinking and I hope you are right. I would have done anything that he asked me without hesitation or regret. And I have never loved another man."

"You didn't have the time to love him, it seems," my aunt said.

"There you are quite quite wrong. Perhaps because you don't know what love is. I loved him from the moment he got off the bus at Chelsea Town Hall, and I love him today. When he was dead I did everything for him—everything—there was no one else to help my poor dear—his wife wouldn't come. There had to be a post-mortem, and she wrote to the authorities to bury him in Boulogne—she didn't want his poor poor mutilated body. So there was only myself and the concierge . . ."

"You have certainly been very constant," my aunt said, but the remark did not sound like a compliment.

"No one else has ever again used that name he called me, Dolly," Miss Paterson said, "but in the war, when I had to use an alias, I let them call me Poupée."

"Why on earth did you have an alias?"

"They were troubled times," Miss Paterson said and she began to look for her gloves.

I resented the way my aunt had behaved to Miss Paterson, and a slow flame of anger still burned in me when we went out to dinner for the second and last time in the deserted station. The gay wave-worn fishing boats lay against the jetty, each with a painted pious phrase across the bridge: DIEU BNÉIT LA FAMILLE and DIEU A BIEN FAIT, and I wondered what comfort the mottoes brought in a strong Channel gale. There was the same smell of oil and fish, the same train from Lyon was awaited by no one, and in the restaurant there was the same disgruntled Englishman with the same companion and the same dog—he made the restaurant seem all the emptier with his presence, as though there had never been a different customer.

My aunt said, "You are very silent, Henry."

"I have a lot to think about," I said.

"You were quite taken by that miserable little woman," Aunt Augusta accused me.

"I was touched to meet someone who loved my father."

"A lot of women loved him."

"I mean a woman who *really* loved him."

"That little sentimental creature? She doesn't know what love is."

"Do you?" I asked, letting my anger out.

"I think I have had rather more experience of it than you," Aunt Augusta replied with calm and careful cruelty. It was true—I hadn't even answered Miss Keene's last letter. My aunt sat opposite me over her sole with an air of perfect satisfaction. She ate the shrimps that went with it one by one before she tackled the sole; she enjoyed the separate taste and she was in no hurry.

Perhaps she did have reason to despise Miss Paterson. I thought of Curran and Monsieur Dambreuse and Mr. Visconti—they lived in my imagination as though she had actually created them: even poor Uncle Jo struggling towards the lavatory. She was one of the life-givers. Even Miss Paterson had come to life, stung by the cruelty of her questions. Perhaps if she ever talked about me to another—I could well imagine what a story she could make out of my dahlias and my silly tenderness for Tooley and my stainless past—even I would come to some sort of life, and the character she drew, I felt sure, would be much more vivid than the real I. It was useless to complain of her cruelty. I had once read, in a book on Charles Dickens, that an author must not be attached to his characters, he must treat them without mercy. In the act of creation there is always, it seems, an awful selfishness. So Dickens's wife and mistress had to suffer so that Dickens could make his novels and his fortune. At least a bank manager's money is not so tainted by egotism. Mine was not a destructive profession. A bank manager doesn't leave a trail of the martyred behind him. Where was Curran now? Did even Wordsworth still survive?

"Have I ever told you," my aunt asked, "of a man called Charles Pottifer? In his way he clung to a dead man as fervently as your Miss Paterson. But in his case the dead man was himself."

"Not tonight, Aunt Augusta," I pleaded. "My father's death is enough of a story for one day."

"And she told it reasonably well," my aunt admitted, "though I think that given her opportunity I would have told it a great deal better. But I warn you—you will be sorry one day that you refused to let me tell you the story I proposed."

"What story?" I asked, thinking of my father.

"The story of Charles Pottifer, of course," my aunt said.

"Another time, Aunt Augusta."

"You are wrong to be so confident in the existence of another time," my aunt replied and called for the bill so loudly that the dog barked back at her from the bar.

CHAPTER 19

My aunt did not return with me to England by the car-ferry as I thought she intended. She told me at breakfast that she was taking a train to Paris. "There are things which I must settle," she said, and I remembered her warning of the night before and wondered—quite wrongly as it turned out if she had a premonition of death.

"Would you like me to go with you?" I asked.

"No," she said. "From the way you spoke to me last night I think you have had enough of my company for a while."

Obviously I had hurt her deeply by refusing to listen to the story of the man called Charles Pottifer.

I saw her off at the station and received the coldest of cold pecks upon the cheek.

"I didn't mean to offend you, Aunt Augusta," I said.

"You resemble your father more than your mother. He believed no story was of interest outside the pages of Walter Scott."

"And my mother?" I asked quickly. Perhaps at last I was to be given a clue.

"She tried in vain to read *Rob Roy*. She loved your

father very dearly and was anxious to please, but *Rob Roy* was going too far."

"Why didn't she marry him?"

"She hadn't the right disposition for a life in Highgate. Will you buy me a *Figaro* before you go?"

When I came back from the bookstall she gave me the keys to her apartment. "If I am away a long time," she said, "I may want you to send me something or just to look in to see that all is well. I will write to the landlord and tell him you have the keys."

I returned to London on the car-ferry. Two days before, from the window of the train, I had watched a golden England spread beside the line—now the picture was very different: England lay damp and cold, as grey as the graveyard, while the train lagged slowly from Dover Town towards Charing Cross under the drenching rain. One window could not be closed properly and a little pool of water collected at the side of the compartment; the heating had not been turned on. In the opposite corner a woman sneezed continuously while I tried to read the *Daily Telegraph*. There was a threatened engineering strike, and the car industry was menaced by a stoppage of cleaners in some key factory which turned out windscreen-wipers. Cars in all the BMC factories waited without wipers on the production line. Export figures were down and so was the pound.

I came at last beyond the court news to the obituaries, but there was little of interest to read in that column. Somebody called Sir Oswald Newman had died at the age of seventy-two; he was the star death in a poor programme. He had been chief arbitrator in a building dispute in the 1950s after retiring as Permanent Secretary in the Ministry of Works. He had married Rosa Urquhart in 1928, by whom he had three sons, and she survived him. His eldest was now Secretary of the International Federation of Thermofactors and an OBE. I thought of my father whispering, "Dolly, my darling," before he died on the floor of the *auberge* in the Haute Ville, too soon to meet Sir Oswald Newman during the building dispute, which would probably not have concerned him anyway. He always kept on good terms with his men—so my mother had told me. Laziness and good nature often go together. There were always Christmas bonuses, and he was never in the mood to fight over the rise of a penny an hour. When I looked out of the window it was not Sir Oswald Newman's England I saw but my father's grave in the smoky rain and Miss Paterson standing before it in prayer, and I envied him his inexplicable quality of drawing women's love. Had Rosa Newman so loved Sir Oswald and her son, the OBE?

I let myself into the house. I had been away two nights, but like a possessive woman it had the histrionic air of being abandoned. Dust collected quickly in autumn even with the windows closed. I knew the routine that I would certainly follow: a telephone call to Chicken, a visit to the dahlias if the rain stopped. Perhaps Major Charge might address a remark to me over the hedge. "Dolly, my darling," my father whispered, dying in the small hotel, as I lay in the Highgate nursery with a night-light beside the bed to drive away the fears which always gathered after my mother—or was it my stepmother?—had pecked me good night. I was afraid of burglars and Indian thugs and snakes and fires and Jack the Ripper, when I should have been afraid of thirty years in a bank and a take-over bid and a premature retirement and the Deuil du Roy Albert.

A month passed, and no news came to me from my aunt. I rang several times, but there was never any reply. I tried to interest myself in a novel of Thackeray's, but it lacked the immediacy of my aunt's stories. As she had foreseen, I even regretted having prevented her telling me the story of Charles Pottifer.

I found myself living now, when I lay awake or
waited in the kitchen for the kettle to boil, or when I
let *The Newcome*s fall shut on my lap, with memories of Curran, Monsieur Dambreuse and Mr. Visconti. They peopled my loneliness. When six weeks
went by without news I became anxious, in case, like
my father, she had died in a foreign land. I even
telephoned to the Saint James and Albany—it was the
first time since I left the bank that I had telephoned
abroad. I was nervous of my poor French when I
spoke into a receiver, as though the errors might be
magnified by the microphone. The receptionist told
me that my aunt was no longer there—she had left
three weeks before for Cherbourg.

"Cherbourg?"

"The boat-train," the receptionist said and the line
was cut before I could ask him what boat.

I feared then that my aunt had left me for good.
She had come into my life only to disturb it. I had
lost the taste for dahlias. When weeds swarmed up I
was tempted to let them grow. Once I even con-
sented, as a possible relief to my tedium, to attend, on
Major Charge's invitation, a political meeting: it
turned out to be a meeting of British Empire Loyalists, and I supposed then that it was Major Charge
who had given the organization my address for their
pamphlets. I saw several of my old clients there,
including the admiral, and I was glad for the first
time that I was in retirement. A bank manager is not
expected to have strong political preferences, particularly eccentric ones, and how quickly the gossip of my
presence would have gone around Southwood. Now,
if my old clients looked at me at all, it was with a
puzzled expression, as though they were uncertain
when it was we had met and on what occasion. Like a
waiter on his day off, I passed virtually unrecognized.
It was an odd feeling for one who had been so much
in the centre of Southwood life. As I went upstairs to

bed I felt myself to be a ghost returning home, transparent as water. Curran was more alive than I was. I was almost surprised to see that my image was visible in the glass.

Perhaps it was to prove the reality of my existence that I began a letter to Miss Keene. I made several drafts before I was satisfied with what I wrote, and the letter I am copying now differs in many small details from the one I dispatched. "My dear Miss Keene," I can read in the draft, but I cut out the "My" in the final version, for it seemed to presume an intimacy which she had never acknowledged and which I had never claimed. "Dear Miss Keene, I am truly distressed that you don't feel properly settled yet in your new home at Koffiefontein, though of course I cannot help feeling a little glad" (I altered the "I" to a "we" in later drafts) "that your thoughts still rest sometimes on our quiet life here in Southwood. I have never known so good a friend as your father, and my thoughts often go back to those pleasant evenings when Sir Alfred sat under the Van de Velde dispensing hospitality, and you sat sewing while he and I finished the wine." (That last phrase I cut from the next draft—there was too much emotion in it barely concealed. ("I have been leading a rather unusual life the last month, much of it in the company of my aunt of whom I wrote to you. We have even gone as far afield together as Istanbul, where I was a good deal disappointed with the famed Santa Sophia. I can say to you—as I couldn't say to my aunt—that I much prefer our own St. John's Church for a religious atmosphere, and I am glad that the vicar doesn't feel it necessary to summon the faithful to prayer by a gramophone record in a minaret. At the beginning of October we paid a visit together to my father's grave. I don't think I ever told you (indeed I only learnt of it recently myself) that he died and was buried in Boulogne by a strange concatenation of circumstances too long to write here. How I wish you were in Southwood that I might tell you of them." That sentence too I thought it prudent to eliminate. "I am reading *The Newcomes* at the moment, but I don't enjoy it as I enjoyed *Esmond*. Perhaps that is the romantic in me. I open Palgrave too from time to time and read over my old favourites." I went on with a sense of hypocrisy: "My books are a good antidote to foreign travel and reinforce the sense of the England I love, but sometimes I wonder whether that England exists still beyond my garden hedge or further than Church Road. Then I think how much harder it must be for you in Koffiefontein to keep the taste of the past. The future here seems to me to have no taste at all: it is like a meal on a menu, which serves only to kill the appetite. If you ever come back to England—" But that was a sentence I never finished, and I can't remember now what I intended to write.

Christmas approached with no news of my aunt, not even by the medium of a Christmas card. A card, of course, arrived from Koffienfontein, a rather unlikely card with an old church seen across an acre of snow, and a comic one from Major Charge which showed goldfish in a bowl being fed by Father Christmas; it was delivered by hand to save the stamp. The local store sent me a tear-off calendar with a different treasure of British art for each month, the colours bright and shiny as though they had been washed in Omo, and on December 23 the postman brought a large envelope which when I opened it at breakfast shed a lot of silvery tinsel into my plate, so that I couldn't finish my marmalade. The tinsel came from an Eiffel Tower which Father Christmas was climbing with his sack over his shoulder. Under the printed *Meilleurs Vœux* was only one name, written in block capitals: WORDSWORTH. He must have seen my aunt in Paris, for how else could he have obtained my address? At the bank I had always used the official

Christmas cards to send to my best clients, with the bank's coat of arms stamped on the cover and inside a picture of the main office in Cheapside or a photograph of the board of directors. Now that I had retired there were few people to whom I posted cards: Miss Keene, of course, Major Charge perforce. I sent one also to my doctor, my dentist, to the vicar of St. John's and my former chief cashier who had become manager of a branch in Nottingham.

A year before my mother had come to me for Christmas dinner, and without the aid of Chicken I had cooked a turkey quite successfully under her directions, then we had sat almost silent, like strangers in a restaurant-car, both of us feeling that we had eaten too much, until she left at ten. Afterwards I had, as was my habit, attended the midnight service with carols at St. John's. This year, since I had no wish to cook a meal for myself alone, I booked a table for dinner at the Abbey Restaurant off Latimer Road. It proved a mistake. I had not realized they were mounting a special menu with turkey and plum pudding to attract the lonely and the nostalgic from all over Southwood. Before I left home I had rung my aunt's number in the vain hope that she might have returned just in time for Christmas, but the bell tolled and tolled in the empty flat, and I could imagine the noise setting all the Venetian glasses atinkle.

The first person I saw when I came into the restaurant, which was a very small one with heavy beams and stained-glass windows and a piece of mistletoe in an undangerous position over the toilet, was the admiral sitting all alone. He had obviously dined early and he wore a scarlet paper crown—a torn cracker lay on his plate with the remains of plum pudding. I bowed to him and he said angrily, "Who are you?" At a table beyond him I could see Major Charge, who was frowning over what looked like a political pamphlet.

"I am Pulling," I said.

"Pulling?"

"Late of the bank."

There was an angry flush below the red paper hat, and an empty Chianti bottle stood on the table. I added, "Happy Christmas, Admiral."

"Good God, man," he said, "haven't you read the news?"

I managed to get by, though the channel between the tables was very narrow, and found to my distress that my table had been reserved next to Major Charge's.

"Good evening, Major," I said. I began to wonder whether I was the only civilian in the place.

"I have a favour to ask of you," Major Charge said.

"Of course . . . any help . . . I am afraid I no longer keep up with the stock market . . ."

"Who's talking about the stock market? You don't suppose I'd have anything to do with the City? They've sold this country down the river. I'm talking about my fish."

Miss Truman interrupted us to take my order. Perhaps to encourage her customers, she was wearing a paper cap, vaguely military in shape but yellow in colour. She was a large boisterous woman who liked to be called Peter; the little restaurant had always seemed too small to contain her and her partner as well—a woman named Nancy who was timid and retiring and perhaps for that reason showed herself only occasionally framed at the service hatch.

Unable to look elsewhere, I made some complimentary reference to her cap.

"Like the old days," she said, looking pleased, and I remembered that she had been an officer in the women's Navy.

How ambiguous my feelings were. I realized in those moments how deep was the disturbance my aunt had caused. This was my familiar world—the little local world of ageing people to which Miss Keene longed to return, where one read of danger only in the newspapers and the deepest change to be expected was a change of government and the biggest scandal— I could remember one defecting clerk who had lost too much money at the Earls Court greyhound track. It was more my country than England could be, for I had never seen the Satanic mills or visited the northern wastes, and in my way I had been happy here; yet I was looking at Peter (Miss Truman) with an ironic eye, as though I had borrowed my aunt's vision and saw with her eyes. Beyond Latimer Road there stretched another world—the world of Wordsworth and Curran and Monsieur Dambreuse and Colonel Hakim and the mysterious Mr. Visconti who had dressed up as a monsignor to escape the Allied troops, yes, and of my father too, saying "Dolly darling" to Miss Paterson with his last breath on the *auberge* floor and gaining a lifelong devotion by dying in her arms. To whom now could I apply for a visa to that land with my aunt gone?

"Will you take the set meal, Mr. Pulling?"

"I don't think I can manage the plum pudding."

"Nancy has made some smashing mince pies."

"Perhaps one," I said, "because it's Christmas."

Miss Truman rolled away with a Tom Bowling stride and I turned to Major Charge. "You were saying?"

"I'm going away for the New Year. To a study group at Chesham. I've got to board my fish. Can't trust them with the daily. I thought of Peter—but she's a woman too, in a way. You can see how she feeds us. Any excuse to pile it on. She would probably do the same with the little buggers."

"You want me to look after your fish?"

"I looked after your dahlias."

And starved them of water, I thought, but I had to say, "Yes, of course, I will."

"I'll bring you the food. Just one teaspoonful once a day. Don't pay any attention if they come guzzling at the glass. They don't know what's good for them."

"I'll harden my heart," I said. I waved away the turtle soup—it was overfamiliar. Too often I had opened a bottle of it when I had no appetite even for eggs. I asked, "What kind of a study group?"

"The problems of empire," he replied, staring at me with eyes enlarged and angry as though I had already made some foolish or unsympathetic reply.

"I thought we had got rid of all those."

"A temporary failure of nerve," he snapped and bayoneted his turkey.

I would certainly have preferred him as a client to Curran. He would never have bothered me about overdrafts: he lived carefully within the limits of his pension: he was an honest man, even if I found his ideas repulsive, and then I thought of Mr. Visconti dancing with my aunt in the reception room of the brothel behind the *Messaggero* after swindling the Vatican and the King of Saudi Arabia and leaving a wide trail of damage behind him in the banks of Italy. Was the secret of lasting youth known only to the criminal mind?

"A man's been looking for you," Major Charge said after a long silence. The admiral got up from his table and made unsteadily for the door. He was still wearing his paper crown, but when his fingers were already on the handle, he remembered it and scrunched it into a ball.

"What man?"

"You'd gone to the post office—or so I imagine. At any rate you turned right not left at the bottom of Southwood Road."

"What did he want?"

"He didn't tell me. He rang and knocked and rang and knocked, making the hell of a din. Even the fish were scared, poor little buggers. There were two of them. I thought I ought to speak to them before they disturbed the whole street."

I don't know why, but I thought at that moment of Wordsworth, a possible message from my aunt . . .

"Was he black?" I asked.

"Black? What an extraordinary question. Of course he wasn't."

"He didn't give a name?"

"Neither of them did. He asked where he could find you, but I had no idea you were planning to come here. You weren't here last year or the year before. I don't think I've ever seen you here before. All I could tell him was that I knew you went to the carol service at Saint John's."

"I wonder who it could be," I said.

I had a deep conviction that I was about to find myself again in Aunt Augusta's world, and my pulse beat with an irrational sense of pleasure. When Miss Truman brought me two mince pies I accepted them both as though I needed them to sustain me for a long voyage. I even helped myself liberally to brandy butter.

"I used real Rémy Martin," Miss Truman said. "You haven't pulled your cracker."

"Pull it with me, Peter," I said with daring. She had a strong wrist, but I got the winning end, and a small plastic object rolled on to the floor. I was glad to see that it was not a hat. Major Charge leapt at it and gave a snort of laughter as merciless as a nose-blowing. He put it to his mouth and breathed hard, making a sound like a raspberry. Then I saw that it was shaped like a tiny po with a whistle in the handle.

"Lower-deck humour," Miss Truman said in a kindly way.

"It's the festive season," Major Charge said. He blew another raspberry. " 'Hark! the herald-angels sing,' " he said in a tone of savagery, as though he were taking some kind of revenge on Christmas Eve and all its impedimenta of holy families and mangers and wise men, a revenge on love, a revenge for some deep disappointment.

I arrived at St. John's Church by a quarter past eleven. The service always began at half past eleven so as to distinguish it from the Roman Catholic Midnight Mass. I had begun to attend when I first became the bank manager, for it gave me a stable family air if I were seen at the service, and though, unlike Aunt Augusta, I have no religious convictions, I could be there without hypocrisy since I have always enjoyed the more poetic aspects of Christianity. Christmas, it seems to me, is a necessary festival; we require a season when we can regret all the flaws in our human relationships: it is the feast of failure, sad but consoling.

For years now I have always sat in the same pew below a stained-glass window which was dedicated in 1887 to the memory of Councillor Trumbull. It shows Christ surrounded by children as he sits in the shade of a very green tree—the text, of course, is "Suffer little children." Councillor Trumbull was responsible for building the square red-brick block with barred windows in Cranmer Road, which, once an orphanage, is now a detention centre for juvenile delinquents.

The carol service began with a gentler version than Major Charge's of "Hark! the Herald-Angels Sing," and then we proceeded to the old favourite, "Good King Wenceslas."

"Deep and crisp and even," the high female voices sang from the gallery—it has always seemed to me a very beautiful line, conveying the landscape of a small country England with no crowds, no traffic, to soil the snow, when even the royal palace stood among the silent and untrodden fields.

"No white Christmas, sir, this year," a voice whispered in my ear from the pew behind, and turning, I saw Detective-Sergeant Sparrow.

"What on earth are you doing here?"

"If you can spare me a moment after the service, sir," he replied, and raising his prayer-book, he sang in a very fine baritone voice:

> "Though the frost was cru-el,
> When a poor man hove in sight"

(perhaps Detective-Sergeant Sparrow, like Miss Truman, had once been in the Navy)

> "Gathering winter fu-u-el."

I looked back at his companion. He was smartly dressed with a lean legal face. He wore a dark grey overcoat and carried an umbrella crooked for safety over his arm—I wondered what he would do with it or with the sharp crease to his trousers when the time came for him to kneel. He didn't seem as much at home in the church as Detective-Sergeant Sparrow. He was not singing and I doubt whether he was praying.

> "Mark my footsteps, good my page,"

the sergeant sang lustily,

> "Tread thou in them boldly,"

and the voices in the gallery rose ardently to the unexpected competition from below.

At last the proper service began, and I was glad when the Athanasian Creed, which they invariably inflict on us at Christmas, was safely over. "As also there are not three incomprehensibles, nor three uncreated: but one uncreated, and one incomprehensible." (Sergeant Sparrow coughed several times in the course of it.)

I intended—it is always my custom at Christmas—to go to Communion. The Anglican Church is not exclusive: Communion is a commemoration service, and I had as much right to commemorate a beautiful legend as any true believer has. The vicar was saying clearly, while the congregation buzzed ambiguously to disguise the fact that they had forgotten the words: "We acknowledge and bewail our manifold sins and wickedness, which we, from time to time, most grievously have committed ..." I noticed that the detective-sergeant, perhaps from professional prudence, did not join in this plea of guilty. "We do earnestly repent, and are heartily sorry for these our misdoings. ..." I had never before noticed how the prayer sounded like the words of an old lag addressing the Bench with a plea for mercy. The presence of Detective-Sergeant Sparrow seemed to alter the whole tone of the service. When I stepped into the nave to go up to the altar I heard an outburst of argumentative whispers in the pew behind me and the words. "You, Sparrow," spoken very forcibly, so that I was not surprised when I saw that it was Detective-Sergeant Sparrow who knelt as my neighbour at the Communion rail. Perhaps they had been uncertain whether I might not take advantage of the Communion to escape through a side-door.

When his turn with the chalice came Detective-Sergeant Sparrow took a very long swig, and I noticed afterwards that more wine had to be fetched before the Communion was finished. When I returned to my seat, the detective-sergeant trod on my heels, and in the pew behind me the whispers broke out again. "My throat's like a grater," I heard the sergeant say. I suppose he was apologizing for his performance with the chalice.

At the end of the service they stood and waited for me at the church door, and Sergeant Sparrow introduced his companion. "Detective-Inspector Woodrow," he said, "Mr. Pulling." He added with awe in a lower voice, "Inspector Woodrow belongs to the Special Branch."

I shook hands after a little hesitation on both sides.

"We were wondering, sir, if you would mind assisting us again," Sergeant Sparrow said. "I told Inspector Woodrow how helpful you had been once before over that jar of pot."

"I suppose you are referring to my mother's urn," I replied with as much coldness as I could muster on Christmas morning.

The congregation poured out on either side. I saw the admiral go by. In his breast-pocket he had a patch of scarlet, which I suppose was the paper cap serving as a handkerchief.

"They told us at the Crown and Anchor," Inspector Woodrow said to me in a stiff unfriendly tone, "that you have your aunt's keys."

"We like to do things nicely," Sergeant Sparrow explained, "with the free consent of all parties concerned. It goes down so much better in court."

"What exactly do you want?" I asked.

"A happy Christmas, Mr. Pulling." The vicar put his hand on my shoulder. "Have I the pleasure of meeting two new parishioners?"

"Mr. Sparrow, Mr. Woodrow, the vicar," I said.

"I hope you all enjoyed our carol service."

"Indeed I did," Sergeant Sparrow said heartily. "If there's one thing I like it's a good tune with words I can understand."

"Just a moment while I find copies of our parish magazine. Quite a bumper Christmas number." The vicar dived back into the dark church looking like a ghost in his surplice.

"You understand, sir," Sergeant Sparrow said, "we could have easily got a search-warrant and made a forcible entry, but besides ruining a good lock—it's a Chubb, very prudent of Miss Bertram—it looks bad in evidence, you understand what I mean, for the good lady. If it comes to evidence. Which we hope will not be the case."

"But what on earth are you looking for? Not pot again surely?"

Inspector Woodrow said in a grave hangman's tone, "We are pursuing an inquiry at the request of Interpol."

The vicar came hurrying back to us, waving copies of the parish magazine. He said, "If you would both just turn to the last page you will find a tear-out subscription form for the coming year. Mr. Pulling already subscribes."

"Thank you, thank you, I am sure," Detective-Sergeant Sparrow said. "I haven't a pen with me at the moment, but just leave it with me. A very tasteful and original design—all that holly and the birds and gravestones."

Inspector Woodrow took his copy with evident reluctance. He held it in front of him as a witness holds a Bible in court, not quite certain what to do with it.

"It's a very *swinging* number," the vicar said. "Oh, forgive me. Poor lady. I'll be back in one sec." He pursued an elderly lady down the path to Latimer Road, calling, "Mrs. Brewster, Mrs. Brewster."

"I think before he returns," Inspector Woodrow said, "we had better go somewhere and discuss things."

Sergeant Sparrow had already opened the parish magazine and was reading it with absorption.

"You can come home with me," I said.

"I would prefer to go to Miss Bertram's with no further delay. We can explain matters in the car."

"Why do you want to go to my aunt's flat?"

"I've told you. There has been an inquiry from Interpol. We don't want to disturb a magistrate on Christmas night. You are next of kin. Your aunt by giving you her keys has left the flat in your care . . ."

"Has something happened to my aunt?"

"It is not impossible." He was never satisfied unless he made four words serve for one. He said sharply, "The vicar is coming back . . . For God's sake, Sparrow, pay attention."

"Now I hope you won't either of you forget your subscription," the vicar said. "It will go to a good cause. We are furnishing a Children's Corner in time for Easter. I would have preferred to call it a chapel, but we have some old Protestant battle-axes in Southwood. I'll let you into a very deep secret. I haven't even told my committee. The other day I obtained in Portobello Road an *original* drawing of Mabel Lucy Atwell's. We shall unveil it at Easter, and I am wondering if we couldn't persuade Prince Andrew . . ."

"I'm afraid, Vicar, we shall have to go," Inspector Woodrow said, "but I hope your Corner will be a great success." It was beginning to rain. He looked at his umbrella, but he didn't open it. Perhaps he was not confident that the neat folds could ever be properly reproduced.

"I will be calling on you both one day very soon," the vicar said, "when I have your addresses on the subscription form."

"Sparrow!" Inspector Woodrow spoke quite sharply.

Sparrow closed the parish magazine with reluctance and followed us at the run because of the rain. As he sat down beside Woodrow in the driver's seat, he explained apologetically, "There's a story called 'Who's Guilty?' I thought it might be a murder story— I like a good murder story—but it was only about an old lady who was unkind to a pop singer. You can't tell anything from titles nowadays."

"Now, Mr. Pulling," Inspector Woodrow said, "when did you last see your aunt?" The phrase sounded vaguely familiar.

"Some weeks—months—ago. In Boulogne. Why?"

"You travel about a great deal with her, don't you?"

"Well . . ."

"When did you last hear from her?"

"I've told you—Boulogne. Do I have to answer these questions?"

"You have your constitutional rights," Detective-Sergeant Sparrow began, "like any citizen. Duties too, of course. A voluntary statement always has a better sound in court. The court takes into account . . ."

"For God's sake, hold your tongue, Sparrow," Inspector Woodrow said. "Aren't you surprised, Mr. Pulling, that you've heard nothing from your aunt since Boulogne?"

"There is nothing about my aunt which surprises me."

"You aren't anxious—in case something might have happened to her?"

"Should I be?"

"She has kept some very queer company. Have you ever heard of a Mr. Visconti?"

"The name," I said, "is somehow familiar."

"A war criminal," Detective-Sergeant Sparrow added unwisely.

"Please keep your eye on the road, Sparrow," the inspector said. "General Abdul—you've heard of General Abdul, I presume?"

". . . Perhaps, yes, I seem to know the name."

"You were with your aunt in Istanbul some time ago. You arrived by train and you were expelled after a few hours. You saw a Colonel Hakim."

"I saw some police officer or other certainly. An absurd mistake."

"General Abdul made a statement before he died."

"Died? Poor fellow. I didn't know. I can't see how his statement can concern me."

"Or your aunt?"

"I'm not my aunt's keeper."

"The statement concerned Mr. Visconti. Interpol has circulated the details. Until now we had always assumed that Mr. Visconti was dead. We had written him off."

"By the way," I said, "before we go any further, I must tell you that I haven't got my aunt's keys with me."

"I had hardly expected that. I wanted only your permission to enter. I assure you that we'll do no damage."

"I'm afraid I can't allow it. The flat is in my charge."

"It would look so much better if it ever came to a jury, Mr. Pulling," Sparrow began, but the inspector interrupted him. "Sparrow. Take the next turning on the left. We will take Mr. Pulling home."

"You can call on me after Christmas," I said, "that is, if you have a search-warrant."

Chapter 20

I had expected the inspector and Detective-Sergeant Sparrow to come and see me, but they didn't even telephone. A picture postcard turned up unexpectedly from Tooley. It was the view of a rather ugly temple in Katmandu and she had written on it, "I am on a marvellous trip. Love, Tooley." I had quite forgotten that I had given her my address. There was no reference to Christmas (the season, I suppose, had passed unnoticed in Nepal), and I felt the more proud of her casual remembrance.

When Boxing Day was over I drove to the Crown and Anchor a little before closing time in the afternoon. I wanted to see the flat in case the inspector turned up with his search-warrant. If there were any discreditable remnants of Wordsworth still lying about the place I wanted to remove them, and I carried a small week-end case with me for the purpose. All my working life I had been strictly loyal to one establishment, the bank, but my loyalty now was drawn in quite another direction. Loyalty to a person inevitably entails loyalty to all the imperfections of a human being, even to the chicanery and immorality from which my aunt was not entirely free. I wondered whether she had ever forged a cheque or robbed a bank, and I smiled at the thought with the tenderness I might have shown in the past to a small eccentricity.

When I reached the Crown and Anchor I looked cautiously in at the window of the saloon bar. Why cautiously? I had every right to be there—it was still opening time. The day was grey with a threat of snow and the customers were all pressing against the bar to get their last refill before three o'clock. I could see the back of the girl, who was still in jodhpurs, and a large hairy hand laid against it. "Another double," "pint of best bitter," "double pink." The clock stood at two minutes to three. It was as though they were whipping up their horses on the last straight before the winning post, and there was a great deal of irregular crowding. I found the right key to open the side door and climbed the stairs. On the second landing, I sat down for a moment on my aunt's sofa. I felt as illicit as a burglar and I listened for footsteps, but of course there was only the buzz and murmur of the bar.

When I opened the door of the flat I found everything in deep darkness. I set an occasional table rocking in the hall and something Venetian tinkled into fragments on the floor. When I drew the curtains the Venetian glasses had no glitter—they had gone dead like unused pearls. There was a scurf of correspondence on the floor among the broken glass, but it consisted mainly of circulars and I didn't bother to examine them for the moment. I went into my aunt's bedroom with a sense of shame—yet hadn't she asked me to see that all was in order? I remembered how meticulously Colonel Hakim had explored the hotel room and how easily he had been outwitted, but I could see no candles anywhere, except in the kitchen, where they were of a normal size and weight— presumably a genuine precaution against an electric failure.

In Wordsworth's room the bed had been stripped and the hideous Walt Disney figures had all been put into drawers. The only decoration left was a framed photograph of Freetown harbour which showed market women in bright dresses with baskets on their heads descending some old steps towards the waterfront. I hadn't noticed it when I came before—perhaps my aunt had hung it there in memory of Wordsworth.

I returned to the sitting-room and began to go through the post. One day my aunt might send me a forwarding address, but in any case I wanted to save anything remotely personal from the scrutiny of Woodrow and Sparrow if they came. My old acquaintance Omo had written, and there were various bills from a laundry, a wine-merchant's, a grocer's. I was surprised not to find a bank statement, but remembering the gold brick and the suitcase stuffed with notes, I thought that perhaps my aunt preferred to keep her resources liquid. In that case, it seemed to me wise to take a closer look among the dresses she had left behind, for it would be dangerous to leave cash about in the empty flat.

Then among the bills I came on something which interested me—a picture postcard from Panama showing a French liner on a very blue sea. The card was written in French, in a tiny economic script to take full advantage of the small space. The writer signed himself with the initials A.D. and he wrote, so far as I could make out, what a *concours de circonstances miraculeux* it had been to find my aunt on the ship after all these years of a *triste séparation* and what a calamity it was that she had left the boat before the end of the cruise and not given him a longer chance to live over again the memories they shared. After her departure A.D.'s lumbago had taken a turn for the worse and the gout had revived in his right toe.

Could this possibly, I wondered, be Monsieur Dambreuse, the gallant lover who had kept two mistresses in the same hotel? If he was alive, then perhaps Curran was alive too. It was as though my aunt's crooked world were destined to a kind of immortality—only my poor father lay certainly dead in the smoke and rain of Boulogne. I admit that a pang of jealousy struck me because on this voyage I had not been my aunt's companion. It was to others that she now recounted her stories.

"Forgive us coming in without ringing, Mr. Pulling," said Detective-Sergeant Sparrow. He stood back to allow Inspector Woodrow to precede him according to protocol into the sitting-room. The inspector was carrying his umbrella, which looked as if it hadn't been opened since I had seen him last.

"Good afternoon," Inspector Woodrow said stiffly. "It is just as well we have found you here."

"The door being open . . ." Sergeant Sparrow said.

"I have a search-warrant," Inspector Woodrow told me before I could ask him, and he held it out for my inspection. "All the same we prefer a member of the family to be present at a search."

"Not wishing to make a commotion," Sergeant Sparrow said, "which would be disagreeable to all, we were waiting in our car across the street till the manager closed the bar, but then seeing you come in, we thought we could do things on the quiet without even the manager knowing. Much nicer for your aunt because there would have been a lot of gossip in the bar tonight, you can be sure of that. You can't trust a barman not to talk to his locals. It's like husband and wife."

While he spoke the inspector was busy examining the room.

"Looking at her mail, eh?" the sergeant asked me. He took the card out of my hand and said, "Panama. Signed A.D. Now you wouldn't have an idea who A.D. is?"

"No."

"You see, it might be an alias. Interpol doesn't get much cooperation in Panama," the sergeant said, "except in the American zone."

"Keep the card, Sparrow," the inspector said, "nonetheless."

"What have you got against my aunt?"

"You know, sir, we err on the side of kindness," Sergeant Sparrow said. "We could have charged her over that Cannabis affair, but seeing what an old lady she was and the coloured man taking off to Paris like that, we let her be. The case wouldn't have stood up well in court anyway. Of course we didn't know a thing then about this undesirable connection of hers."

"What connection?"

I wondered if they had arranged their two parts beforehand: the sergeant being told to keep me occupied while the inspector searched the flat, as he was now doing.

"This man Visconti, sir. An Italian as you might surmise with a name like that. He's a viper."

"All this glass," the inspector said. "Curious stuff. It's like a museum."

"Venetian glass. My aunt worked once in Venice. I expect a lot were gifts—from her clients."

"Very valuable? Collectors' pieces?"

"I wouldn't have thought so."

"Works of art?"

"It's a matter of taste," I said.

"Miss Bertram knew a lot about art, I daresay. Any pictures?"

"I don't think so. Only a photo of Freetown in the spare room."

"Why Freetown?"

"Wordsworth came from there."

"Who's Wordsworth?"

"The black valet," Sergeant Sparrow said. "The

one who took off to France when we found the pot."

They trailed from room to room and I followed them. I thought that Woodrow was less thorough in his search than Colonel Hakim. I had the impression that he expected nothing and was only anxious to make a formal report to Interpol that every effort had been made. Every now and then he tossed me a question without looking round. "Has your aunt ever mentioned this fellow Visconti?"

"Oh yes, many times."

"Is he alive, would you say?"

"I don't know."

"Any idea if they are still in contact?"

"I wouldn't think so."

"The old viper would be over eighty by now," Sergeant Sparrow said. "Nearer ninety, I'd guess."

"It seems a bit late to be chasing him even if he *is* alive," I said. We had left my aunt's room and entered Wordsworth's.

"That's one of the troubles of Interpol," Sergeant Sparrow said. "Too many files. It's not real police work they do. Not one of them has ever been on the beat. It's a civil service. Like Somerset House."

"They do their duty, Sparrow," Woodrow said. He took down the photo of Freetown harbour and turned it over. Then he hung it up again. "It's a good-looking frame," he said. "Cost more than the photograph."

"Italian too from the look of it," I said, "like the glass."

"Perhaps given her by the man Visconti?" Sergeant Sparrow asked.

"There's no indication on the back," the inspector said. "I had hoped for an inscription. Interpol haven't even a specimen of his signature—leave alone finger-prints." He consulted a piece of paper.

"Have you ever heard your aunt mention any of these names—Tiberio Titi?"

"No."

"Stradano? Passerati? Cossa?"

"She's never spoken to me very much about her Italian friends."

"These weren't friends," Inspector Woodrow said. "Leonardo da Vinci?"

"No."

He began to go through the rooms all over again, but I could tell that it was only for form's sake. At the door he gave me a telephone number. "If you hear from your aunt," he said, "if you ever do, please ring us at once."

"I promise nothing."

"We only want to ask her a few questions," Sergeant Sparrow said. "There's no charge against her."

"I'm glad to hear it."

"It is even possible," Inspector Woodrow said, "that she might be in serious personal danger. From her unfortunate associations."

"Particularly from that viper Visconti," Sergeant Sparrow chimed in.

"Why do you keep on calling him a viper?"

Sergeant Sparrow said, "It's the only description Interpol has given us. They haven't so much as a passport photo. But he was once described as a viper by the Chief of Police in Rome in 1945. All their war records were destroyed, the chief's dead, and we don't know now whether viper was a physical description or what you might call a moral judgement."

"At least," the inspector said, "we now have a postcard from Panama."

"It's something for the files," Detective-Sergeant Sparrow explained to me.

When I double-locked the door and followed them, I was left with the sad impression that my aunt might be dead and the most interesting part of my life might be over. I had waited a long while for it to arrive, and it had not lasted very long.

PART II

CHAPTER 1

While the ship was tugged out into the yellow tidal rush and the untidy skyscrapers and the castellated customs house jerked away, as though they rather than the ship were at the end of the rope, I thought of that distant day's depression and of how wrong my fears had proved. It was eight on a July morning and the sea-birds wailed like the cats in Latimer Road and the clouds were heavy with coming rain. There was one break of sunlight over La Plata which gave the dull river a single silver streak, but the brightest spot in the sombre scape of water and shore was the flames from gas pipes flapping against the black sky. There were four days ahead of me, up the Plata, the Paraná and the Paraguay, before I joined my aunt, and I left the Argentine winter for my overheated cabin and began to hang up my clothes and arrange my books and papers into a semblance of home.

More than half a year passed after my encounter with the detectives before I received any news of my aunt. I had become convinced of her death by that time, and once in a dream I was badly frightened by a creature crawling across the floor towards me with broken legs which swung like a snake's tail. It was going to pull me down within reach of its teeth, and

I was paralysed with terror like a bird before a snake. When I woke I remembered, Mr. Visconti, though I believe it is a cobra and not a viper which is supposed to paralyse birds.

During that empty time I received one more letter from Miss Keene. She wrote in her own hand, for a clumsy servant had broken the keyboard of her typewriter. "I was just going to write," she said, "how stupid and clumsy these blacks are, and then I remembered how you and my father had discussed racialism one night at dinner and I felt as though I were betraying our old house in Southwood and the companionship of those days. Sometimes I fear that I am going to be quite assimilated. In Koffiefontein the Prime Minister no longer seems the monster we thought him at home: indeed he's criticized here sometimes as an old-fashioned liberal. I find myself when I meet a tourist from England explaining apartheid so convincingly. I don't want to be assimilated, and yet if I am to make my life here . . ." The broken sentence sounded like an appeal which she was too shy to make clear. There followed the gossip of the farm: a dinner party to neighbours who lived more than a hundred miles away, and then one paragraph which I found a little disturbing: "I have met a Mr. Hughes, a land surveyor, and he wants to marry me (please don't laugh at me). He is a kind man in his late fifties, a widower with a teen-age daughter whom I like well enough. I don't know what to do. It would be the final assimilation, wouldn't it? I've always had a silly dream of one day coming back to Southwood and finding the old house empty (how I miss that dark rhododendron walk) and beginning my life all over again. I am afraid of talking to anyone here about Mr. Hughes—they would all be too encouraging. I wish you were not so far away, for I know you would counsel me wisely."

Was I wrong to read an appeal in that last sentence, a desperate appeal in spite of its calm wording, an appeal for some decisive telegram "come back to Southwood and marry me"? Who knows whether I might not have sent one in my loneliness if a letter had not arrived which drove poor Miss Keene right out of my mind?

It was from my aunt, written on stiff aristocratic note-paper bearing simply a scarlet rose and the name Lancaster with no address, like the title of a noble family. Only when I read a little way into the letter did I realize that Lancaster was the name of an hotel. My aunt made no appeal; she simply issued a command, and there was no explanation of her long silence. "I have decided," she wrote, "not to return to Europe and I am giving up my apartment over the Crown and Anchor at the end of the next quarter. I would be glad if you would pack what clothes there may be there and dispose of all the furniture. On second thoughts, however, keep the photograph of Freetown harbour for me as a memento of dear Wordsworth and bring it with you." (She had not even told me where to come at that point of the letter or asked me if it were possible.) "Preserve it in its frame, which has great sentimental value because it was given me by Mr. V. I enclose a cheque on my account at the Crédit Suisse, Berne, which will be sufficient for a first-class ticket to Buenos Aires. Come as soon as you can, for I get no younger. I do not suffer from gout like an old friend whom I met the other day on a packet boat, but I feel nonetheless a certain stiffness in the joints. I want very much to have with me a member of my family whom I can trust in this rather bizarre country, not the less bizarre for having a shop called Harrods round the corner from the hotel, though it is less well stocked, I fear, than in the Brompton Road."

I telegraphed to Miss Keene, JOINING MY AUNT IN BUENOS AIRES SHORTLY. WILL WRITE, and set about selling the furniture. The Venetian glass, I am afraid, went for a song. When all was sold at Harrods' auction rooms (I had some dispute with the landlord of the Crown and Anchor over the sofa on the landing) I received enough for my return ticket and fifty pounds in travellers' cheques, so I did not cash my aunt's draft on the Swiss bank and I paid the little that was over into my own account, for I thought it better for her to have no assets in England if she planned not to return.

But as for joining my aunt in Buenos Aires, my forecast had been too optimistic. There was no one to meet me at the airport, and when I arrived at the Lancaster Hotel I found only my room reserved and a letter. "I am sorry not to be here to greet you," she wrote, "but I have had to move on urgently to Paraguay, where an old friend of mine is in some distress. I have left you a ticket for the river-boat. For reasons too complicated to explain now I do not wish you to take a plane to Asunción. I cannot give you an address, but I will see that you are met."

It was a highly unsatisfactory arrangement, but what could I do? I hadn't sufficient funds to stay in Buenos Aires until I heard from her again, and I felt it impossible to return to England, when I had travelled so far on her money, but I took the precaution of changing her single ticket to Asunción into a return.

I propped the photograph of Freetown harbour in its expensive frame at the back of my dressing-table and supported it with books on either side. I had brought with me, among more ephemeral literature, Palgrave's *Golden Treasury*, the collected poems of Tennyson and Browning, and at the last minute I had added *Rob Roy*, perhaps because it contained the only photograph I possessed of my aunt. When I opened the book now the pages naturally divided at the photograph, and I found myself thinking not for the first time that the happy smile, the young breasts, the curve of her body in the old-fashioned bathing costume were like the suggestion of a budding maternity. The memory of Visconti's son as he took her in his arms on Milan platform hurt me a little, and I looked out of my porthole, to escape my thoughts, into the winter day and saw a tall lean sad grey man gazing back at me. My window gave on to the bows and he turned quickly away to watch the ship's wake, embarrassed at having been noticed. I finished my unpacking and went down to the bar.

There was the restlessness of departure about the ship. Lunch, as I learnt, was to be served at the curious hour of eleven-thirty, but until that time the passengers could no more settle than can the passengers on a Channel crossing. They came up and down the stairs, they looked at the bar and inspected the bottles and went away again without ordering a drink. They streamed into the dining-room and out again, they sat down for a moment at a table in the lounge, then rose to look through a porthole at the monotonous river scene which was to be with us for the next four days. I was the only one to take a drink. There was no sherry, so I took a gin and tonic, but the gin was Argentinian, though the name was English, and had a foreign flavour. The low wooded shore of what I took to be Uruguay unrolled in the misty rain which now began to clear the decks. The water of the river was the colour of coffee with too much milk.

An old man who must have been well into his eighties reached a decision and sat down beside me. He asked me a question in Spanish which I couldn't answer. *"No hablo español, señor,"* I said, but this scrap of Spanish which I had learnt from a phrase-book he took as an encouragement and at once began to deliver a small lecture, removing from his pocket a large magnifying glass and laying it down between us. I tried to escape by paying my bill, but he grabbed it from my hand and stuck it under his own glass, at the same time ordering the barman to refill mine. I have never been in the habit of taking two drinks before lunch, and I definitely did not like the taste of the gin, but for lack of Spanish I had to submit.

He was making some demand on me, but I could not guess what. The words *el favor* were repeated several times, and when he saw I didn't understand, he held out his own hand as a demonstration and began to examine it through the magnifying glass. A voice said, "Can I be of any help?" and turning, I saw the sad lean man who had watched me through my porthole.

I said, "I don't understand what this gentleman wants."

"His hobby is reading hands. He says he's never had the opportunity to read an American's."

"Tell him I'm English."

"He says the same applies. I don't think he sees much difference. We are both Anglo-Saxon."

There was nothing I could do but hold out my hand. The old man examined it with extreme care through the magnifying glass. "He asks me to translate, but maybe you'd rather I didn't. It's kind of personal, a fortune."

"I don't mind," I said, and I thought of Hatty and her tea-leaves and how she had foreseen my travels in her best Lapsang Souchong.

"He says you have come from a long way off."

"That's a bit obvious, isn't it?"

"But your travels are nearly over."

"That can hardly be true. I have to go back home."

"He sees a reunion of someone very close to you. Your wife perhaps."

"I have no wife."

"He says it could be your mother."

"She's dead. At least . . ."

"You have had a great deal of money in your care. But no longer."

"At any rate he's scored there. I was in a bank."

"He sees a death—but it's far away from your heart-line and your life-line. It's not an important death. Perhaps a stranger's."

"Do you believe in this nonsense?" I asked the American.

"No, I guess not, but I try to keep an open mind. My name's O'Toole. James O'Toole."

"Mine's Pulling—Henry," I said. In the background the old man continued his report in Spanish. He seemed not to care whether it was translated or not. He had pulled out a notebook and was writing things down.

"You a Londoner?"

"Yes."

"I come from Philadelphia. He wants me to tell you that yours is the nine hundred and seventy-second hand he's studied. Sorry, nine hundred and seventy-fifth." The old man closed his notebook with an air of satisfaction. Then he shook hands with me and thanked me, paid for the drinks, bowed and departed. The magnifying glass bulged in his pocket like a gun.

"Mind if I join you?" the American asked. He wore an English tweed coat and a pair of old grey flannel trousers: thin and melancholy, he looked as English as I did; there were small lines bitten by care around the eyes and mouth, and like a man who has lost his way, he had a habit of looking this way and that with anxiety. He had nothing in common with the Americans whom I had met in England, noisy and self-confident, with the young unlined faces of children romping and shouting to one another across the nursery floor.

He said, "You going to Asunción too?"

"Yes."

"There's nowhere else on this trip worth a visit. Corrientes isn't too bad—if you don't spend a night. Formosa—that's a dump. Only smugglers get off there, though they do talk of the fishing. I guess you're not a smuggler?"

"No. You seem to know these parts well."

"Too well," he said. "You on vacation?"

"I suppose so. Yes."

"Going to see the Iguazú Falls? Lots of people go there. If you do, better stay on the Brazilian side. Only good hotel."

"Are they worth a visit?"

"Maybe. If you like that kind of thing. Just a lot of water if you ask me."

The barman obviously knew the American well, for he had made him a dry Martini without a word said, and he drank it now morosely and without pleasure. "It's not like Gordon's," he said. He took a slow look at me, almost as if he were memorizing my features. "I took you for a business-man, Henry," he said. "Vacationing all by yourself? Not much fun. Strange country. And you don't speak the language—not that Spanish is any good outside the city. In the country they all speak Guaraní."

"Do you?"

"A smattering." I noticed he asked questions more than he answered them, and when he gave me information it was the kind of information which I could have obtained from any guide-book. "Picturesque ruins," he said, "old Jesuit settlements. They appeal to you, Henry?"

I felt he wouldn't be satisfied until I had told him more. What was the harm? I wasn't carrying a gold brick or a suitcase stuffed with notes. As he said, I was no smuggler. "I am visiting an old relation of mine," I said and added, "James." I could see he wanted that too.

"My friends call me Tooley," he said automatically, and it was quite a while before in my mind the coin fell.

"Are you in business here?"

"Not exactly," he said. "I do research work. Social research. You know the sort of thing, Henry. Cost of living. Malnutrition. Degree of illiteracy. Have a drink."

"Two is all I can take, Tooley," I said, and it was only at the repetition of the name that I remembered, remembered Tooley. He pushed his own glass forward for another.

"Do you find things easy in Paraguay? I've read in the papers you Americans have a lot of trouble in South America."

"Not in Paraguay," he said. "We and the General are like that." He raised his thumb and forefinger and then transferred them to his refilled glass.

"He's quite a tough dictator, so they tell me."

"It's what the country needs, Henry. A strong hand. Don't mistake me though. I keep out of politics. Simple research. That's my line."

"Have you published anything?"

"Oh," he replied vaguely, "reports. Technical. They wouldn't interest you, Henry."

It was inevitable that when the bell rang we should go into lunch together. We shared the table with two other men. One was a grey-faced man in a blue city suit who was on a diet (the steward, who knew him well, brought him a special dish of boiled vegetables which he looked at carefully before eating, twitching the end of his nose and his upper lip like a rabbit). The other was a fat old priest with rogue eyes who looked rather like Winston Churchill. I was amused

to watch O'Toole set about the two of them. Before
we had finished our bad liver *pâté*, he had found
that the priest had a parish in a village near Corrientes,
on the Argentine side of the border, and before
we had eaten our equally bad pasta he had broken a
little way into the taciturnity of the man with the
nose like a rabbit's. He was apparently a business-
man returning to Formosa. When he mentioned Formosa, O'Toole looked at me and gave a little nod of
confirmation: he had placed him.

"Now I'd guess you to be a pharmacist?" he said,
leading him on.

The man had little English, but he understood
that. He looked at O'Toole and twitched his nose. I
thought he was not going to reply, but out the phrase
came with all its international ambiguity, "Import-
export."

The priest for some reason began to speak of flying
saucers. They swarmed over Argentina, so it seemed
—perhaps if we had clear nights we would observe
one from the boat.

"You really believe in them?" I asked, and the old
priest in his excitement abandoned his little English
altogether.

"He says," O'Toole explained, "that you must
have seen yesterday's *Nación*. Twelve cars were
stopped coming from Mar del Plata to Buenos Aires
on Monday night. When a flying saucer passes overhead a car-engine stops. The reverend father believes
they have a divine origin." He translated almost as
rapidly as the other talked. "Recently a couple who
were driving to Mar del Plata for the weekend were
surrounded by a cloud. The car stopped and when
the cloud dispersed they found they were in Mexico
near Acapulco."

"And he believed even that?"

"Sure. They all do. Once a week on the radio at
Buenos Aires you can hear a programme all about

flying saucers. Who's seen them that week and where. Our friend here says it may be the explanation of the flying house of Loretto. It was just picked up in Palestine, like those people on the road to Mar del Plata, and dumped down in Italy."

They served us a tough steak and afterwards oranges. The priest lapsed into silence and ate with a slight frown. Perhaps he felt in the presence of unbelievers. The business-man pushed back his plate of boiled vegetables and excused himself. I asked my neighbour what I had been longing to ask all through the meal: "Are you married, Tooley?"

"Yeah. Sort of."

"You've got a daughter?"

"Sure. Why? She's studying in London."

"She's in Katmandu," I said.

"Katmandu! Why, that's Nepal."

The lines of anxiety deepened. "That's a hell of a thing to tell me," he said. "How do you know?" I told him about the Orient Express, but I left out any references to the young man. I said she was with a group of students, which was true when I last saw her. He said, "What can I do, Henry? I've got my work. I can't go chasing round the world. Lucinda doesn't know the worry she gives."

"Lucinda?"

"Her mother chose the name," he said with bitterness.

"She calls herself Tooley now, like you."

"She does? That's new."

"She seemed to have a great admiration for you."

"I let her go to England," he said. "I thought she'd be safe there. But Katmandu!" He pushed away the orange which he had so carefully sliced. "Where's she living? I doubt if there's a good hotel in the place. If there's a Hilton at least you know where you are. What shall I do, Henry?"

"She'll be all right," I said without conviction.

"I could send a cable to the embassy—I suppose there's an embassy." He got up abruptly and said, "I've got to take a leak."

I followed him out of the dining-room and down a corridor to the lavatory. There we stood side by side in silence. I noticed his lips moving—perhaps, I thought, he was having an imaginary dialogue with his daughter. We left the lavatory together, and without a word he sat down on a bench on the port side of the deck. It was no longer raining, but it was grey and cold. There was nothing to see but some small trees growing at the edge of the dirty river, an occasional hut, and through the trees an expanse of brown scrub stretching to the horizon without a hill in sight.

"Argentina?" I asked to break the silence.

"It's all Argentina," he said, "till we reach the Paraguay river our last day." He took out a pocket-book and made some notes. They seemed to be figures. When he had finished he said, "Excuse me. It's a record I keep."

"Research?"

"Kind of a study I'm making."

"Your daughter told me you were in the CIA."

He turned on me his sad and anxious eyes. "She's a romantic," he said. "She imagines things."

"Is the CIA romantic?"

"A kid thinks so. I guess she saw some report of mine marked SECRET. Anything's secret that goes to a government department. Even malnutrition in Asunción."

I wasn't sure which of them I believed.

He asked me with an air of helplessness, "What would you do, Henry?"

I said, "If you were really in the CIA you could probably find out how she was from one of your men there. You must have a man in Katmandu."

"If I were really in the CIA," he said, "I wouldn't want to get them mixed up in my private affairs. Have you any children, Henry?"

"No."

"You are a lucky man. People talk about the age of reason. There's no such thing. When you have a child you are condemned to be a father for life. They go away from you. You can't go away from them."

"How would I know?"

He brooded awhile, staring out over the scrub which never changed. The boat moved slowly against the strong flow to the sea. He said, "My dad was all against the divorce—for the sake of the child. But there are limits to what a man can take—she began to bring her boy-friends home. She was corrupting Lucinda."

"She didn't succeed," I said.

Next morning I missed O'Toole: he didn't appear at breakfast, and I looked for him in vain upon the deck. There was a heavy mist over the river which the sun took a long time to disperse. I felt a little lonely without my only contact. Everyone else was settling into a shipboard relation: even a few flirtations had begun. Two old men paced the deck fiercely, showing off their physical fitness. There was something obscene to me about their rapid regular walk—they seemed to be indicating to all the women they passed that they were still in full possession of their powers. They wore slit jackets in imitation of the English—they had probably bought them at Harrods—and they reminded me of Major Charge.

We had pulled up at a town called Rosario during the night (the voices, the shouts, the noise of chains had entered my dreams and made them dreams of violence some while before I woke), and now the river, when the mist rose, had changed its character. The water was sprinkled with islands, and there were cliffs and sand bars and strange birds piping and whispering beside us. I experienced far more the sensation of travel than when I passed all the crowded frontiers in the Orient Express. The river was low, and a rumour spread that we might not be able to get beyond Corrientes because the expected rains of winter had not come. A sailor on the bridge was continually heaving the lead. We were within half a metre, the priest told me, of the ship's draught, and he moved on to spread despondency further.

I began for the first time seriously to read *Rob Roy*, but the moving scenery was a distraction. I would begin a page while the shore was half a mile away, and when I lifted my eyes after a few paragraphs, it had approached within a stone's throw—or was it an island? At the beginning of the next page I looked again, and the water was now nearly a mile wide. A Czech sat down beside me. He spoke English and I was content to close *Rob Roy* and listen to him. He was a man who, having once known prison, enjoyed freedom to the full. His mother had died under the Nazis, his father under the Communists, he had escaped to Austria and married an Austrian girl. His training had been scientific, and when he decided to settle in the Argentine he had borrowed the money to start a plastics factory. He said, "I looked around first in Brazil and Uruguay and Venezuela. One thing I noticed. Everywhere but in the Argentine they used straws for cold drinks. Not in the Argentine. I thought I'd make my fortune. I made two million plastic straws and I couldn't sell a hundred. You want a straw? You can have two million for free. There they are stacked in my factory today. The Argentines are so conservative they won't drink through a straw. I was very nearly bankrupt, I can tell you," he said happily.

"So what do you do now?"

He gave me a cheerful grin. He seemed one of the happiest men I had ever met. He had shed his past fears and failures and sorrows more completely than most of us can do. He said, "I manufacture plastic

material and let other fools risk their money on what
they make with it."

The man with the rabbit nose went twitching by,
grey as the grey morning. "He gets off at Formosa," I
said.

"Ah, a smuggler," the Czech said and laughed and
went on his way.

I began to read *Rob Roy* again while the leads-
man called the sounding. "You must remember my
father well; for as your own was a member of the
mercantile house, you knew him from infancy. Yet
you hardly saw him in his best days, before age and
infirmity had quenched his ardent spirit of enterprise
and speculation." I thought of my father lying in his
bath in his clothes, just as later he lay in his Bol-
logne coffin, and giving me his impossible instructions, and I wondered why I felt an affection for him,
while I felt none for my faultless mother who had
brought me up with rigid care and found me my first
situation in a bank. I had never built the plinth
among the dahlias and before I left home I had
thrown away the empty urn. Suddenly a memory
came back to me of an angry voice. I had woken up,
as I sometimes did, afraid that the house was on fire
and that I had been abandoned. I had climbed out of
bed and sat down at the top of the stairs, reassured by
the voice below. It didn't matter how angry it was: it
was there: I was not alone and there was no smell of
burning. "Go away," the voice said, "if you want to,
but I'll keep the child."

A low reasonable voice, which I recognized as my
father's, said, "I *am* his father," and the woman I
knew as my mother slammed back like a closing door,
"And who's to say that I'm not his mother?"

"Good morning," O'Toole said, sitting down beside
me. "Did you sleep well?"

"Yes. And you?"

He shook his head. "I kept on thinking of Lucinda," he said. He took out his notebook and again began to write down his mysterious columns of numerals.

"Research?" I asked.

"Oh," he said, "this is not official."

"Making a bet on the ship's run?"

"No, no. I'm not a betting man." He gave me one of his habitual looks of melancholy and anxiety. "I've never told anyone about this, Henry," he said. "It would seem kind of funny to most people, I guess. The fact is I count while I'm pissing and then I write down how long I've taken and what time it is. Do you realize we spend more than one whole day a year pissing?"

"Good heavens," I said.

"I can prove it, Henry. Look here." He opened his notebook and showed me a page. His writing went something like this:

July 28	
7.15	0.17
10.45	0.37
12.30	0.50
13.15	0.32
13.40	0.50
14.05	0.20
15.45	0.37
18.40	0.28
10.30	? Forgot to time
	4 m. 31 sec

He said, "You've only got to multiply by seven. That makes half an hour a week. Twenty-six hours a year. Of course shipboard life isn't quite average. There's more drinking between meals. And beer keeps on repeating. Look at this time here—one minute, fifty-five seconds. That's more than the average, but then I've noted down two gins. There's a lot of variations too I haven't accounted for, and from now on I'm going to make a note of the temperature too. Here's July twenty-fifth—six minutes, nine seconds n.c.—that stands for 'not complete.' I went out to dinner in BA and left my notebook at home. And here's July twenty-seventh—only three minutes twelve seconds in all, but, if you remember, there was a very cold north wind on July twenty-fifth and I went out to dinner without an overcoat."

"Are you drawing any conclusions?" I asked.

"That's not my job," he said. "I'm no expert. I just report the facts and any data—like the gins and the weather—that seem to have a bearing. It's for others to draw the conclusions."

"Who are the others?"

"Well, I thought when I had completed six months' research I'd get in touch with a urinary specialist. You don't know what he mightn't be able to read into these figures. Those guys deal all the time with the sick. It's important to them to know what happens in the case of an average fellow."

"And you are the average fellow?"

"Yes. I'm a hundred per cent healthy, Henry. I have to be in my job. They give me the works every so often."

"The CIA?" I asked.

"You're kidding, Henry. You can't believe that crazy girl."

He fell into a sad silence as he thought of her, leaning forward with his chin in his hand. An island with the appearance of a gigantic alligator floated downstream with its snout extending along the water. Pale green fishing boats drifted downstream faster than our engines could drive us against the current— they passed rapidly like little racing cars. Each fisherman was surrounded by floating blocks of wood to which his lines were attached. Rivers branched off into the grey misty interior, wider than the Thames at Westminister but going nowhere at all.

He asked, "And she really called herself Tooley?"

"Yes, Tooley."

"I guess she must think of me sometimes?" he said with a sort of questioning hope.

CHAPTER 3

It was two days later that we came to Formosa, on a day which was as humid as all the others had been. The heat broke on the cheek like little bubbles of water. We had turned off the great Paraná river the night before near Corrientes, and now we were on the Paraguay. Fifty yards across the water from the Argentinian Formosa the other country lay, sodden and empty. The import-export man went ashore in his dark city suit carrying a new suitcase. He went with rapid steps, looking at his watch like the rabbit in *Alice in Wonderland*. It certainly seemed an ideal town for smugglers, with only a river to cross. In Paraguay I could see only a crumbling hut, a pig and a small girl.

I was tired of walking the deck, so I went ashore too. It was a Sunday and quite a crowd had collected to see the boat come in. There was a pervading smell of orange petals, but it was the only sweet thing about Formosa. One long avenue was lined with oranges and trees bearing rose-coloured flowers, which I learnt later to be *lapachos*. The side streets petered out a few yards away into a niggardly wild nature of mud and scrub. Everything to do with government, business, justice or amusement lay in the one avenue: a tourist hotel of grey cement on the water's edge had been half-built, for what tourists? little shops selling Coca-Cola; a cinema which advertised an Italian Western; two hairdressers; a garage with one wrecked car; a *cantina*. The only house of more than one story was the hotel, and the only old and beautiful building in the long avenue proved, as I came closer to it, to be the prison. There were fountains all down the avenue but they didn't play.

The avenue must lead me somewhere, I thought, but I was wrong. I passed the bust of a bearded man called Urquiza, who, judging from the carved inscription, must have had something to do with liberation—from what?—and ahead of me I saw rise up above the orange trees and the *lapachos* a marble man upon a marble horse who was certainly General San Martín—Buenos Aires had made me familiar with his features and I had seen him upon the seafront at Boulogne too. The statue closed the avenue as the Arc de Triomphe closes the Champs-Elysées; I expected some further avenue beyond, but when I reached the statue I found the hero sat on his horse in a waste of mud at the farthest limit of the town. No strollers came so far, and the road went no farther. Only a starving dog, like a skeleton from the Natural History Museum, picked his way timorously across the dirt and the rain pools towards me and San Martín. I began to walk back.

If I describe this ignoble little town in such detail, it is because it was the scene of a long dialogue I held with myself which was interrupted only by a surprising encounter. I had begun, as I passed the first hairdresser, to think of Miss Keene and her letter of shy appeal which surely deserved a better response than my brief telegram, and then in this humid place, where the only serious business or entertainment was certainly crime, and even the national bank had to be defended on a Sunday afternoon by a guard

with an automatic rifle, I thought of my home in
Southwood, of my garden, of Major Charge trumpet-
ing across the fence, and of the sweet sound of the
bells from Church Road. But I remembered Southwood now with a kind of friendly tolerance—as the
place which Miss Keene should never have left, the
place where Miss Keene was happy, the place where I
myself no longer belonged. It was as though I had
escaped from an open prison, had been snatched
away, provided with a rope ladder and a waiting car,
into my aunt's world, the world of the unexpected
character and the unforeseen event. There the rabbit-
faced smuggler was at home, the Czech with his two
million plastic straws, and poor O'Toole busy making
a record of his urine.

I passed the end of a street called Rua Dean Fur-
nes which petered away like all the others into no-
man's-land, and I stayed a moment outside the gover-
nor's house, which was painted with a pink wash. On
the veranda were two unoccupied chaises-longues and
the windows were wide open on an empty room with
a portrait of a military man, the President, I suppose,
and a row of empty chairs lined up against the wall
like a firing squad. The sentry made a small movement with his automatic rifle and I moved on towards
the national bank, where another sentry made the
same warning movement when I paused.

That morning in my bunk I had read Wordsworth's great ode in Palgrave's *Golden Treasury*.
Palgrave, like Scott, carried signs of my father's reading in the form of dog-eared pages, and knowing so
little about him, I had followed every clue and so
learned to enjoy what he had enjoyed. Thus when I
first entered the bank as junior clerk I had thought of
it in Wordsworth's terms as a "prison-house"—what
was it my father had found a prison, so that he
double-marked the passage? Perhaps our home, and
my stepmother and I had been the warders.

One's life is more formed, I sometimes think, by books than by human beings: it is out of books one learns about love and pain at second hand. Even if we have the happy chance to fall in love, it is because we have been conditioned by what we have read, and if I had never known love at all, perhaps it was because my father's library had not contained the right books. (I don't think there was much passionate love in Marion Crawford, and only a shadow of it in Walter Scott.)

I can remember very little of the vision preceding the prison-house: it must have faded very early "into the light of common day," but it seemed to me, as I put Palgrave down beside my bunk and thought of my aunt, that she for one had never allowed the vision to fade. Perhaps a sense of morality is the sad compensation we learn to enjoy, like a remission for good conduct. In the vision there is no morality. I had been born as a result of what my stepmother would have called an immoral act, an act of darkness. I had begun in immoral freedom. Why then should I have found myself in a prison-house? My real mother had certainly not been imprisoned anywhere.

It's too late now, I said to Miss Keene, signalling to me desperately from Koffiefontein, I'm no longer there, where you think I am. Perhaps we might have comforted ourselves once and been content in our prison cell, but I'm not the same man you regarded with a touch of tenderness over the tatting. I have escaped. I don't resemble whatever identikit portrait you have of me. I walked back towards the landing stage, and looking behind me, I saw the canine skeleton on my tracks. I suppose to that dog any stranger represented hope.

"Hi, man," a voice called. "You in number-one hurry?" and Wordsworth was suddenly there a few yards away. He had risen from a bench beside the bust of the liberator Urquiza and advanced towards

me with both hands out and his face slashed open
with the wide wound of his grin. "Man, you not
forget old Wordsworth?" he asked, wringing both my
hands, and laughing so loudly and deeply that he
sprayed my face with his happiness.

"Why, Wordsworth," I said with equal pleasure,
"what on earth are you doing here?"

"My lil bebi gel," he said, "she tell me go off
Formosa and wait for Mr. Pullen come."

I noticed that he was every bit as smartly dressed
now as the rabbit-nosed importer and he too carried a
very new suitcase.

"How is my aunt, Wordsworth?"

"She pretty O.K.," he said, but there was a look of
distress in his eyes and he added, "She dance one hell
too much. Ar tell her she no bebi gel no more. Ef she
no go stop . . . Man, she got me real worried."

"Are you coming on the boat with me?"

"Ar sure am, Mr. Pullen. You lef everyting to old
Wordsworth. Ar know the customs fellows in
Asunción. Some good guys. Some bad like hell. You
lef me talk. We don wan no humbug."

"I'm not *smuggling* anything, Wordsworth." The
noise of the ship's siren summoned us, wailing up
from the river.

"Man, you lef everyting to old Wordsworth. Ar jus
gone tak a look at that boat and ar see a real bad guy
there. We gotta be careful."

"Careful of what, Wordsworth?"

"You in good hands, Mr. Pullen. You lef old Wordsworth be now."

He suddenly took my fingers and pressed them.
"You got that picture, Mr. Pullen?"

"You mean of Freetown harbour? Yes, I've got
that."

He gave a sigh of satisfaction. "Ar lak you, Mr.
Pullen. You allays straight with old Wordsworth.
Now you go for boat." I was just leaving him when

he added, "You got CTC for Wordsworth?" and I gave him what coins I had in my pocket. Whatever trouble he might have caused me in that dead old world of mine, I was overjoyed to see him now.

They were carrying the last cargo on to the ship through the black iron doors open in the side. I made my way through the steerage quarters, where women with Indian faces sat around suckling their children and climbed the rusting stairs to the first-class. I never noticed Wordsworth come on board, and at dinner he was nowhere to be seen. I supposed that he was travelling in the steerage and saving for other purposes the difference in the fare, for I was quite certain that my aunt would have given him a first-class ticket.

After dinner O'Toole suggested a drink in his cabin. "I've got some good bourbon," he said, and though I have never been a spirit-drinker, preferring a glass of sherry before a meal or a glass of port after it, I accepted his invitation gladly, for it was our last night together on board. Again the spirit of restlessness had taken over all the passengers in the ship, and they seemed touched with a kind of mania. In the saloon an amateur band had begun to play, and a sailor with hairy legs and arms, dressed inadequately as a woman, had whirled in a dance between the tables, demanding a partner. Now in the captain's cabin, which was close to O'Toole's, someone was playing the guitar and a woman squealed. It wasn't what you expected to hear from a captain's quarters.

"No one will sleep tonight," O'Toole remarked, pouring out the bourbon.

"If you don't mind," I said, "a lot more soda."

"We've made it. I thought we were going to be stuck fast at Corrientes. The rain is damn late this year," and as though to soften his rebuke of the weather there came a long peal of thunder which almost drowned the music of the guitar.

"What did you think of Formosa?" O'Toole asked.

"There wasn't much to see. Except the prison. A fine colonial building."

"Not so good inside," O'Toole said. A splash of lightning was flung over the wall and made the cabin lights flicker. "Met a friend, didn't you?"

"A friend?"

"I saw you talking to a coloured guy."

What was it that made me cautious, for I liked O'Toole? I said, "Oh, he wanted money. I didn't see you on shore."

"I was up on the bridge," O'Toole said, "looking through the captain's glasses." He changed course abruptly. "I can't get over you knowing my daughter, Henry. You can't imagine how I miss that girl. You never told me how she looked."

"She looked fine. She's a very pretty girl."

"Yeah," he said, "so was her mother. If I ever married again I'd marry a plain girl." He brooded a long time over the bourbon, and I looked around his cabin. He had made no attempt, as I had made the first day, to make it a temporary home. His suitcases lay on the floor filled with clothes; he had not bothered to hang them. A razor beside the wash-basin and a Bantam book beside his bed seemed to be the extent of his unpacking. Suddenly the rain hit the deck outside like a cloudburst.

"I guess winter's here all right," he said.

"Winter in July."

"I've gotten used to it," he said. "I haven't seen the snow for six years."

"You've been out here for six years?"

"No, but I was in Thailand before this."

"Doing research?"

"Yeah. Sort of . . ." If he was usually as tongue-tied as this it must have taken him a long time to unearth every fact he required.

"How are the urine statistics?"

"More than four minutes thirty seconds today," he said. He added glumly. "And I haven't reached the end," lifting the bourbon. When the next peal of thunder had trembled out he went on, obviously straining after any subject to fill the pause, "So you didn't like Formosa?"

"No. Of course it may be all right for fishing," I said.

."Fishing!" he exclaimed with scorn. "Smuggling is what you mean."

"I keep on hearing all the time about smuggling. Smuggling what?"

"It's the national industry of Paraguay," he said. "It brings in nearly as much as the maté and a lot more than hiding war criminals with Swiss bank accounts. And a darn sight more than my research."

"What have they got to smuggle?"

"Scotch whisky and American cigarettes. You get yourself an agent in Panama who buys wholesale and he flies the stuff down to Asunción. They are marked GOODS IN TRANSIT, see. You pay only a small duty at the international airport and you transfer the crates to a private plane. You'd be surprised to see how many private Dakotas there are now in Asunción. Then your pilot takes off to Argentina just across the river. At some *estancia* a few hundred kilometres from BA you touch down—they nearly all have private landing grounds. Not built for Dakotas perhaps, but that's the pilot's risk. You unload into trucks and there you are. You've got your distributors waiting with their tongues hanging out. The government makes them thirsty with duties of a hundred and twenty per cent."

"And Formosa?"

"Oh, Formosa's for the small guy working himself up on the river traffic. All the goods that arrive from Panama don't go on in the Dakota. What do the police care if some of the crates stay behind? You'll buy Scotch cheaper in the stores at Asunción than you will in London and the street boys will sell you good American cigarettes at cut-rate. All you need's a rowboat and a contact. One day, though, you'll get tired of that game—perhaps a bullet's come too close— and you'll buy a share in a Dakota and then you're in the big money. You tempted, Henry?"

"I didn't have the right training at the bank," I said, but I thought of my aunt and her suitcases stuffed with notes and her gold brick—perhaps there was something in my blood to which a career like that might once have appealed. "You know a lot about it," I said.

"It's part of my sociological research."

"Did you never think of researching a bit deeper?" The frontier spirit, Tooley." I teased him only because I liked him. I could never have teased Major Charge or the admiral in that way.

He gave me a long sad look, as though he wanted to answer me quite truthfully. "You don't save enough money in a job like mine to buy a Dakota. And the risks are big too, Henry, for a foreigner. These guys fall out sometimes and then there's hijacking. Or the police get greedy. It's easy to disappear in Paraguay—not necessarily disappear either. Who's going to make a fuss about an odd body or two? The General keeps the peace—that's what people want after the civil war they had—and a dead man makes no trouble for anyone. They don't have coroners in Paraguay."

"So you prefer life to the frontier spirit, Tooley."

"I know I'm not much good for my girl three thousand miles away, Henry, but at least she gets her monthly cheque. A dead man can't write a cheque."

"And I suppose the CIA aren't interested?"

"You shouldn't believe that nonsense, Henry. I told you—Lucinda's romantic. She wants an exciting father, and what's she got? She's saddled with me. So she has to invent things. A report on malnutrition's not romantic."

"I think you ought to bring her home, Tooley."

"Where's home?" he said, and I looked around the cabin and wondered too. I don't know why I wasn't quite convinced. He was a great deal more reliable than she was.

I left him with his Old Forester and returned to my cabin on the opposite deck. O'Toole was port and I was starboard. I looked out at Paraguay and he looked out at Argentina. The guitar was still playing in the captain's cabin and someone was singing in a language I couldn't recognize—perhaps it was Guaraní. I hadn't locked my door, and yet it wouldn't open when I pushed. I had to put my shoulder to it to make it give. Through the crack I saw Wordsworth. He faced the door and he had a knife in his hand. When he saw who it was he held the knife down.

"Come in, boss," he said in a whisper.

"How can I come in?"

He had wedged the door with a chair. He removed it now and let me in.

"Ar got to be careful, Mr. Pullen," he said.

"Careful of what?"

"Too much bad people on this boat, too much humbug."

His knife was a boy's knife with three blades and a corkscrew and a tin-opener and something for taking stones out of horses' hoofs—cutlers are conservative and so are schoolboys. Wordsworth closed it and put it in his pocket.

"Well," I said, "what do you want, you happy shepherd boy?"

He shook his head. "Oh, she's a wonder, your auntie. No one ever talk to Wordsworth like that befo. Why, she come right up to me in the street outside the movie palace an she say, clear like day, 'Thou child of joy.' Ar love your auntie, Mr. Pullen. Ar ready to die for her any time she raise a finger an say, 'Wordsworth, you go die.' "

"Yes, yes," I said, "that's fine, but what are you doing barricaded in my cabin?"

"Ar come for the picture," he said.

"Couldn't you wait till we get ashore?"

"Your auntie say bring that picture safe, Wordsworth, double quick, or you no come here no more."

A suspicion returned to me. Could the frame, like the candle, be made of gold? Or did the photograph cover some notes of a very high denomination? Neither seemed likely, but neither was impossible with my aunt.

"Ar got friends in customs," Wordsworth said, "they no humbug me, but, Mr. Pullen, you a stranger here."

"It's only a photograph of Freetown harbour."

"Ya'as, Mr. Pullen. But your auntie say . . ."

"All right. Take it then. Where are you sleeping?

Wordsworth jerked his thumb at the floor. "Ar more comfortable down below there, Mr. Pullen. The folks thar they sing an dance an have good time. They don wear no cravats an they no don go wash befo meals. Ar don like soap with my chop."

"Have a cigarette, Wordsworth."

"If you don't mind, Mr. Pullen, I smoke this here."

He pulled a ragged reconstructed cigarette out of a crumpled pocket.

"Still on pot, Wordsworth?"

"Well, it's a sort of medicine, Mr. Pullen. Arm not too well these days. Ar got a lot o' worry."

"Worry about what?"

"Your auntie, Mr. Pullen. She allays safe with old Wordsworth. Ar no cost her nothing. But she got a fellah now—he cost her plenty plenty. An he too old for her, Mr. Pullen. Your auntie no chicken. She need a young fellah."

"You aren't exactly young yourself, Wordsworth."

"Ar no got ma big feet in no tomb, Mr. Pullen, lak

that one. Ar no trust that fellah. When we come here he plenty sick. He say, 'Please Wordsworth, please Wordsworth,' an he mak all the sugar in the world melt in his mouth. He live in low-class hotel, but he ain got no money. They go to turn him out an, man, he were plenty scared to go. When your auntie come he cry like a lil bebi. He no man, sure he no man, but he plenty plenty mean. He say sweet things all right all right, but he allays act mean. What wan she leave Wordsworth for a mean man like him? Tell me that, man, tell me that." He let his great bulk down on my bed and he began to weep. It was like a spring forcing its hard way to the surface, spilling out of the crevices of a rock.

"Wordsworth," I said, "are you jealous of Aunt Augusta?"

"Man," he said, "she war my bebi gel. Now she gon bust ma heart in bits."

"Poor Wordsworth." There was nothing more I could say.

"She wan me quit," Wordsworth said. "She wan me for come bring you, and then she wan me quit. She say, "I give you biggest CTC you ever saw, you go back Freetown and find a gel,' but I no wan her money, Mr. Pullen, I no wan Freetown no more, and I no wan any gel. I love our auntie. I wan for to stay with her like the song say: 'Abide with me; fast falls the eventide; the darkness deepens: oh, with me abide. . . . Tears have no bitterness,' but man, these tears are bitter, tha's for sure."

"Wherever did you learn that hymn, Wordsworth?"

"We allays sang that in Saint George's cathedral in Freetown. 'Fast falls the eventide.' Plenty sad songs like that we sang there, an they all mak me think now of my bebi gel. 'Here lingrin still we ask for nought but simply worship thee.' Man, it's true. But now she wan me to quit, an go right away an never see her no more."

"Who is this man she's with, Wordsworth?"

"I won spik his name. My tongue burn up if I spik his name. Oh, man, I bin faithful to your auntie long time now."

It was to distract him from his misery and not to reproach him that I said, "You remember that girl in Paris?"

"That one who wan do jig-jig?"

"No, no, not that one. The young girl on the train."

"Oh ya'as. Sure. I member her."

"You gave her pot," I said.

"Sure. Why not? Very good medicine. You don think I do anytin bad with her? Why, man, she was the ship that gone by one day. She too young for old Wordsworth."

"Her father's on the boat now."

He looked at me with astonishment. "You don say!"

"He was asking me about you. He saw us on shore."

"What he look lak?"

"He's as tall as you but very thin. He looks unhappy and worried and he wears a tweed sports coat."

"Oh, God Almighty! I know *him*. I seen him plenty in Asunción. You got to be bloody careful of *him*."

"He says he's doing social-research work."

"What that mean?"

"He investigates things."

"Oh, man, you're right there. I tell you sometin. Your auntie's fellah—he don like that man around."

I had meant to distract him, and I had certainly succeeded. He pressed my hand hard when he left me, carrying the picture concealed under his shirt. He said, "Man, you know what you are to Wordsworth. You help of the helpless, Mr. Pullen. O abide with me."

When I went up on deck after breakfast we were already approaching Asunción. Red cliffs were honeycombed with caves. Half-ruined huts stood at the very edge of the cliff and naked children with the pot-bellies of malnutrition stared down on us as the boat passed, moving like an overfed man who picks his slow way home after a heavy meal, giving little belches on the siren. Above the huts, like a medieval castle dominating some wretched village of mud and wattle, stood the great white bastions of Shell.

O'Toole came and stood beside me as the immigration officers arrived on board. He asked, "Can I be of any help? Give you a lift or anything?"

"Thank you very much, but I think I shall be met."

The steerage passengers were going ashore. He said, "If you want any help at any time . . . I know most of the ropes. You'll find me at the embassy. They call me a second secretary. It's convenient."

"You're very kind."

"You are a friend of Lucinda . . ." he said. "Katmandu seems a hell of a long way off. Maybe some mail will have come in."

"Is she a good correspondent?"

"She writes me picture postcards," he said. He leant forward on the rail. "Isn't that your friend?" he asked.

"What friend?"

I looked at the steerage queue on the gangway and saw Wordsworth.

"The man who spoke to you on shore."

I said, "All coloured men look very much alike to me at that distance."

"It's not often you see an African here," he said. "I guess it's your friend."

When at last the formalities were over and I stood beside my luggage on the corner of a street named after Benjamin Constant, I looked around awhile in vain for Wordsworth. Families exchanged greetings and drove away in cars. The Czech plastics manufacturer offered me a lift in his taxi. A small boy wanted to clean my shoes and another tried to sell me American cigarettes. A long colonnaded street, which sloped uphill in front of me, was full of liquor shops, and old women sat against the wall with baskets of bread and fruit. In spite of the dirt and fumes of old cars, the air was sweet with orange blossom.

Somebody whistled, and I turned to see Wordsworth getting out of a taxi. He lifted my two heavy suitcases as though they were empty cardboard boxes. "Ar look for friend," he said, "too plenty humbug here." I had never before been driven in quite such a decrepit taxi. The lining was torn and the stuffing leaked out of the seat. Wordsworth punched at it to make it more comfortable. Then he made motions to the driver which the man seemed to understand. "We drive aroun a bit," Wordsworth said. "Ar wan to see if they lef us alone." He looked out of the window, while the taxi ground and shook. All the other taxis which passed us were smart enough, and sometimes the drivers shouted what I

took to be insults to our old man, who had a white
moustache and a hat without a crown.

"Suppose we're *not* left alone," I said, "what do we
do?"

"We tak bloody good care," Wordsworth said
vaguely.

"You seem to have chosen the oldest taxi."

Soldiers were goose-stepping in front of the cathedral, and a very early tank stood on a plinth up on
the greensward. The orange trees were everywhere,
some in fruit and some in blossom.

"He good friend of mine."

"You talk Spanish?" I asked.

"No. He don know no Spanish."

"What does he talk?"

"He talk Indian lingo."

"How do you make him understand?"

"Ar give him smokes," Wordsworth said. "He lak
pot."

Except for the skyscraper of a new hotel, it was a
very Victorian town. One soon ceased to notice the
cars—they were an anachronism; there were mule
carts and sometimes men on horses, there was a little
white castellated Baptist church, a college built like a
neo-Gothic abbey, and when we reached the residen-
tial quarter I saw big stone houses with bosky gardens
and pillared porticos above stone steps which reminded me of the oldest part of Southwood, but in Southwood the houses would have been split into flats and
the grey stone would have been whitewashed and the
roofs would have bristled with television masts. In
place of the orange and banana trees, I would have
seen neglected rhododendrons and threadbare lawns.

"What is the name of my aunt's friend, Wordsworth?" I asked.

"Ar don remember," Wordsworth said. "Ar don
wanta remember. Ar wanta forget."

A little crumbling house with corinthian pillars and broken windows was called SCHOOL OF ARCHITECTURE on a board which had been split by the seasons, but, however tumbledown the houses, the flowers were everywhere. A bush of jasmine blossomed with white and blue flowers on the same bush.

"We stop here," Wordsworth said and he shook the driver's shoulder.

It was an enormous house with a great untidy lawn which ended in a dark green fuzz of trees, a small wood of banana, orange, lemon, grapefruit, *lapacho*. On the two sides visible to me through the gates wide stone steps led up to separate entrances. The walls were blotched with lichen and were four stories high.

"It's a millionaire's house," I said.

"You jus wait," Wordsworth replied.

The iron gates were rusty and padlocked. Worn pineapples were carved on the gateposts, but the gates, draped with barbed wire, had lost their dignity. A millionaire may once have lived there, I thought, but no longer.

Wordsworth led me round the corner of the street and we approached the house from the back through a little door which he locked behind him and through the grove of sweet-smelling trees and bushes. "Hi!" he called to the great square block of stone, "hi!" and got no response. The house in its solidity and its silence reminded me of the great family tombs in the cemetery at Boulogne. This was a journey's end too.

"Your auntie she got a bit deaf," Wordsworth said. "She no young no more, no more." He spoke regretfully, as though he had known her as a girl, and yet she had been over seventy when she picked him up outside the Grenada Palace. We went up one flight of stone steps and into the hall of the house.

Paved with cracked marble, the big hall was unfurnished. The windows had been shuttered and the only light came from a bare globe in the ceiling. There was no chair, no table, no sofa, no pictures. The one sign of human occupation was a mop which leant against one wall, but it might have been left there a generation ago by someone hired to tidy up after the furniture-removers had departed.

"Hi!" Wordsworth shouted. "Hi! Mr. Pullen be here," and I heard the click of high heels along a passage overhead. A flight of pink marble stairs rose to the first floor, and at the head of them my aunt appeared. The light was too dim to see her clearly, and it may have been my imagination which read into her voice an older, more tremulous tone than I had remembered. "Why, Henry," she said, "you are welcome home." She came slowly down the stairs, and perhaps it was the bad light which caused her to clutch at the banister. "I am so sorry," she said, "that Mr. Visconti is not here to greet you. I had expected him yesterday."

"Mr. Visconti?"

"Yes," my aunt said, "Mr. Visconti. We are happily reunited. Did you bring the picture safely?"

"Ar got it," Wordsworth said, holding up his new suitcase.

"Mr. Visconti will be relieved. He was afraid of the customs. You look well, Henry," she said, kissing my cheek and leaving on the air a smell of lavender. "Come, let me show you your room." She led me up to the first landing, which was as bare as the hall, and opened a door. This room at least contained a bed and a chair and a cupboard, though nothing else. My aunt may have thought some explanation was needed, for she said, "The furniture will be arriving any day now." I opened another door and saw a room which was empty except for two mattresses laid together on the floor and a dressing-table and stool that looked new. "I have given you the bed," my aunt said, "but I couldn't do without my dressing-table."

"Is this your room?"

"Sometimes I miss my Venetian glass, but when the curtains go up and the furniture arrives ... You must be hungry, Henry. Wordsworth will bring your bags. I have a little meal prepared."

I could no longer be surprised by the furnishing of the dining-room—an immense room which had been lit once by three chandeliers; the wires sprouted like weeds out of holes in the ceiling. There was a table but no cloth, and the chairs were packing-cases. "It's all a little rough," my aunt said, "but when Mr. Visconti returns you will see how soon we shall get things in order." The meal came out of tins, and there was a sweet red wine of local origin which tasted like an evil medicine of childhood. I thought of my first-class ticket on the boat with shame.

"When Mr. Visconti is back," Aunt Augusta said, "we plan to give you a party. A house like this is made for parties. We shall have a barbecue with an ox roasted whole in the garden, and there will be coloured lights in the trees, and music, of course, for dancing. A harp and a guitar—that is the fashion here. The polka and the galop are the national dances. I shall invite the Chief of Police, the Jesuit Provincial (for his conversation of course), the British Ambassador and his wife. The Italian Ambassador, no—it would not be tactful. We must find some pretty girls for you, Henry." A splinter from the packing-case scratched my thigh.

I said, "You will need a little furniture first, Aunt Augusta."

"That goes without saying. I regret that I cannot ask the Italian Ambassador—he is such a handsome man, but under the circumstances ... I shall have to tell you something, Henry, that only Wordsworth knows ..."

"Where is Wordsworth now?"

"In the kitchen. Mr. Visconti prefers us to eat alone. As I was going to say, Henry, when you interrupted me, Mr. Visconti has taken to an Argentine passport and he is known here as Mr. Izquierdo."

"I am not altogether surprised, Aunt Augusta." I told her how the two detectives had searched her flat. "General Abdul is dead, by the way."

"I rather expected that. Did they take anything away?"

"Nothing except a picture postcard from Panama."

"Why did they want that?"

"They thought it might have something to do with Mr. Visconti."

"How absurd the police always seem to be. The card must have been sent by Monsieur Dambreuse. I met him on the boat going out to Buenos Aires. Poor man, he had aged a great deal. I didn't even recognize him until he began to tell me about his metallurgical company and his family in Toulouse."

"And he hadn't recognized you?"

"That is not so surprising. In those days, when we were living at the Saint James and Albany, I had black hair, not red. Red was Mr. Visconti's favorite colour. I kept red especially for him."

"The police were acting for Interpol," I said.

"It's absurd of them to treat Mr. Visconti like a common war criminal. There are lots of such men hidden around here. Martin Bormann is just across the border in Brazil and the unspeakable Dr. Mengele of Auschwitz is said to be with the army near the Bolivian border. Why doesn't Interpol do anything about *them*? Mr. Visconti was always very kind to Jews. Even when he had those dealings with Saudi Arabia. Why should he be chased out of the Argentine, where he was doing quite well in the antique business? There was an American in Buenos Aires who made the most impertinent inquiries, Mr. Visconti told me. Mr. Visconti had sold a picture to a private purchaser in the States, and this American, who claimed to be a representative of the Metropolitan Museum, said the picture had been looted . . ."

"Was the man's name O'Toole by any chance?"

"It was."

"He's here in Asunción now."

"Yes, I know that. But he is not finding people so cooperative here. After all, the General has German blood."

"He was with me on the boat and he told me he was doing social research."

"That's quite untrue. Like the Metropolitan Museum. He's in the CIA."

"He's Tooley's father."

"Tooley?"

"The girl on the Orient Express."

"How very interesting. I wonder if that could be of any use to us," my aunt reflected. "You say he was on the boat with you?"

"Yes."

"He may have been following you. Such a fuss about a few pictures. I seem to remember that you and his daughter became great friends on the train. And there was all that business of the pregnancy . . ."

"Aunt Augusta, that had nothing to do with me."

"Rather a pity," Aunt Augusta said, "under the circumstances."

Wordsworth came into the room wearing the butcher's apron in which I had first seen him in the flat above the Crown and Anchor. Then his services in washing up had been recognized and praised, but I could tell they were taken for granted now.

"Chop finished?"

"We will have our coffee in the garden," my aunt said grandly.

We sat down in the meagre shade of a banana tree. The air was sweet with orange and jasmine, and the moon swam palely in the pale blue daylight sky. It looked as worn and thin as an old coin, and the craters were the same colour as the sky, so that one seemed to be looking through holes at the universe behind. There was no sound of traffic. The clip-clop of a horse belonged to the same ancient world of silence.

"Yes, it's very peaceful," my aunt said, "only an occasional gunshot after dark. The police are sometimes trigger-happy. I forget whether it's one lump or two."

"I wish you would tell me a little more, Aunt Augusta. I can't help being puzzled. This big house and no furniture . . . and Wordsworth here with you."

"I brought him from Paris," Aunt Augusta said. "I was travelling with rather a lot of ready money—nearly everything I had left, though I kept enough in Berne to pay for your ticket. A frail old lady like myself needed a bodyguard." It was the first time I had ever heard her admit to being old.

"You could have taken me with you."

"I wasn't sure about your attitude to certain things. You were rather shocked, you remember, about that gold bar in Istanbul. What a pity General Abdul made a mess of the affair. We could have done now with the twenty-five per cent."

"Where has all your money gone, Aunt Augusta? You haven't even a bed to sleep in."

"The mattresses are perfectly comfortable, and I have always found a soft bed enervating. When I arrived here poor Mr. Visconti was in a very low state. He was living on credit in a really horrible little hotel. All his money had gone on his new passport and bribes to the police. God knows how Dr. Mengele manages, but I expect he has a numbered account in Switzerland. I only arrived just in time. He was sick too, poor fellow, from living mainly on *mandioca*."

"So you gave him your money a second time, Aunt Augusta?"

"Of course, what do you expect? He needed it. We bought this house for a song (someone was murdered here twenty years ago and people are very superstitious) and what was left has been well invested now. We have a half share in a very promising enterprise."

"A Dakota by any chance?"

My aunt gave a little excited giggle. "Mr. Visconti will tell you all about it himself."

"Where is he?"

"He meant to be back yesterday, but there has been a lot of rain and the roads are very bad." She looked with pride at the empty shell of her house. She said, "You won't know this place in a week's time. When the chandeliers are hung in the hall, and the furniture arrives. I so wanted it to be ready before you came, but there were delays in Panama. A lot always depends on Panama."

"And what about the police?"

"Oh, they won't interfere with an established business," my aunt said.

All the same, another day passed and Mr. Visconti had not returned from wherever he was. My aunt slept late on her mattresses, Wordsworth was busy cleaning, and I walked around the town. Preparations were in progress for some festival. There were decorated cars of pretty girls parked at street corners. Outside the cathedral and the military academy, which faced each other over the little memorial tank, squads of soldiers goose-stepped. There were pictures of the General everywhere—sometimes in uniform and sometimes in civilian clothes looking like the amiable well-fed host of a Bavarian *Bierstube*. There had been unpleasant stories in Buenos Aires about his early rule—enemies tossed out of airplanes into the jungle, bodies washed up on the Argentine shore of the two great rivers with their hands and feet bound with wire, but there were cheap cigarettes on the street and cheap whisky in the stores and no income tax to pay (so my aunt had told me) and even the bribes were not unreasonable if one were doing well and could pay regularly, and the oranges lay under the trees hardly worth the bother of gathering when they were threepence a dozen in the market, and everywhere there was the smell of flowers. I hoped that Mr. Visconti's investment would prove a success. There were worse places than this to end one's days.

But when I returned home the second evening Mr. Visconti was not there, and my aunt was having a bitter argument with Wordsworth. As I crossed the lawn I could hear her voice sounding hollowly from the empty hall at the head of the garden steps. "I am not your bebi gel, Wordsworth, any more. Understand that. I have kept enough money for you to return to Europe . . ."

"Ar no wan yo money," Wordsworth's voice replied.

"You've taken plenty of my money in the past. The CTCs you've had from me and all my friends . . ."

"Ar tak yo money them times because you lov me, you slip with me, you lak jig-jig with Wordsworth. Now you no slip with me, you no lov me, I no wan your damn money. You give it *him*. He tak everytin you got. When you got noting at all, you come to Wordsworth, and ar work for you and ar slip with you an you lov me and you lak jig-jig all same last time."

I stood at the bottom of the steps. I couldn't turn my back and walk away. They would have seen me.

"Don't you understand, Wordsworth, all that's finished now I have Mr. Visconti back. Mr. Visconti wants you to go, and I want what he wants."

"He be feared of Wordsworth."

"Dear, dear Wordsworth, it's you who should be afraid. I want you to leave now—today—don't you understand that?"

"O.K.," Wordsworth said, "ar go. You ask me an ar go. Ar no feared of *that* man. But you no slip with me no more an ar go." My aunt made a movement as though she wished to embrace him, but Wordsworth turned away from her and came down the steps. He didn't even see me, though I was only a step away. "Good-bye, Wordsworth," I said and held out my hand. I had a fifty-dollar note concealed in it. Wordsworth looked at the note but he didn't take it. He said, "Good-bye, Mr. Pullen. Man, the darkness deepens, sure thing, sure thing, she no abide with me." He pressed my left hand, which was moneyless, and went off down the garden.

My aunt came out on to the steps to see the last of him.

"How will you do without him in this big house?" I asked.

"Staff are easy to come by and much cheaper than Wordsworth with all his CTCs. Oh, I'm sorry for poor Wordsworth," she added, "but he was only a stop-gap. Everything has been a stop-gap since Mr. Visconti and I were separated."

"You must love Visconti a great deal. Is he worth it?"

"To me he is. I like men who are untouchable. I've never wanted a man who needed me, Henry. A need is a claim. I thought that Wordsworth wanted my money and the comfort I gave him at the Crown and Anchor, but there's not much comfort for anyone here and you saw how he wouldn't even take a CTC. I'm disappointed in Wordsworth." She added as though it were relevant, "Your father was pretty untouchable too."

"All the same, I found your photograph in *Rob Roy*."

"Perhaps he wasn't untouchable enough," she said, and she added with venom in her voice, "Think of the little schoolteacher and 'Dolly, darling,' and dying in *her* arms."

The house was twice as empty now that Wordsworth had gone and we were alone. We ate our evening meal almost in silence, and I drank too much of the heavy sweet medicinal wine. Once we heard the distant sound of a car and my aunt went at once to the big windows which gave on to the garden. The single globe on the enormous ceiling hardly stretched that far, so that she looked slim and young in her dark dress, and in the obscurity I would never have taken her for an old woman. She quoted at me with a scared smile:

> "She only said, 'The night is dreary,
>   He cometh not,' she said."

She added, "Your father taught me that."

"Yes, I learnt it from him too—in a way. He turned down that page in Palgrave."

"And no doubt he taught it to Dolly darling," she said. "Can't you imagine her reciting it over the grave in Boulogne like a prayer?"

"*You* are not untouchable, Aunt Augusta."

"That's why I need a man who is. Two touchables together, what a terrible life they always make of it, two people suffering, afraid to speak, afraid to act, afraid of hurting. Life can be bearable when it's only one who suffers. It's easy to put up with your own suffering, but not someone else's. I'm not afraid of making Mr. Visconti suffer. I wouldn't know how. I have a wonderful feeling of freedom. I can say what I like, and it will never get under that thick dago skin of his."

"And if he makes you suffer?"

"It's only for a little time, Henry. Like now. When he doesn't come and I don't know what's keeping him, and I fear . . ."

"There can't be anything seriously wrong. If there had been an accident you would have heard from the police."

"My dear, this is Paraguay. I am afraid of the police."

"Then why do you stay here?"

"Mr. Visconti hasn't all that much choice. I daresay he might be safe in Brazil if he had enough money. Perhaps when he's made a fortune, we can move there. Mr. Visconti has always wanted to make a fortune, and he believes he can at last make one here. He has come close to making a fortune so many times. There was Saudi Arabia and then there were the Germans . . ."

"If he makes one now he won't have very long to enjoy it."

"That's not the point. He'll die happy if it's there. Stacked gold bars. (He has always had a fancy for gold bars.) He'll have done what he set out to do."

"Why did you want me to come, Aunt Augusta?"

"You are the only family I have, Henry—and you can be of great use to Mr. Visconti."

It was not an idea which appealed to me greatly.

"I can't speak a word of Spanish," I said.

"Mr. Visconti wants somebody he can trust to keep the books. Accounts have always been his weak point."

I looked around the empty room. The bare globe flickered with an approaching storm. The packing-case scratched hard against my thigh. I thought of the two mattresses and the dressing-table upstairs. The books didn't seem to need very much accounting. I said, "I planned to leave after I had seen you."

"Leave? Why?"

"I was thinking that perhaps it's almost time I settled down."

"What else have you been doing? For far too long."

"And married, I was going to say."

"At your age?"

"I'm not nearly as old as Mr. Visconti."

A gust of rain splashed against the windows. I began to tell my aunt about Miss Keene and of the evening when I had nearly proposed to her.

"You are suffering from loneliness," my aunt said. "That's all. You won't be lonely here."

"I really think Miss Keene loves me a little. I get a bit of pleasure from the thought that perhaps I could make her happy." I was arguing without conviction, waiting for my aunt's denial, and even hoping for it.

"In a year," my aunt said, "what would you two have to talk about? She would sit over her tatting—I didn't realize that anyone still tatted—and you would read gardening catalogues, and then when the silence was almost unbearable she would begin to tell you a story of Koffiefontein which you had heard a dozen times before. Do you know what you'll think about when you can't sleep in your double bed? Not of women. You don't care enough about them, or you wouldn't even consider marrying Miss Keene. You will think how every day you are getting a little closer to death. It will stand there as close as the bedroom wall. And you'll become more and more afraid of the wall because nothing can prevent you coming nearer and nearer to it every night while you try to sleep and Miss Keene reads. What does Miss Keene read?"

"You may be right, Aunt Augusta, but isn't it the same everywhere at our age?"

"Not here it isn't. Tomorrow you may be shot in the street by a policeman because you haven't understood Guaraní, or a man may knife you in a *cantina* because you can't speak Spanish and he thinks you are acting in a superior way. Next week, when we have our Dakota, perhaps it will crash with you over Argentina. (Mr. Visconti is too old to fly with the pilot.) My dear Henry, if you live with us, you won't be edging day by day across to any last wall. The wall will find you of its own accord without your help, and every day you live will seem to you a kind of victory. 'I was too sharp for it that time,' you will say, when night comes, and afterwards you'll sleep well." She said, "I only hope the wall hasn't found Mr. Visconti. If it has I will have to go out and look for it myself."

CHAPTER 5

The far-off murmur of great crowds woke me next
morning; I thought at first that I was back in
Brighton and that the sea was turning the shingle.
My aunt was already up and had prepared breakfast
with grapefruit picked in the garden. From the town
came snatches of music.

"What's happening?"

"It's the National Day. Wordsworth warned me,
but I had forgotten. If you go into town carry something red."

"Why?"

"It's the colour of the governing party. The Liberal
Party is blue, but it's unhealthy to carry blue. No one
does."

"I haven't got anything red."

"I've got a red scarf."

"I can hardly wear a woman's scarf."

"Stuff it in your breast pocket. It will look like a
handkerchief."

"Won't you come into town with me, Aunt Augusta?"

"No. I must wait for Mr. Visconti. He will come
today for sure. Or at least he'll send a message."

I needn't have been shy of wearing the scarf. Most men in the street wore red scarves round their necks, and many scarves were printed with a picture of the General. Only the bourgeois confined themselves to a handkerchief, and some to a handkerchief barely on display at all but pressed in the hand and showing only through the knuckles—perhaps they would rather have carried blue. There were red flags everywhere: you would have thought the town had been taken over by the Communists, but red here was the colour of conservatism. I was held up continually at street crossings by processions of women in red scarves carrying portraits of the General and slogans about the great Colorado Party. Groups of gauchos came riding into town with scarlet reins. A drunk man fell out of a tavern door and lay face down in the road with the general's genial face spread over his back as the horses picked their way across him. Decorated cars carrying pretty girls with scarlet camellia blossoms in their hair went by. Even the sun looked red through the morning mist.

The movement of the crowd edged me towards the Avenue of Mariscal Lopez, where the processions were passing. Across the road were stands reserved for the government and the diplomats. I could recognize the general taking the salute, and the stand next door must have been that of the American Embassy, for in the back row I could see my friend O'Toole pressed into a corner by a stout military attaché. I waved to him and I think he must have seen me because he gave a shy smile and spoke to the fat man at his side. Then a procession passed and I lost sight of him.

It was a procession of elderly men in shabby suits— a few were on crutches and some had lost an arm. They carried banners representing their old units. They had fought in the Chaco war, and once a year, I suppose, they had this moment of pride. They looked more human than the colonels who followed them, standing upright in their cars, in dress uniforms with gold tassels and epaulettes, all with black moustaches and all quite indistinguishable; the colonels looked like painted skittles waiting for a ball to bowl them over.

After an hour I had had enough of watching and walked into the centre of town, to the new skyscraper hotel, to buy an English-language newspaper, but there was only a five-day-old *New York Times*. A man spoke to me in a confidential voice before I went into the hotel; he had a distinguished intellectual air; he might have been a diplomat or a university professor. "I beg your pardon," I said.

"Any U.S. dollars?" he asked me rapidly, and when I shook my head (for I had no desire to break any local currency laws) he walked away. Unfortunately when I emerged again from the hotel with my newspaper he was back on the opposite pavement and failed to recognize me. "Any U.S. dollars?" he whispered. I said no again and he glared at me with an air of disgust and disdain, as though I had been playing a childish practical joke.

I walked back towards the edge of town and my aunt's house, interrupted at street corners by the tag end of processions. A palatial house covered in banners bore a number of scarlet placards; it was probably the headquarters of the Colorado Party. Stout men in city suits who sweated in the morning sun climbed up and down the wide steps wearing red scarves. One of them stopped and demanded, or so I supposed, what I wanted. "Colorado?" I asked.

"Yes. Are you American?"

I was glad to find someone who spoke English. He had the face of an amiable bulldog, but he needed a shave.

"No," I said, "I'm English."

He gave a short bark which did not sound amiable at all, and at that moment, perhaps because of the heat, the sun and the scent of flowers, I was overcome by a fit of sneezing. Without thinking, I drew my aunt's red scarf from my breast pocket and blew my nose. It was most unfortunate. I found myself sitting on the pavement without knowing how I got there, and my nose streamed with blood. Fat men surrounded me, all of them in dark suits and all with the faces of bulldogs. Others like them appeared on the balcony of the Colorado house and looked down at me with curiosity and disapproval. I heard the word *"inglés"* repeated often, and then a policeman yanked me on to my feet. Afterwards I was to think how lucky I had been; if I had blown my nose near a group of gauchos I might well have received a knife in the ribs.

Several fat men accompanied me to the police station, including the one who had struck me. He carried my aunt's scarf, the evidence of a crime. "It's all a mistake," I assured him.

"Mistake?" His English was very limited.

At the police station—a very imposing building, built to withstand a siege—everyone began to speak at once with noise and fury. I felt at a loss how to behave. I kept on repeating *"inglés"* without effect. Once I tried "ambassador," but it wasn't in their vocabulary. The police officer was young and worried—I imagine his superior officers were all at the parade. When I said *"inglés"* for the third time and "ambassador" for the second he hit me but without conviction—a blow which hardly hurt me at all. I was discovering something new. Physical violence, like the dentist's drill, is seldom as bad as one fears.

I tried "mistake" again, but no one could translate that word. The scarf was handed from one to another, and a patch of snot was pointed out to the officer. He picked up what looked like an identity card and waved it at me. I suppose he was demanding my passport. I said, "I left it at home," and three or four people began to argue. Perhaps they were disagreeing on the meaning of what I said.

Oddly enough, it was the man who had struck me who proved most sympathetic. My nose was still bleeding and he gave me his handkerchief. It was not very clean and I feared blood poisoning, but I didn't want to reject his help, so I dabbed rather tentatively at my nose and then offered him his handkerchief back again. He waved it away with a gesture of generosity. Then he wrote something on a piece of paper and showed it me. I read the name of a street and a number. He pointed at the floor and then pointed at me and held out the pencil. Everyone pressed nearer with great curiosity. I shook my head. I knew how to walk to my aunt's house, but I had no idea of the name of the street. My friend—I was beginning to think of him as that—wrote down the name of three hotels. I shook my head.

Then I spoilt everything. For some unknown reason, standing beside the officer's desk in the hot and crowded room, with an armed sentry at the door, my mind went suddenly back to the morning of my stepmother's funeral, the chapel full of distant relatives, and the voice of my aunt breaking the reverent whisper: "I was present once at a premature cremation." I had looked forward to the funeral as a break in the orderly routine of my retirement and what a break it had proved. I had been worried, I remembered, about the rain falling on my lawn-mower. I began to laugh, and when I laughed all the enmity returned. I was again the insolent foreigner who had blown his nose on the flag of the Colorado Party. My first assailant snatched away his handkerchief, and the officer, pushing aside those who stood in his way, strode to my side and gave me a severe cuff on my right ear which began to bleed in its turn. Desperately trying to find the name of anyone they might know, I let out Mr. Visconti's alias. "Señor Izquierdo," I said with no effect at all, and then, "Señor O'Toole." The officer paused with his hand raised to strike again and I tried, "Embassy—Americano."

Something about those words worked, though I was not sure whether the working was in my favour. Two policemen were summoned and I was pushed down a corridor and locked into a cell. I could hear the officer telephoning and I could only hope that Tooley's father really knew the ropes. There was nothing to sit on in the cell—only a piece of sacking under a barred window too high for me to see anything but a patch of monotonous sky. Somebody had written on the wall in Spanish—perhaps a prayer, perhaps an obscenity, I couldn't tell. I sat down on the sacking and prepared for a long wait. The wall opposite me reminded me of what my aunt had said: I trained myself to be thankful that the wall seemed to keep its distance.

To pass the time I took out my pen and began to doodle on the whitewash. I put down my initials and was irritated, as often before, because they represented a famous sauce; then I wrote the date of my birth, 1913, with a dash against it where someone else could fill in the date of my death. It occurred to me to record a family history—it would help to pass the time if I were to have a long stay, so I wrote down my father's death in 1923 and my stepmother's less than a year ago. I knew nothing of my grandparents, so the only relative left me was my aunt. She had been born somewhere around 1895, and I put a question mark after the year. It occurred to me to try to work out my aunt's history on the wall, which had already begun to take on a more friendly family air. I didn't entirely believe all her stories and perhaps I might discover a chronological flaw. She had seen me at my baptism and never again, so she must have left my father's house somewhere around 1913, when she was eighteen—it could not have been long after the snapshot had been taken. There had been the period with Curran in Brighton—that must surely have been after the First World War, so I put Dogs' Church 1919 with another question mark. Curran had left her, she had gone to Paris, and there in the establishment in the Rue de Provence she had met Mr. Visconti— perhaps about the same time as my father died in Boulogne. She would have been in her twenties then. I began to work on the Italian period, her travels between Milan and Venice, Uncle Jo's death, her life with Mr. Visconti, which had been interrupted by the failure of his Saudi Arabia scheme. I put tentatively the date 1937 against Paris and Monsieur Dambreuse, for she had returned to Italy and been reunited with Mr. Visconti at the house behind the *Messaggero* before the outbreak of the Second War. Of the last twenty years of her life I knew nothing before the arrival of Wordsworth. I had to admit that I had found nothing intrinsically false in the chronology. There was ample time for all she had told me to happen and a great deal more besides. I began to speculate on the nature of the quarrel with my so-called mother. It must have occurred round about the time of the pretended pregnancy—if that story were true ... The door of the cell was thrown open and a policeman brought in a chair. It seemed a kindly action, and I got up from the sacking to take advantage of it, but the policeman pushed me roughly away. O'Toole came in. He looked embarrassed. "You seem to be in trouble, Henry," he said.

"It's all a mistake. I sneezed and then I happened to blow my nose . . ."

"On the Colorado colours outside the Colorado HQ."

"Yes. But I thought it was my handkerchief."

"You are in an awful spot."

"I suppose I am."

"You could easily have a ten-year sentence. Do you mind if I sit down? I've been standing for hours at that damn parade."

"Of course. Please."

"I could ask for another chair."

"Don't bother. I'm getting used to this sack."

"I guess what makes it worse," O'Toole said, "is that you did it on their National Day. It seems kind of provocative. Otherwise they might have been content to expel you. What made you ask for me?"

"You said you knew the ropes and they didn't seem to understand 'English Embassy.' "

"Your people don't count for very much here, I'm afraid. We provide their arms—and then there's the new hydroelectric station we are helping them to build ... not far from the Iguazú Falls. It will serve Brazil too—but Brazil will have to pay them royalties. Great thing for the country."

"Very interesting," I said with some bitterness.

"Of course I'd like to help you," O'Toole said. "You are a friend of Lucinda's. I've had a postcard from her, by the way. She's not in Katmandu. She's in Vientiane. I don't know why."

"Look, O'Toole," I said, "if you can't do anything else, you might at least ring up the British Embassy. If I'm to have ten years in prison I'd like a bed and a chair."

"Sure," O'Toole said, "I can arrange all that. I guess I could arrange your release too—the Chief of Police is a good friend of mine ..."

"I think my aunt knows him too," I said.

"Don't bank on that. You see, we've had some fresh information about your relative. The police don't want to act—I guess some money has passed—but we're bringing pressure on them. You seem to be mixed up with some pretty shady characters, Henry."

"My aunt's an old lady of seventy-five." I glanced at the notes I had made on the wall: Rue de Provence,

Milan, *Messaggero*. I would have certainly called her career shady myself nine months ago, and yet now there seemed nothing so very wrong in her *curriculum vitae*, nothing so wrong as thirty years in a bank. "I don't see what you can have against her," I said.

"Your friend, that black fellow, came to see us."

"I'm certain he told you nothing against my aunt."

"That's right, he didn't, but he had plenty to say about Mr. Izquierdo. So I persuaded the police to keep him out of circulation awhile."

"Is that part of your social research?" I asked. "Perhaps he suffered from malnutrition."

"I guess I sort of lied to you, Henry," he said, looking ashamed again.

"Are you in the CIA, like Tooley told me?"

"Well ... kind of ... not exactly," he said, clinging to his torn rag of deception like a blown-out umbrella in a high wind.

"What did Wordsworth tell you?"

"He was in a pretty bitter mood. If your aunt hadn't been so old I'd have said it was love. He seemed jealous of this guy Izquierdo."

"Where's Wordsworth now?"

"He's sticking around. He wants to see your aunt again when things blow over."

"Are they likely to blow over?"

"Well, Henry, they could. If everyone were reasonable."

"Even my sneeze?"

"I guess so. As for Mr. Izquierdo's smuggling racket—no one cares a devalued dime about that if only he'd be reasonable. Now *you* know Mr. I."

"I've never met him."

"Maybe you know him under another name?"

"No," I said.

O'Toole sighed. "Henry," he said, "I want to help you. Any friend of Lucinda can count on me. We can have this whole thing tied up in a few hours. Visconti's not important, not like Mengele or Bormann."

"I thought we were talking about Izquierdo."

"You and I and your friend Wordsworth know it's the same man. So do the police, but they protect these guys—anyway till they run out of cash. Visconti nearly ran out of cash, but then Miss Bertram arrived and paid up."

"I don't know a thing," I said. "I'm simply here on a visit."

"I guess there was a good reason why Wordsworth met you in Formosa, Henry. Anyway, I'd like to have a word with your aunt and a word from you might make it easier for me. If I persuaded the police to let you go, you and I could see her together . . ."

"What exactly are you after,"

"She must be anxious about Visconti by this time. I can reassure her. They'll only hold him in jail a few days till I give the word."

"Are you offering her some kind of bargain? I warn you, she won't do anything to hurt Mr. Visconti."

"I just want to talk to her, Henry. With you there. She mightn't trust me alone."

I was feeling very cramped on the sacking, and I saw no reason not to agree.

He said, "It may take an hour or two to get you released. Everything is disorganized today." He stood up.

"How are the statistics, O'Toole?"

"This parade's put everything out. I was afraid to drink any coffee for breakfast. All these hours of standing without taking a leak. I ought to cancel today altogether. It's not what you'd call a normal day."

It took him more than an hour or two to persuade them to let me go, but they forgot to take the chair from the cell after he'd gone and they brought me some thin gruel, and these I took for favourable signs. To my own surprise, I wasn't bored, though there was nothing I could usefully add to the history on the wall, except two problematical dates for Tunis and Havana. I began in my head to compose a letter to Miss Keene describing my present circumstances: "I have insulted the ruling party of Paraguay and I'm mixed up with a war criminal wanted by Interpol. For the first offence the maximum penalty is ten years. I am in a small cell, ten feet by six, and I have nothing to sleep on but a piece of sacking. I have no idea what is going to happen next, but I confess I am not altogether unhappy, I am too deeply interested." I would never really write the letter, for she would be quite unable to reconcile the writer with the man she had known.

It was quite dark outside when at last they came to release me. I was led back down the corridor and through the office, and there they solemnly returned me my aunt's red scarf, and the young officer slapped my back in a friendly way, urging me through into the street where O'Toole waited for me in an ancient Cadillac. He said, "I'm sorry. It took longer than I thought. I'm afraid Miss Bertram will be nervous about you too."

"I don't think I count much beside Mr. Visconti."

"Blood's thicker than water, Henry."

"Water's not the term to use for Mr. Visconti."

There were only two lights on in the house. As we came through the trees at the bottom of the garden someone flashed a light on our faces, but the light went out before I could see who held the torch. I looked back from the lawn and could see nothing.

"Are you having the place watched?" I asked.

"Not me, Henry."

I could tell that he was uneasy. He put his hand inside his jacket.

"Are you armed?" I said.

"One has to take precautions."

"Against an old lady? My aunt's the only one here."

"You can never be sure."

We went forward across the lawn and climbed the steps. The globe in the dining-room shone down on two empty glasses and an empty bottle of champagne. It was still cold to the touch when I picked it up. When I put it down I knocked over one of the glasses and the sound rang through the house. My aunt must have been in the kitchen, for she came at once to the door.

"Where on earth have you been, Henry?"

"In prison. Mr. O'Toole helped me to get out."

"I never expected to see Mr. O'Toole in my house. Not after what he did to Mr. Izquierdo in Argentina. So you are Mr. O'Toole."

"Yes, Miss Bertram. I thought it would be a good thing if we could have a friendly talk. I know how anxious you must be about Mr. Visconti."

"I'm not in the least anxious about Mr. Visconti."

"I thought perhaps . . . that not knowing where he was . . . all this long delay . . ."

"I know perfectly well where he is," my aunt said. "He's in the lavatory." The flush of water could not have come more exactly on cue.

CHAPTER 6

I waited with excited curiosity to see Mr. Visconti. Not many men can have been so loved or have been forgiven so much, and I had an image in my mind's eye to fit the part, of an Italian tall and dark and lean, as aristocratic as his name. But the man who came through the door to meet us was short and fat and bald; when he held his hand out to me I saw that his little finger had been broken and this made his hand resemble a bird's claw. He had soft brown eyes quite without expression. One could read into them whatever one liked. If my aunt read love, I felt sure that O'Toole read dishonesty.

"So here you are at last, Henry," Mr. Visconti said. "Your aunt has been anxious." He spoke English very well with practically no accent.

O'Toole said, "You are Mr. Visconti?"

"My name is Izquierdo. To whom have I the pleasure . . . ?"

"My name's O'Toole."

"In that case," Mr. Visconti said with a smile which was rendered phony by a large gap in his front teeth, " 'pleasure' is not the word I ought to use."

"I thought you were safe in jail."

"The police and I came to an understanding."

O'Toole said, "That's what I've come here for—an understanding."

"An understanding is always possible," Mr. Visconti said, as though he were quoting from a well-known source—perhaps from Machiavelli, "if there are equal advantages on either side."

"I guess there are in this case."

"I think," Mr. Visconti said to my aunt, "there are still two bottles of champagne left in the kitchen."

"*Two* bottles?" my aunt asked.

"There are four of us, my dear." He turned to me and said, "It is not the best champagne. It has travelled a long way and rather roughly by way of Panama."

"Then I suppose," O'Toole said, "your arrangements with Panama are now okay."

"Exactly," Mr. Visconti said. "When the police arrested me at your suggestion they thought they were once again arresting a poor man. I was able to convince them that I am now again potentially a man of means."

My aunt came in from the kitchen carrying the champagne. "And glasses," Mr. Visconti said, "you have forgotten the glasses."

I watched Aunt Augusta with fascination. I had never seen her taking orders from anyone before.

"Sit down, sit down, my friends," Mr. Visconti said. "You must forgive the rough nature of our chairs. We have passed through a period of some privation, but all our difficulties, I hope, are over. Soon we shall be able to entertain our friends in proper fashion. Mr. O'Toole, I raise my glass to the United States. I have no ill feelings towards you or your great country."

"That's big of you," O'Toole said. "But tell me, who's the man in the garden?"

"In my position I have to take precautions."

"He didn't stop us."

"Only against my enemies."

"Which do you prefer to be called, Izquierdo or Visconti?" O'Toole asked.

"By this time I have grown quite accustomed to both. Let us finish this bottle and open another. Champagne, if you are seeking the truth, is better than a lie-detector. It encourages a man to be expansive, even reckless, while lie-detectors are only a challenge to tell lies successfully."

"You've had experience of them?" O'Toole asked.

"I had a session with one before I left BA. The results, I suspect, were not very useful to the police—or to you. You received them, I imagine? I had prepared myself beforehand very carefully. They strapped two rubber belts around my arms and I thought at first they were taking my blood pressure. Perhaps they were doing that among other things. They warned me that however much I lied the machine would always tell the truth. You can imagine my reaction to that. Scepticism is inbred in a Catholic. First they asked me a number of innocent questions, such as what was my favourite food, and did I become breathless going upstairs? As I answered those innocent questions I thought very hard of what a joy it would one day be for me to see again my dear friend here and my heart beat and my pulses jumped, and they couldn't understand what was making me so excited about walking upstairs or eating cannelloni. Then they allowed me to calm down and afterwards they shot the name Visconti at me. 'Are you Visconti?' 'You're Visconti, the war criminal,' but that had no effect on me at all because I had trained my old daily woman to call me Visconti in the morning when she drew the curtains. 'Visconti, you war criminal, wake up.' It had become a homely phrase to me, meaning 'Your coffee is ready.' After that they went back to the question about going upstairs and this time I was very calm, but when they asked me why I liked cannelloni, I thought of my darling and I got excited again, so that at the next question, which was a serious one, the cardiogram—if that's what it was called—became much calmer because I stopped thinking of my dear. In the end they were in quite a rage—both with the machine and with me. You notice how champagne makes me talk. I am in the mood to tell you everything."

"I've come here to propose an arrangement, Mr. Visconti. I'd hoped to have you out of circulation for a while so that I could convince Miss Bertram in your absence."

"I would have agreed to nothing," my aunt said, "until I had talked to Mr. Visconti."

"We could still make a pack of trouble for you here. Every time we put pressure on the police it would cost you money in bribes. Now suppose we persuaded Interpol to close the files on you and we told the police we were not interested any more, that you were free to come and go . . ."

"I wouldn't entirely trust you," Mr. Visconti said, "I would prefer to stop here. Besides I am making friends."

"Sure, stay, if you want to. The police wouldn't be able to blackmail you any more."

"It's an interesting proposal," Mr. Visconti said. "You obviously imagine I have something to offer you in return? Let me fill your glass again."

"We are prepared to do a deal," O'Toole said.

"I'm a business-man," Mr. Visconti replied. "In my time I've had dealings with many governments. Saudi Arabia, Turkey, the Vatican."

"And the Gestapo."

"They were not gentlemen," Mr. Visconti said. "Force of circumstances alone impelled me." His way of speaking reminded me of Aunt Augusta's. They must have grown together with the years. "You realize, of course, I've had other offers of a private nature."

"A man in your position can't afford private offers. Unless you deal with us, you'll never be able to live in this house of yours. I wouldn't bother about buying the furniture."

"The furniture," Mr. Visconti said, "is no longer a problem. My Dakota did not return empty yesterday from Argentina. Miss Bertram had already arranged with Harrods at Buenos Aires to deliver the furniture to a friend's *estancia*. So many chandeliers for so many cigarettes. The bed was an expensive item. How many cases of whisky did we pay, my dear? To my friend, of course, not to Harrods. An honourable firm. It takes a lot of whisky or cigarettes in these days to furnish a few essential rooms, and I admit frankly that I could do with a little ready cash. A beefsteak is sometimes more necessary than a chandelier. Panama cannot deliver again for two weeks. I'm in the position of a sound business with good prospects, but short of petty cash."

"I'm offering you security," O'Toole said, "not money."

"I'm used to being insecure. It doesn't worry me. In my situation cash alone has a tongue."

I was wondering what kind of an overdraft I would have granted Mr. Visconti on his say-so alone, when my aunt took my hand. "I think," she whispered to me, "that we should leave Mr. Visconti alone with Mr. O'Toole." Aloud she said to me, "Henry, come with me a moment. I've got something to show you."

"Has Mr. Visconti any Jewish blood?" I asked when we were outside the room.

"No," Aunt Augusta said, "Saracen perhaps. He always got on well with the Saudi Arabians. Do you like him, Henry?" she asked with an appeal which touched me under the circumstances. She was not a woman who found it easy to make an appeal.

"It's early for me to judge," I said. "He doesn't seem to me very trustworthy."

"If he were, would I have loved him, Henry?"

She led me through the kitchen—one chair, a drying rack, an ancient gas stove, tins of food stacked upon the floor—to the back of the house. The yard was full of wooden crates. My aunt said with pride. "You see our furniture. Enough for two bedrooms and a dining-room. A little garden furniture too for our celebration."

"And for the food and drink?"

"That is what Mr. Visconti is discussing now."

"Does he really expect the CIA to pay for your party? What happened to all the money you had in Paris, Aunt Augusta?"

"It was very expensive settling with the police, and then I had to find a house worthy of Mr. Visconti's position."

"Has he got one?"

"He has walked in his time with cardinals and Arabian princes," Aunt Augusta said. "You don't imagine that a little country like Paraguay will hold him down for long."

A light went on at the bottom of the garden and then was extinguished. "Who is it prowling there?" I asked.

"Mr. Visconti doesn't altogether trust his partner. He has been betrayed too often." I couldn't help wondering how many he had himself betrayed: my aunt, his wife, those cardinals and princes, even the Gestapo.

My aunt sat down on one of the smaller crates. She said, "I am so happy, Henry, that you are here and Mr. Visconti is safely returned. Perhaps I am getting a little old, for I shall be quite content with a spell of family life. You and me and Mr. Visconti working together . . ."

"Smuggling cigarettes and whisky?"

"Yes."

"And the bodyguard in the garden."

"I wouldn't want my days to *peter* out, Henry, with no interest in them at all."

Mr. Visconti's voice called from somewhere in the vast house. "My dear, my dear. Can you hear me?"

"Yes."

"Fetch me the picture, dear."

My aunt rose. "The deal, I think, must have been concluded," she said. "Come, Henry." But I let her go without me. I walked away from the house towards the trees. The stars were so brilliant in the low sky that I must have been easily visible to anyone watching from the trees. A small warm breeze blew around me the scent of orange and jasmine. It was as though I had plunged my head into a box of cut flowers. As I entered the shade a light flashed on my face and went out again, but this time I was ready for it and I knew exactly where the man stood. I had kept a match ready and I struck it. I saw leaning against a *lapacho* a little old man with long moustaches; his mouth had fallen open with surprise and perplexity so that I could see the toothless gums before the match burnt down. *"Buenas noches,"* I said, which was one of the few expressions I had picked up from my phrase-book, and he mumbled something in reply. I turned to go back and stumbled on the uneven ground and he flashed on his torch to aid me. I thought to myself that Mr. Visconti could not as yet afford much in the way of a bodyguard. Perhaps with the second load from Panama he would be able to afford something better.

In the dining-room I found all three of them, gathered round the picture. I recognized it from the frame, for it had been propped in my cabin for four days.

"I don't understand," O'Toole said.

"Nor do I," said Mr. Visconti. "I expected a photograph of the Venus of Milo."

"You know that I can't stand torsos, dear," Aunt Augusta said. "I told you about that murder on the *chemin de fer*. I found this photograph in Wordsworth's room."

O'Toole said, "I don't understand what in hell all this is about. What murder on the *chemin de fer*?"

"It's too long a story to tell you now," Aunt Augusta said. "Besides, Henry knows it, and he doesn't care for my stories."

"That's not true," I said. "I was simply tired that night in Boulogne . . ."

"Look," O'Toole said, "I'm not interested in what happened in Boulogne. I made an offer for a picture which Mr. Visconti here stole . . ."

"I did not steal it," Mr. Visconti said. "The prince gave it me quite voluntarily to present to Field-Marshal Goering in recognition . . ."

"Oh sure, sure, we know all that. The prince didn't give you a photo of a lot of African women . . ."

"It should have been the Venus of Milo," Mr. Visconti said, shaking his head in perplexity. "You had no need to change it, dear. It was a very fine photograph."

"It should have been a drawing of Leonardo da Vinci's," O'Toole replied.

"What did you do with the photograph?" Mr. Visconti asked.

"I threw it away. I won't have any torsos to remind me . . ."

"I'll have you pulled in again in the morning," O'Toole threatened, "whatever bribes you pay. The Ambassador himself . . ."

"Ten thousand dollars was the agreed price, but I'll accept payment in the local currency if it's more convenient."

"For a photograph of a lot of black women," O'Toole said.

"If you really want the photograph I would throw it in with the other."

"What other?"

"The prince's picture."

Mr. Visconti turned the frame over and began to tear away the backing. My aunt said, "Would anyone like some whisky?"

"Not after the champagne, dear."

Mr. Visconti removed a small drawing which had been hidden behind the photograph of Freetown. It could not have been more than eight inches by six. O'Toole looked at it with wonder. Mr. Visconti said, "There you are. Is anything wrong?"

"I guess I thought it would be a Madonna."

"Leonardo was not primarily interested in Madonnas. He was the chief engineer of the Pope's army. Alexander VI. You know about Alexander?"

"I'm not a Roman Catholic," O'Toole said.

"He was the Borgia Pope."

"A bad guy?"

"In some respects," Mr. Visconti said, "he resembled my patron, the late Marshal Goering. Now this, as you can see, is an ingenious device for attacking the walls of a city. A sort of dredge, very much the same as they use on building sites today, though motivated by human power. It grabs out the foundations of a wall and throws the stones up to this catapult, which projects them into the city. In fact, you bombard the city with its own walls. Ingenious, isn't it?"

"Ten thousand dollars for this ... Would it work?"

"I'm no engineer," Mr. Visconti said. "I cannot judge it practically, but I challenge anyone today to make so beautiful a drawing of a dredge."

"I guess you're right," O'Toole said and added with reverence, "So this is the real McCoy. We've been looking for this and for you for nearly twenty years."

"And where does it go now?"

"The prince died in prison, so I guess we hand it over to the Italian government." He gave a sigh. I don't know whether it was of disillusion or satisfaction.

"You may keep the frame," Mr. Visconti said kindly.

I went with O'Toole down through the garden to the gate. There was no sign now of the old bodyguard. O'Toole said, "It goes against the grain to see the U.S. government pay ten thousand dollars for a stolen picture."

"It would be difficult to prove," I said. "Perhaps it was a sort of present to Goering. I wonder why they shut the prince up."

We stood together by his car. He said, "I got a letter today from Lucinda. The first in nine months. She writes about a boy-friend of hers. She says they are hitch-hiking to Goa because Vientiane wasn't right for him."

"He's a painter," I explained.

"A painter?" He put the Leonardo carefully on the back seat.

"He paints pictures of Heinz soup tins."

"You are joking."

"Leonardo drew a dredge and you paid ten thousand dollars for it."

"I guess I'll never understand art," O'Toole said. "Where's Goa?"

"On the coast of India."

"That girl's one hell of an anxiety," he said, but if she hadn't existed, I thought, he'd have been anxious just the same. Anxieties, in his case, would always settle on him like flies on an open wound.

"Thanks for getting me out of the jail," I said.

"Any friend of Lucinda's . . ."

"Give my love to Tooley when you write."

"I'm putting your friend Wordsworth on the next boat. Why don't you go with him?"

"My family . . ."

"Visconti's no relation of yours. He's not your type, Henry."

"My aunt . . ."

"An aunt's not all that close. An aunt's not a mother." He couldn't get his starter to work. He said, "It's time they gave me a newer car. Think about it, Henry."

"I will."

I found Mr. Visconti laughing when I returned, my aunt watching him with disapproval.

"What's up?"

"I told him ten thousand dollars was too little for a Leonardo."

"It didn't belong to him," I said. "And he's got security as well. The file's closed."

"Mr. Visconti," my aunt said, "has never cared about security."

"The boat goes back the day after tomorrow. O'Toole is putting Wordsworth on board. He wants me to go with him."

"She said I ought to have asked double," Mr. Visconti said, "for a Leonardo."

"So you should have."

"But it's not a Leonardo at all. It's only a copy," Mr. Visconti said. "That's why they shut the prince up." He was a little breathless with laughter. He said, "It was nearly a perfect copy. The prince was afraid of thieves and he kept the original in a bank. Unfortunately the bank was obliterated by the American air force. No one knew, except the prince, that the Leonardo was obliterated too."

"If it was so good a copy how could the Gestapo tell?" I asked.

"The prince was a very old man," Mr. Visconti said with all the pride of his mere eighty years. "When I came to see him—on behalf of the Marshal—he pleaded for his picture. He told me it was only a copy and I wouldn't believe him. Then he showed me. If you look through a magnifying glass at the cog-wheel of the dredge you can see the forger's initials in looking-glass writing. I kept the drawing in memory of the prince, because I thought it might prove useful one day."

"You told the Gestapo?"

"I couldn't trust them not to have it examined by an expert," Mr. Visconti said. "He hadn't long to live. He was very old."

"As you are now."

"He had nothing to live for," Mr. Visconti said, "and I have your aunt."

I looked at Aunt Augusta. The corner of her mouth twitched. "It was very wrong of you," was all she said, "very, very wrong."

Mr. Visconti rose, and picking up the photograph of Freetown, he tore it in small pieces. "And now to our well-earned rest," he said.

"I wanted to send that back to Wordsworth," my aunt protested, but Mr. Visconti put his arm around her and they went up the marble staircase side by side, like any old couple who had continued to love each other through a long and difficult life.

CHAPTER 7

"They described you as a viper," I said to Mr. Visconti.

"They?"

"Well, in fact, it was not the detectives: it was the Chief of Police in Rome."

"A Fascist," Mr. Visconti said.

"In 1945?"

"Ah, a collaborator then."

"The war was over."

"A collaborator nonetheless. One collaborates always with the victorious side. One supports the losing." It sounded again like a quotation from Machiavelli.

We were drinking champagne together in the garden, for the house at the moment was impossible. Men were carrying furniture. Other men were up ladders. Electricians were repairing lights and hanging chandeliers. My aunt was very much in charge.

"I preferred flight to a new form of collaboration," Mr. Visconti said. "One can never tell who will win in the end. Collaboration is always a temporary measure. It's not that I care much for security, but I like to survive. Now if the *Questore* had described me as a rat, I would have had no objection. Indeed I have a great fellow feeling for rats. The future of the world lies with the rat. God, at least as I imagine him, created a number of possibilities in case some of his prototypes failed—that is the meaning of evolution. One species would survive, another would die out. I have never understood why Protestants objected so much to the ideas of Darwin. Perhaps if he had concentrated on the evolution of sheep and goats he would have appealed to the religious sense."

"But rats . . ." I objected.

"Rats are highly intelligent creatures. If we want to find out anything new about the human body we experiment on rats. Rats indeed are ahead of us indisputably in one respect—they live underground. We only began to live underground during the last war. Rats have understood the danger of surface life for thousands of years. When the atom bomb falls the rats will survive. What a wonderful empty world it will be for them, though I hope they will be wise enough to stay below. I can imagine them evolving very quickly. I hope they don't repeat our mistake and invent the wheel."

"It's odd all the same how much we hate them," I said. I had drunk three glasses of champagne and I found that I could talk to Mr. Visconti as freely as I had talked to Tooley. "We call a coward a rat, and yet it is we who are the cowards. We are afraid of them."

"The *Questore* may not have been afraid of me, but perhaps he had an uneasy sense that I would outlive him. It is an uncomfortable form of envy which is experienced only by those in a really secure position. I don't feel it about you, although you are much younger than I am, because we live here in an equally blessed state of insecurity. You go first? I go first? Mr. O'Toole goes first? It all depends on who is the best rat. That is why in a modern war old men read the casualty lists with a certain smug satisfaction. They may survive longer than their grandchildren."

"I met a rat once in my garden," I said and allowed Mr. Visconti to refill my glass. "He was standing motionless so as not to be seen in the flower-bed. His fur looked fluffy like a bird who has blown out its feathers against the cold. He wasn't repulsive like a smooth rat. Without thinking, I threw a stone at him. I missed him and I expected him to run, but instead he only limped away. One of his legs must have been broken. There was a hole in the hedge and he made for it very slowly. Once he stopped exhausted and peered over his shoulder at me. He looked rejected, and I was sorry for him. I couldn't throw another stone. He limped on to the hole and went through it. There was a cat in the next garden and I knew he didn't stand a chance. He had such dignity, going to his death. I felt ashamed of myself all that morning."

"It does you credit," Mr. Visconti said. "Speaking as an honorary rat on behalf of other rats, I forgive the stone. Have another glass."

"I'm not used to champagne in the morning."

"There is nothing more useful that we can do at the moment than put ourselves in a good humour. My wife is quite happy in the house preparing for her party."

"Your wife?"

"Yes, I speak prematurely, but last night we decided to marry. Now that the sexual urge is behind us, marriage presents no danger of infidelity or boredom."

"You lived a long time without marriage."

"Our life has been what the French call *mouvementé*. Now I can leave a great deal of the burden of work to you. My partner needs watching, but you can leave him to me. And I will look after relations with the police. The Chief of Police is coming tomorrow night. He has a charming daughter, by the way.

It's a pity you are not a Catholic, he would make a valuable father-in-law, but perhaps we could remedy that."

"You talk as if I were settling here for life."

"I know that 'for life' has a rather lugubrious sound, as in the term 'imprisonment for life,' but here you know 'for life' can so easily mean for a day, for a week, for a month. And you won't die in a traffic accident."

"You speak as though I were a young man looking for adventure. O'Toole wants me to take the boat tomorrow."

"But you are one of the family now," Mr. Visconti replied, putting his hand like a bird's claw on my knee and digging a little with his fingers to retain a grip. "I feel towards you very like a father." His smile, which he must have meant to be a tender one, was not of the kind which one associates with paternity: the missing teeth ruined it. He must have seen me looking at his mouth, for he explained, "I had very good dentures once. Some magnificent gold work. It's the only form of jewelry a man can wear that women fully appreciate. Dear things, they like to put their lips on gold. Unfortunately the Nazis were acquisitive that way, and although I tried to remain on friendly terms, I thought it safer to have the teeth removed. There was an officer of the Gestapo who had a drawer full of teeth. I noticed that he always looked me in the mouth, not the eyes."

"How did you explain their absence?"

"I told them I had exchanged them for cigarettes. I cannot think what I would have done without those teeth when I had to run away. Before I reached Milan and Mario's Jesuits I was down to my last tooth."

Aunt Augusta joined us from the house. "I could do with a glass myself," she said. "I hope it's not going to rain tomorrow. I'm keeping the dining-room empty for dancing in case. Your room is looking quite furnished, Henry. Everything is a little slow because there are misunderstandings. I keep on using Italian words, and they don't understand. I find myself looking round for Wordsworth to explain. He had a way of explaining . . ."

"I thought we had agreed, dear, that his name was not to be spoken."

"I know, but it's so absurd to inconvenience ourselves with jealousies at our age. Do you know, Henry, Mr. Visconti was quite disturbed when I told him that I met Achille on the boat? Poor Achille. He couldn't move for gout."

"I like the dead to stay dead," Mr. Visconti said.

"Unlike Pottifer," my aunt replied and laughed.

"Who was Pottifer?" I asked.

"I was going to tell you at Boulogne, but you wouldn't listen."

"Tell me now."

"There are too many things to see about."

I could see that the only way to atone for my conduct in the restaurant of the Gare Maritime was to beg her to tell me. "Please, Aunt Augusta, I want to know . . ." I felt like a child pretending interest in a story to delay bedtime. What was it that I was delaying? Perhaps the moment when I had finally to decide to catch the boat home, to find again my dahlias and Major Charge, to reply to Miss Keene's letter, or to pass the border into my aunt's world where I had lived till now as a tourist only. It seemed to me, watching the champagne from Panama shooting up its bubbles like balls dancing on water at a fair, inconceivable that I could abandon forever the region of Colonel Hakim and Curran and O'Toole . . .

"What are you smiling at?" Aunt Augusta asked.

"I was thinking of O'Toole flying off today to Washington with the fake Leonardo."

"Not today. There are no planes to the north. He will be at the party tomorrow night. I asked him before he left. When once he had got what he wanted he was quite a charming man. Good-looking in a sad way."

"But perhaps today when he has time to examine the drawing . . ."

"Mr. O'Toole is no art expert," Mr. Visconti said. "The man who did that forgery was a genius. He was quite illiterate. A peasant on the prince's estate, but with a wonderful hand and eye. The prince never knew what a treasure he had living there until the police descended—that was in the early days of Mussolini—and arrested the man. He was making counterfeit notes. He had rigged up a little printing works at the back of the estate forge. They were extraordinarily good, his forgeries, but he didn't know his own value: he gave them away to his fellow labourers. The prince could never understand how it was his people had become so prosperous—there wasn't a labourer without a radio set. In socialist circles the prince gained a high reputation as an enlightened employer—they even wanted him to stand as a deputy. Then all the peasants began buying refrigerators and even motor-cycles. And of course they went too far . . . somebody bought a Fiat. And the paper the forger used wasn't up to the mark. When the man came out of prison the prince welcomed him back, and he was very careful to give him the correct materials for copying the Leonardo."

"Extraordinary. And you say he was illiterate?"

"It really helped him with the forging. He had no preconceived idea for example of how a letter was written. A letter was simply an abstract shape. It's easier to copy something with no meaning."

The heat of the morning deepened, and the smell of flowers. We had nearly finished the bottle of champagne. The lotos land, I thought.

To hear each other's whispered speech,
Eating the lotos day by day.

What were the lines about "the long-leaved flowers weep?" It was the trees which wept here, golden tears. I heard an orange strike the ground. It rolled a few inches and lay among a dozen others.

"What are you thinking, dear?"

"Tennyson has always been my favourite poet. I used to believe there was something Tennysonian in Southwood. The old church perhaps, the rhododendrons, Miss Keene sewing. I always liked his lines:

Then take the broidery frame, and add
A crimson to the quaint Macaw

although of course it wasn't embroidery she did."

"Are you missing Southwood even here?"

"No," I said, "there was another Tennyson and I find him here more than there.

"Death is the end of life, ah, why should life
all labour be?"

"Mr. Pottifer didn't believe that—that death was the end of life."

"A lot of people don't."

"Yes, but he took positive action."

I realized that Aunt Augusta passionately wanted to tell me about Pottifer. I caught Mr. Visconti's eye and he gave a very slight shrug. "Who was Pottifer?" I asked my aunt.

"He was an income-tax consultant," Aunt Augusta said and fell silent.

"Is that all?"

"He was a very proud man."

I could tell that my remark in Boulogne still rankled and that I would have to drag the story out of her piecemeal.

"Yes?"

"He had formerly been employed by the Inland Revenue—a tax inspector."

The sun shone down on the orange trees, the lemon and the grapefruit. Under the rosy *lapachos* grew the blue and white flowers on the same bush of jasmine. Mr. Visconti poured what was left of the champagne into our three glasses. The transparent moon was dropping over the horizon. Somerset House, income tax . . . They were as distant as the Mare Crisium or the Mare Humorum on the pale globe in the sky.

"Please tell me about him, Aunt Augusta," I said reluctantly.

"He had the idea," my aunt said, "of prolonging his life after death by means of the answering service of the general post office. Not very convenient for his clients, of whom I was one. It was when I was separated for the second time from Mr. Visconti by war. In Italy I had never been accustomed to pay taxes. They came as a rude shock to me. Especially as the little income I had was regarded as unearned. When I think of those endless tours, Rome, Milan, Florence, Venice before Jo died and I joined forces with Visconti . . ."

"A happy day for me, dear," Mr. Visconti said, "but you were telling Henry about the man Pottifer."

"I have to give a little background or Henry wouldn't understand about the company."

"What company?" I asked.

"It was invented by Mr. Pottifer to take care of my case and that of a few other ladies in my position. It was called Meerkat Products Ltd. We were appointed directors and our incomes (unearned indeed!) were put down as directors' fees. The fees appeared on the books and helped the company to show what Mr. Pottifer always called a healthy little loss. In those days, the bigger the loss, the more valuable the company when the time came to sell it. I never understood why."

"Your aunt is not a business-woman," Mr. Visconti said with tenderness.

"I trusted Mr. Pottifer and I was right to trust him. During his years as an inspector he had developed quite a hatred for the office he served. He would do anything to help anyone about tax. He was very proud of his ability to circumvent a new law. He always went into purdah for three weeks after a new Finance Act."

"What was Meerkat and what did it produce?"

"It produced nothing or we might have shown a profit. When Mr. Pottifer died I did look up Meerkat in the dictionary. It said a small South African mammal like an ichneumon. As I didn't know what an ichneumon was, I looked that up too. Apparently it was something which destroyed crocodile's eggs—I would have thought an unproductive occupation. I think the tax inspectors probably thought that it was a province in India."

Two men came down into the garden carrying a black metal frame.

"What's that, dear?"

"The barbecue."

"It looks enormous."

"It has to be if it's to roast an ox whole."

I said, "You haven't told me about the answering service."

"It was most awkward," my aunt said, "income-tax demands came in—exorbitant as usual—and every time I tried to telephone to Mr. Pottifer I heard the answering service, 'Mr. Pottifer is at a meeting of the Commissioners. He will call you back.' This went on for nearly a fortnight, and then it occurred to me to ring him up at one in the morning. The answer was just the same: 'Mr. Pottifer is at a meeting of the Commissioners ...' Then I knew something was wrong. It all came out in the end. He had been dead for three weeks, but in his will he had insisted that his brother should keep on the telephone and make an arrangement with the answering service."

"But why?"

"I think the reason lay partly in his idea of immortality, but I think too it belonged to his war against the Inland Revenue. He was a great believer in delaying tactics. 'Never answer all their questions,' he would say. 'Make them write again. And be ambiguous. You can always decide what you mean later according to circumstances. The bigger the file the bigger the work. Personnel frequently change. A newcomer has to start looking at the file from the beginning. Office space is limited. In the end it's easier for them to give in.' Sometimes, if the inspector was pressing very hard, he told me that it was time to fling in a reference to a nonexisting letter. He would write sharply, 'You seem to have paid no attention to my letter of April 6, 1963.' A whole month might pass before the inspector admitted he could find no trace of it. Mr. Pottifer would send in a carbon copy of the letter containing a reference which again the inspector would be unable to trace. If he was a newcomer to the district, of course he blamed his predecessor; otherwise, after a few years of Mr. Pottifer, he was quite liable to have a nervous breakdown. I think when Mr. Pottifer planned to carry on after death (of course there was no notice in the papers and the funeral was very quiet) he had these delaying tactics in mind. He didn't think of the inconvenience to his clients, only of the inconvenience to the inspector."

Aunt Augusta gave a deep sigh, as ambiguous as one of Pottifer's letters. I couldn't tell whether it was of melancholy for Pottifer's death or of satisfaction in having at last told the story she had begun in the Gare Maritime at Boulogne.

"In this blessed land of Paraguay," Mr. Visconti spoke as though he were adding a moral to the story, "there is no income tax and no evasions are necessary."

"Mr. Pottifer would not have been happy here," Aunt Augusta said.

That night, as I was preparing to undress, she came to my room. She sat down on the bed. "It's quite comfortable here now, isn't it?" she asked me.

"Very comfortable."

She noticed at once the photograph of herself which I had taken from *Rob Roy* and stuck into a corner of a looking-glass. A bedroom without a photograph always seems to indicate a heartless occupant, for one needs the presence of others when one falls asleep, standing around as Matthew, Mark, Luke and John used to in childhood. "Where did that come from?" Aunt Augusta asked.

"I found it in a book."

"Your father took it."

"I thought so."

"It was a very happy day," she said. "There weren't many happy days at that time. There were so many arguments about *your* future."

"Mine?"

"And you weren't even born. Now again I wish that I could know your future. Are you going to stay with us? You are so evasive."

"It's too late for the boat now."

"There's sure to be an empty cabin."

"I don't think I want three days with poor Wordsworth."

"There are planes . . ."

"Exactly," I said, "so you see I needn't make up my mind. I can go next week, or the week after. We can wait and see how things go."

"I have always thought that one day we might be together."

"Always, Aunt Augusta? We've known each other for less than a year."

"Why do you suppose I came to the funeral?"

"It was your sister's funeral."

"Yes, of course, I had forgotten that."

"There's plenty of time to make plans," I said. "You may not even want to settle here yourself. After all you are a great traveller, Aunt Augusta."

"This is my journey's end," Aunt Augusta said. "Perhaps travel for me was always a substitute. I never wanted to travel as long as Mr. Visconti was there. What is there in Southwood which draws you back?"

The question had been in my mind for several days and now I did my best to answer it. I spoke of my dahlias, I even talked of Major Charge and his goldfish. The rain began to fall, rustling through the trees in the garden: a grapefruit tumbled heavily to earth. I spoke of the last evening with Miss Keene and her sad undecided letter from Koffiefontein. Even the admiral stalked through my memories, flushed with Chianti and wearing a scarlet paper cap. Packages of Omo were left on the doorstep. I felt a sense of relief as a patient must feel under Pentothal, and I let my random thoughts dictate my words. I spoke of Chicken and of Peter and Nancy in the Abbey Restaurant in Latimer Road, of the bells of Saint John's Church and the tablet to Councillor Trumbull, the patron of the grim orphanage. I sat on the bed beside my aunt and she put her arm round me while I went over the uneventful story of my life. "I've been very happy." I concluded as though it needed an excuse.

"Yes, dear, yes, I know," she said.

I told her how very kind to me Sir Alfred Keene had been, and I told her of the bank and of how Sir Alfred threatened to remove his account if I did not remain as manager.

"My darling boy," she said, "all that is over now," and she stroked my forehead with her old hand as though I were a schoolboy who had run away from school and she was promising me that I would never have to return, that all my difficulties were over, that I could stay at home.

I was sunk deep in my middle age. All the same I laid my head against her breast. "I had been happy," I said, "but I have been so bored for so long."

The party was larger than I had conceived possible after seeing my aunt alone in the empty unfurnished house, and I could only explain it by the fact that not one real friend was present among all the hundred guests, unless one could call O'Toole a friend. As more and more guests assembled I wondered from what highways and hedges Mr. Visconti had drummed them up. The street was lined with cars, among them two armoured ones, for the Chief of Police had arrived, as promised, bringing with him a very fat and ugly wife and a beautiful daughter called Camilla. Even the young officer who had arrested me was there, and he gave me a hearty slap on the back to show that there was no ill feeling on his part. (I had still a piece of plaster on my ear where he had struck me on the earlier occasion.) I think Mr. Visconti must have visited every hotel bar in town, and the most passing acquaintances had been invited to bring their friends. The party was to be his apotheosis. After it no one would ever care to remember the former Mr. Visconti who had lain sick and impoverished in a mean hotel by the yellow Victorian station.

The great gates had been cleaned of rust and flung open; the chandeliers sparkled in the *sala,* lights were turned on in even the empty rooms, while coloured globes had been strung from tree to tree and over the boards of the dance-floor laid on the grass. On the terrace two musicians tuned a guitar and a harp. O'Toole was there, the Czech who had failed to sell two million plastic straws had brought his wife from the Hotel Guaraní, and suddenly I saw moving inconspicuously through the crowd and disappearing again as though into some warren in the garden the export-import merchant who had shared our table on the boat, grey and thin, twitching his rabbit nose. On the lawn the ox steamed and crackled on its iron frame, and the smell of roasting meat chased away the perfume of orange and jasmine.

My memories of the party are very confused, perhaps because I helped myself rather liberally to champagne before dinner. There were more women than men, as so often happens in Paraguay, where the male population has been reduced by two terrible wars, and I found myself on more than one occasion dancing or speaking with the beautiful Camilla. The musicians played mainly polkas and galops, the steps of which were unknown to me, and I was astonished to see how my aunt and Mr. Visconti picked them up on the spot by a kind of second nature. Whenever I looked among the dancers, on the lawn or in the *sala,* they were there. Camilla who could speak very little English tried in vain to teach me: it was too much a matter of duty on her part for me to respond. I said, "I am glad I am not in prison tonight."

"How?"

"That young man over there put me in a cell."

"How?"

"Do you see this plaster? That's where he hit me."

I was trying to make light conversation, but when there was a pause in the music she hastened away.

O'Toole was suddenly at my side. He said, "It's a great party. Great. I wish Lucinda could have been

here. She'd have found it great too. There's the
Dutch Ambassador talking to your aunt. I saw your
British Ambassador just now. And the Nicaraguan. I
wonder how Mr. Visconti corralled the diplomatic
corps. I guess it's his name—if it is his real name.
There's not much to do in Asunción, and I suppose if
you get an invitation from a guy called Visconti . . ."

"Have you seen Wordsworth?" I asked. "I half-
expected him to turn up as well."

"He'll be on the boat by now. They sail at six, as
soon as it's light. I guess he wouldn't be very welcome
here as things are."

"No."

The guests were crowding to the steps of the terrace, clapping and crying "Brava." I saw Camilla up
there dancing with a bottle balanced on her head.
Mr. Visconti pulled at my arm and said, "Henry, I
want you to meet our representative in Formosa." I
turned and held out my hand to the man with the
grey rabbit face.

"We were on the boat together coming from
Buenos Aires," I reminded him, but of course he
spoke no English.

"He handles our river-borne traffic," Mr. Visconti
said, as though he were talking about some great
legal enterprise. "You will be seeing a lot of each
other. Now come and meet the Chief of Police."

The Chief of Police spoke English with an American accent. He told me he had studied in Chicago. I
said, "You have a beautiful daughter."

He made a bow and said, "She has a beautiful
mother."

"She tried to teach me to dance, but I have no ear
for music and your dances are new to me."

"The polka and the galop. They are our national
dances."

"The names sound very Victorian," I said. I had

meant it as a compliment, but he moved abruptly away.

The charcoal under the ox was turning black, and there was little left of the ox but a skeleton. It had been a good dinner. We had sat on benches in the garden before trestle tables and carried our plates to the barbecue. I had noticed how a stout man who sat beside me refilled his plate four times with huge steaks. "You have a good appetite," I said.

He ate like a good trencherman in a Victorian illustration, with the elbows stuck out and the head well down and a napkin tucked in his collar. He said, "This is nothing. At home I eat eight kilos of beef a day. A man needs strength."

"What do you do?" I asked.

"I am the chief customs officer," he said. He pointed with his fork down the table to a slim pale girl who looked scarcely eighteen. "My daughter," he said. "I tell her to eat more meat, but she is obstinate like her mother."

"Which is her mother?"

"She died. In the Civil War. She had no resistance. She did not eat meat."

Now in the small hours I found him again beside me. He put his arm around my shoulders and squeezed me as if we were old friends. He said, "Here is Maria. My daughter. She speaks English good. You must dance with her. Tell her she must eat more meat."

We walked away together. I said, "Your father says he eats eight kilos of meat a day."

"Yes. That is true," she said.

"I don't know your dances, I'm afraid."

"It does not matter. I have danced enough."

We walked towards the trees and I found two chairs. A photographer stopped beside us and held up his flash. Her face was startlingly white and her eyes looked frightened in the glare. Then everything faded out and I could hardly see her. "How old are you?" I asked.

"Fourteen," she said.

"Your father thinks you should eat more meat."

"I do not care for meat," she said.

"What do you like?"

"Poetry. English poetry. I like English poetry very much." She recited very seriously, " 'Hearts of oak are our ships, Hearts of oak are our men.' " She added, "And 'Lord Ullin's Daughter.' " She said, "I cry often when I read 'Lord Ullin's Daughter.' "

"And Tennyson?"

"Yes, I know Lord Tennyson too." She was gaining confidence, finding an interest we shared. "He is sad also. I like very much sad things."

The guests crowded the floor as the harpist and the guitarist played another polka: we could see beyond the terrace through the windows of the *sala* the ebb and flow of the dancers. I quoted "Maud" in my turn to the customs officer's daughter: " 'The brief night goes in babble and revel and wine.' "

"I do not know that poem. Is it sad?"

"It's a very long poem, and it ends very sadly." I tried to remember some of the sad lines, but the only one that came to my mind was: "I hate the dreadful hollow behind the little wood," which had little meaning out of context. I said, "If you like I will lend it to you. I have the collected poems of Tennyson here with me."

O'Toole came towards us and I saw a chance of escaping, for I was feeling very tired and my ear hurt. I said, "This is Maria. She is studying English literature like your daughter." He was a sad and serious man. They would get on well together. It was nearly two in the morning. I wanted to find some unobtrusive corner where I could sleep awhile, but halfway across the lawn I found the Czech in conversation with Mr. Visconti. Mr. Visconti said, "Henry, we have an offer."

"An offer?"

"This gentleman has two million plastic straws which he would let us have at half the cost price."

"That's nearly the whole population of Paraguay," I said.

"I am not thinking of Paraguay."

The Czech said with a smile, "If you could persuade them to drink maté through a plastic straw . . ." He wasn't taking the business discussion very seriously, but I could see that Mr. Visconti's imagination had taken wings—I was reminded of Aunt Augusta when she began to embroider one of her anecdotes. It was probably the sound of that very round *de luxe* number—two million—that had excited Mr. Visconti.

He said, "I was thinking of Panama. If our agent there could get them into the Canal Zone. Think of all those American sailors and tourists . . ."

"Do American sailors take soft drinks?" the Czech asked.

"Have you never heard," Mr. Visconti said, "that beer is much more intoxicating drunk through a straw?"

"Surely that is only a legend."

"There speaks a Protestant," Mr. Visconti said. "Any Catholic knows that a legend which is believed has the same value and effect as the truth. Look at the cult of the saints."

"But the Americans may be Protestants."

"Then we produce medical evidence. That is the modern form of the legend. The toxic effect of imbibing alcohol through a straw. There is a Doctor Rodriguez here who would help me. The statistics of cancer of the liver. Suppose we could persuade the Panama government to prohibit the sale of straws with alcoholic drink. The straws would be sold illicitly from under the counter. The demand would be tremendous. Remote danger is a great attraction. From the profits I would found the Visconti Research Institute..."

"But these are *plastic* straws."

"We can call them *cured* straws; there will be articles showing that the cure is quite useless like filters on cigarettes."

I left the two of them to their discussion. As I skirted the dance-floor I saw my aunt dancing the galop with the Chief of Police: nothing seemed to tire her. The Chief's daughter Camilla was in the arms of the customs officer, but the dancers had thinned out and a car with a CD plate was driving away.

I found a chair in the yard behind the kitchen, where a few crates of furniture still remained unopened, and almost immediately I fell asleep. I dreamt that the rabbit-nosed man was feeling my pulse and telling Mr. Visconti that I was dead of the fluke —whatever that might mean. I tried to speak out to prove that I was alive, but Mr. Visconti commanded some shadowy figures in the background, in a jumbled phrase from "Maud," to bury me deeper, only a little deeper. I tried to cry out to my aunt, who stood there pregnant in a bathing dress, holding Mr. Visconti's hand, and I woke gasping for breath and for words and heard the sound of the harp and the guitar playing on.

I looked at my watch and saw that it was nearly four. Sunrise was not far off, the lights had been turned out in the garden, and the flowers seemed to breathe their scent more deeply in the small chill of the dawn. I felt oddly elated to be alive, and I knew in a moment of decision that I would never see Major Charge again, nor the dahlias, the empty urn, the packet of Omo on the doorstep or a letter from Miss Keene. I walked down towards the little wood of fruit trees nursing my decision close to my heart—I think even then I knew there would be a price to pay for it. The dancers who remained must all be in the *sala* now, for the lawn was empty, and there were no cars left outside the gates so far as I could see, though I heard the sound of one receding down the road towards the city. Again lines from "Maud" came to mind in the early sweet-scented morning: "Low on the sand and loud on the stone the last wheel echoes away." It was as though I were safely back in the Victorian world where I had been taught by my father's books to feel more at home than in our modern day. The wood sloped down towards the road and up again to the back gate, and as I entered the little hollow I trod on something hard. I stooped down and picked the object up. It was Wordsworth's knife. The tool for taking stones out of a horse's hoof was open —perhaps he had meant to open the blade and in his hurry he had made an error. I struck a match and before the flame went out I saw the body on the ground and the black face starred with white orange petals, which had been blown from the trees in the small breeze of early morning.

I knelt down and felt for the pulse in the heart. There was no life in the black body, and my hand was wet from the wound I couldn't see. "Poor Wordsworth," I said aloud with some idea of showing to his murderer if he were anywhere near by that Wordsworth had a friend. I though how his bizarre love for an old woman had taken him from the doors of the Grenada cinema, where he used to stand so proudly in his uniform, to die on the wet grass near the Paraguay river, but I knew that if this was the price he had to pay, he would have paid it gladly. He was a romantic, and in the only form of poetry he knew, the poetry which he had learnt at St. George's Cathedral, Freetown, he would have found the right words to express his love and his death. I could

imagine him at the last, refusing to admit that she
had dismissed him forever, reciting a hymn to keep
his courage up as he walked towards the house
through the hollow in the little wood:

> "If I ask Her to receive me,
>   Will she say me nay?
> Not till earth and not till heav'n
>   Pass away."

The sentiment had always been sincere even if the
changes in the words were unliturgical.

There was no sound except my own breathing. I
closed the knife and put it in my pocket. Had he
drawn it when he first entered the grounds with the
intention of attacking Visconti? I preferred to think
otherwise—that he had come with the simple purpose
of appealing to his love once more before abandon-
ing hope and that when he heard someone move
among the trees he had drawn the knife hurriedly in
self-defence, pointing at his unseen enemy the useless
tool for horses' hoofs.

I went slowly back towards the house to break the
news as gently as I might to Aunt Augusta. The
musicians were still playing on the terrace, they were
tired out and almost falling asleep over their instru-
ments, but when I entered the *sala* there remained
only one couple—my aunt and Mr. Visconti. I was
reminded of the house behind the *Messaggero* where
they had met after a long separation and danced
together between the sofas while the prostitutes
watched with amazement. They were dancing a slow
waltz now and they never saw me enter, two old
people bound in the deep incurable egotism of passion. They had turned off the lights, and in the big
room illumined only from the terrace there rested
pools of darkness between the windows. As they
moved I lost their faces and found them again. At

one moment the shadows gave my aunt a deceptive air of youth: she looked like the young woman in my father's photograph pregnant with happiness, and at another I recognized the old woman who had faced Miss Paterson with such merciless cruelty and jealousy.

I called out to her as she went by, "Aunt Augusta," but she didn't answer to the name; there was no sign that she even heard me. They danced on in their tireless passion into the shadows.

I took a few steps farther into the room as they returned towards me, calling to her a second time, "Mother, Wordsworth's dead." She only looked over her partner's shoulder and said, "Yes, dear, all in good time, but can't you see that now I am dancing with Mr. Visconti?"

A flashbulb broke the shadows up. I have the photograph still—all three of us are petrified by the lightning flash into a family group: you can see the great gap in Visconti's teeth as he smiles towards me like an accomplice. I have my hand thrown out in a frozen appeal, and my mother is regarding me with an expression of tenderness and reproof. I have cut from the print another face which I hadn't realized was in the room with us, the face of a little old man with long moustaches. He had been first with the news, and Mr. Visconti sacked him later at my insistence (my mother took no part in the dispute, which she said was a matter to be settled between men), so Wordsworth did not go entirely unavenged.

Not that I have time to think of the poor fellow very much. Mr. Visconti has not yet made a fortune, and our import-export business takes more and more of my time. We have had our ups and downs, and the photographs of what we call the great party and of our distinguished guests have proved useful more than once. We own a complete Dakota now, for our partner was accidentally shot dead by a policeman because he couldn't make himself understood in Guaraní, and most of my spare time is spent in learning that language. Next year, when she is sixteen, I am to marry the daughter of the chief of customs, a union which has the approval of Mr. Visconti and her father. There is, of course, a considerable difference in our ages, but she is a gentle and obedient child, and often in the warm scented evening we read Browning together.

> God's in his heaven—
> All's right with the world!

ABOUT THE AUTHOR

GRAHAM GREENE was born in England in 1904. He served on the staff of the London TIMES and the SPECTATOR. In World War II he was a member of the foreign office with special duties in West Africa. His first novel was *The Man Within*. He has written several thrillers, including *The Third Man* and *Our Man in Havana*. His more serious novels are notable for their subtle characterization and accomplished craftsmanship.

A number of Greene's novels and short stories have had successful motion picture adaptations, and two of his plays, *The Living Room* and *The Potting Shed*, were produced on Broadway. In 1952, Graham Greene was given the Catholic Literary Award for *The End of the Affair*. His most recent novels are *A Burnt-Out Case, The Comedians* and *Travels with My Aunt*.

by
GRAHAM GREENE

These words appear on the title pages of some of the finest fiction of the century. *Saturday Review* called Graham Greene "One of the finest craftsmen of story-telling in our time." All of the books below show his unique gift for subtle characterization, taut narrative, and brilliant description.

☐ TRAVELS WITH MY AUNT   (T5786—$1.50)

☐ MAY WE BORROW YOUR HUSBAND? (N4357—95¢)

☐ THE COMEDIANS   (Q5802—$1.25)

☐ BRIGHTON ROCK   (S3644—75¢)

☐ THE END OF THE AFFAIR   (N5762—95¢)

☐ THE POWER & THE GLORY   (Q5804—$1.25)

☐ A BURNT-OUT CASE   (N5825—95¢)

☐ THE HEART OF THE MATTER   (Q6670—$1.25)

☐ THE QUIET AMERICAN   (N6726—95¢)

☐ TWENTY-ONE STORIES   (N6673—95¢)

☐ OUR MAN IN HAVANA   (S3632—75¢)

Ask for them at your local bookseller or use this handy coupon:

BANTAM BESTSELLERS

OUTSTANDING BOOKS NOW AVAILABLE
AT A FRACTION
OF THEIR ORIGINAL COST!

☐ THE LOVE MACHINE by Jacqueline Susann. The new #1 bestselling sensation by the author of VALLEY OF THE DOLLS.　(T5400—$1.50)

☐ AIRPORT by Arthur Hailey. The tremendous national bestseller about a snowbound airport by the author of HOTEL.　(T3982—$1.50)

☐ PORTNOY'S COMPLAINT by Philip Roth. The Controversial #1 national bestseller, the year's most talked about book. By the author of GOOD-BYE, COLUMBUS.　(T4899—$1.50)

☐ AN AFFAIR OF HONOR by Robert Wilder. The major novel of a 20th century buccaneer who corrupted an island paradise.　(Q5591—$1.25)

☐ THE INTERCOM CONSPIRACY by Eric Ambler. A high-tension non-stop thriller that's impossible to put down. Or forget!　(N5594—95¢)

☐ LOVEY CHILDS by John O'Hara. The story of a rich girl with all the right connections and all the wrong ideas. An O'Hara masterpiece!
　(Q5688—$1.25)

☐ IN A WILD SANCTUARY by William Harrison. The powerful story of four bright young grad students and their bizarre deal with death.
　(N5615—95¢)

☐ MAGISTER LUDI by Hermann Hesse. Formerly titled "The Glass Bead Game," this Is Hesse's masterpiece now appearing for the first time in mass paperback.　(T5555—$1.50)

Buy them wherever Bantam Bestsellers are sold or use this handy coupon:

Bantam Books, Inc., Dept. GA1F, Room 2450, 666 Fifth Ave., N.Y., N.Y. 10019

Please send me the titles checked above. I am enclosing $_____
(Check or money order—no currency or C.O.D.'s, please. If less than 5 books, add 10¢ per book for postage and handling.)

NAME_____

ADDRESS_____

CITY_____STATE_____ZIP_____
Please allow about four weeks for delivery.　　　　GA1F—12/70